The Chase

VE June 14

Also by Debra White Smith

TEXAS HEAT
TEXAS PURSUIT

The Chase

LONE STAR INTRIGUE, BOOK THREE

DEBRA WHITE SMITH

AVON
INSPIRE
An Imprint of HarperCollins*Publishers*

THE CHASE. Copyright © 2011 by Debra White Smith. All rights reserved. Printed in the United States of America. No part of this book may be used or reproduced in any manner whatsoever without written permission except in the case of brief quotations embodied in critical articles and reviews. For information address HarperCollins Publishers, 10 East 53rd Street, New York, NY 10022.

HarperCollins books may be purchased for educational, business, or sales promotional use. For information please write: Special Markets Department, HarperCollins Publishers, 10 East 53rd Street, New York, NY 10022.

FIRST EDITION

Library of Congress Cataloging-in-Publication Data has been applied for.

ISBN 978-0-06-149326-3

11 12 13 14 15   OV/RRD   10 9 8 7 6 5 4 3 2 1

The Chase

CHAPTER ONE

Ryan Mansfield's boots crunched against the loose gravel scattered along the wide highway shoulder. He approached the stopped SUV with as much caution as determination. Last year, he'd been sucked into a shoot-out when an angry driver didn't think he deserved a ticket, let alone a citation for driving while intoxicated. The night had a way of bringing that memory into haunting focus.

His flashlight's beam snaked across the pavement as he glanced toward the horizon west of Highway 69. Dusk was disappearing, and a creamy moon hung from the sky like a ballroom chandelier. The November cool sucked all the haze from the air, leaving room for stars to dazzle. Ryan stopped a shiver and wondered if Shelly would ever understand just how lonely he was without her . . . and how much the long, autumn nights sharpened his loneliness.

Forcing himself to focus on the task at hand, he paused near the driver's side as the tinted window slid down.

The worried eyes that peered up at him didn't belong to a threatening stranger but to the woman he knew better than any other.

"Shelly! Good grief! I was just . . ." Ryan blurted and stopped himself from admitting he'd been thinking of her.

The dashboard's glow heightened her petite features, and Ryan wished he could tell her how pretty she was.

"Ryan!" she exclaimed.

"Daddy! Daddy!" Sean's face appeared near Shelly and then the back door popped open. "Daddy!"

"Sean! No!" Shelly ordered.

"It's okay. I've got him," Ryan said and scooped his son into his arms. Sean's damp hair smelled of shampoo, and Ryan tousled it.

"How's my champ?" he asked, hugging his son tight.

"I'm going home with you!" Sean declared.

"No . . . we're going to Granna's to spend the night, remember?" Shelly said. "It's Granna's birthday tomorrow, and she's taking you to the fair." Her focus shifted to Jack. "That's what Mom's 'getting from Sean' for her birthday." Shelly drew invisible quotes in the air.

Ryan smiled and patted his son's back. "Sounds like the best gift in the world to me."

Sean's hold on Ryan's neck increased. "Please, Daddy!" he begged. "I still wanta go home with you."

"You're going to Daddy's *next* weekend," Shelly insisted.

Ryan sized up her determined expression and knew this was one weekend she couldn't relent. They'd amazingly managed to juggle parenting duties for two years now with a cooperation that had escaped every other element of their marriage. Somehow, they'd set aside their own preferences for what was best for Sean. As a result, Shelly gave Ryan more than his share of the dad-time the courts had outlined.

They'd adopted Sean as a newborn when Shelly's unstable sister gave birth out of wedlock. The stress of a baby hadn't helped their self-centered marriage—but even a tumultuous union couldn't change the fierce love they both felt for Sean. Ryan and Shelly never had a biological child, but he couldn't imagine loving one more than he loved his son . . . and Shelly claimed she felt the same.

With a lump in his throat, Ryan chuckled and tried to make light of the awkward situation. "Just wait until next weekend, okay? And then the week after that it's Thanksgiving, and we'll be together all week. We're going fishing at Uncle Jack's and horseback riding . . . and maybe even camping."

The patrol car's flashing lights illuminated the expectation in Sean's widened eyes. "Camping?" he exclaimed. "You promise?"

"You bet," Ryan said, "but you've got to cooperate with your mom now. I think she's in a hurry," he added on a dry note and eyed his ex-wife.

"Uh . . ." Shelly glanced down and then lifted her gaze. "I was supposed to be at Mom's an hour ago. You aren't going to give me a ticket, are you, Ryan?" Her question held an incredulous note, and her big brown eyes begged him to let her off.

He hesitated . . . only because he didn't want her to know just how much her request affected him. Truth was, all chances for a ticket had vanished the second he saw her.

"What's the deal with this SUV anyway?" Ryan asked. "I thought you were still driving the minivan."

"This is Tim's. He's letting me borrow it while the van is in the shop. Something with the transmission. It's been a wild week. My alarm system on the house malfunctioned, maybe due to a family of squirrels up in the attic. Then the dog next door got out and chewed up Sean's shoes, which he'd left outside." Shelly waved aside the problems, and her engagement ring flickered blue in the flash of the patrol car's blinking lights. "All I know is Dad's taking care of the alarm and Tim's taking care of the van."

"Oh," Ryan said, his voice flat. *Daddy always did take care of everything*, he thought and didn't even want to consider Tim. Over the past few months he'd come to despise the name "Tim." Last week, he'd even snapped at some poor guy bagging his groceries, just because his name badge said "Tim."

"You should really get the alarm system fixed ASAP," Ryan encouraged. "I don't mind taking care of it. Your dad lives an hour away."

"I know. I just hated to, well, bother you." She looked away.

Or didn't want me involved, Ryan thought and tried not to wince.

"Dr. Tim gave me a new baseball glove." Sean wiggled in his arms and reached for the door handle. "Here—I'll show it to you!"

Ryan stopped short of refusing his son's offer, simply because he sensed how proud Sean was of his new gift. Once Sean opened the van's door and settled onto the backseat, he lifted the glove for his father's inspection. "See?"

"Very nice," Ryan said, running his fingertips across the high-grade leather. *The thing must have cost the price of a root canal*, he thought and wondered if there was no end to the dentist's money. The best Ryan could have ever done on his salary was a Walmart special.

He clicked his son's seat belt in place and kissed his forehead. "Listen, you be good for your mom, okay?" he said, his voice thick. "And I'll see you next weekend."

"And then camping the next?"

"Right-O, champ." He doubled his fist, and Sean bumped the top with his own fist.

After shutting the door, he shifted back to Shelly's window and attempted to soften the admonishment he couldn't hold at bay. "Try to keep the speed down, you hear? Your mom can wait. She's waited before. Besides, I kinda like that little guy in the back."

"You only clocked me ten miles over the speed limit," she groused.

"Lots of people in the grave have said the same thing."

"That's the speed limit not far up the road anyway."

"Yeah, but the road here has a lot more twists and turns."

Shelly cut him an upward glance and then studied the steering wheel.

Ryan considered another remark, but decided to stop the exchange before it got out of hand. A pause stretched to awkward, and he said, "Well, I guess I'll e-mail you next week, and we can set up a time for me to get Sean."

"Oh sure," she said before Ryan walked away from the vehicle.

"And, thanks . . ." The offer of gratitude was so soft, Ryan wondered if he'd imagined it. He glanced back. Her faint smile held a hint of the appreciation in her voice.

He lifted his brows to prompt an explanation.

"You know," she continued, "for not writing a ticket."

"Why would you think I'd give you a ticket this time? I didn't the last time," Ryan replied, and could have bitten his tongue in half for the slip that referenced their first meeting.

Shelly turned her head as if she had no clue his words had been loaded with the memory of their initial flirtation after Ryan issued Shelly's warning. And Ryan didn't tell her she twisted his heart even more tonight than she had the day he stopped her for speeding more than ten years ago.

When she remained silent, Ryan trudged back to his squad car and thought it odd that she would believe he'd actually issue her a ticket. After all, Shelly was his wife . . . or at least, she used to be. Problem was, somebody forgot to tell Ryan's heart the "used-to-be's" weren't still in effect. In his heart, she was as much his wife as she was the day they each said, "I do."

The vehicle's flashing lights reminded him of the squad car that escorted them out of town on their wedding night. Eager to switch off the lights, he paused by the door, waited until an approaching vehicle whizzed past, and watched Shelly pull away. Sean's face appeared in the back window. He waved, and then rested his hand against the window.

He's gotten out of his seat belt! Ryan thought and prepared to call Shelly on her cell phone if she didn't immediately refasten it. Ryan returned the wave. *Fasten your seat belt, Buddy,* he mouthed, hoping Sean could read his lips.

The vehicle slowed and pulled back to the shoulder. Sean's face disappeared, and Ryan knew Shelly was enforcing the seat belt rule. Even though she pushed the speed limit here and there, she was a stickler about wearing belts.

"At least I can count on that much," he sighed. Ryan opened the door, dropped behind the wheel, and turned off the flashing lights. Another long night on the highway awaited him. He'd asked for a change to nightshift last year when he realized working nights stopped him from sitting in an empty house once the sun went down.

"Oh God," he prayed. "I know I'm the one who blew it . . . but please, somehow, bring her back to me." Ryan lowered his forehead to the steering wheel and groaned over the next words, *"Please, please* stop her marriage to Tim Aldridge. Oh Lord, I need a miracle."

Shelly Mansfield rolled over and opened one eye. According to the digital alarm's glaring red numbers, she had only five minutes left to sleep. Groaning, she pulled the comforter up to her nose and wished for another hour. While she enjoyed serving on the church praise team, it robbed her of the extra sleep she'd normally get. The team met for practice an hour before Sunday school.

Of course, that also meant she and Tim had another hour together on Sundays, since he also sang on the team. Occasionally, they were assigned a duet, and everyone said they sounded professional. A drowsy smile overtook Shelly. She enjoyed mingling her voice with Tim's and could hardly wait until they would fully mingle their lives as one—just three short months away.

Ryan's disapproving expression floated across her mind, and Shelly tried to purge him from her thoughts. When she rolled down her window Friday night, Shelly hadn't expected Ryan. She also hadn't expected to be taken aback by just how good he looked, standing in the shadows in his uniform like a new love who only had eyes for her. But then, Ryan Mansfield always had been a good-looking man— one that turned female heads in any crowd. She squeezed her eyes tight and reminded herself that that had been the problem in their marriage. Ryan had turned one too many heads and finally gave in.

Shelly had just been getting over the devastation when he claimed that he'd found the Lord and wanted to reconcile. But by then, she and Tim were getting acquainted. On top of that, Shelly doubted she could ever trust him again. He was one of those men who became more attractive with age. The more attractive he became, the more women noticed. The more women noticed . . .

Just as they had the last two nights, the old emotions stirred anew . . . betrayal, devastation, confusion—emotions rooted in love gone wrong. The torment of it all had driven her to take the natural sleep aid that her doctor had recommended during and after the divorce two years ago. The stress of her marriage falling apart and Ryan's moving in with his girlfriend had robbed Shelly of precious slumber to the point that she'd welcomed a cure. In the last year, she'd only needed the sleep aid sporadically. Seeing Ryan ensured that the last two nights were some of those nights.

Shelly dragged herself up from the clutches of grogginess. "I refuse to let him get to me today," she muttered and shoved aside the covers. She'd spent a whole year with a counselor, sorting out her wounds and trying to heal. Shelly Mansfield had finished wallowing in the pain a long time ago.

The alarm's squawk accompanied her feet touching the carpet. As she turned off the buzzer, her gaze slid to the other side of the bed. It was empty. Despite her admonishments that Sean should sleep in his own room, he often crawled into her bed in the wee hours. Most the time he claimed he didn't remember moving to her bed. A time or two in the last few months, she'd found him curled up on the floor in his room . . . or on the sofa. The pediatrician attributed it to sleepwalking. Shelly immediately installed some child-proof locks on the doors leading outside.

"He was probably too tired from yesterday to even sleepwalk," she mumbled while thrusting her feet into satin slippers and donning the matching robe. The fair had certainly exhausted Shelly, but insomnia had prevailed even in the face of exhaustion. If not for her dedication to the praise team, she'd have spent another night with her parents and slept in this morning.

The smell of fresh coffee lured her down the hallway; and Shelly was thankful that last night she'd remembered to set the automatic unit for a fresh brew.

Nearing Sean's room, Shelly detoured long enough to make certain he was still in his bed. But only a few steps into the chilled room revealed the bed was empty. Shelly stepped to the light switch, flipped it up, and scanned the floor. Still no Sean. Assuming he must have landed on the couch this time, Shelly swiveled toward the hallway, but stopped. Something was wrong. As her disoriented mind grappled for logic, her nose grew colder.

Shelly touched her cheeks. For some reason, the room was cooler than the hallway. She twisted back around. Her gaze darted to the window. The curtains printed with toy trains shifted with the sound of autumn's breeze dancing among the backyard oaks.

She rushed to the curtains, shoved them aside, and stared at the opened window. "Oh no," she gasped. "No, no, no!" Her desperate mind insisted Sean must have somehow crawled out the window in his sleep. But as she looked up she spotted a precise square cut out of the pane. The resulting hole was just large enough for someone to reach through and unlatch the lock.

CHAPTER TWO

Ryan pulled his Ford truck into the country church grassy parking area, grabbed the grocery bag full of breakfast food, and stepped from his vehicle. Once a month the church hosted a breakfast before Sunday school. Ryan had volunteered to cook this month's meal.

He rounded the truck and went straight toward the fellowship hall, which was nestled behind the white-frame country church he'd begun attending with Jack and Charli since shortly after they married the summer before last. Now Ryan was considered as much a part of the Bullard, Texas, congregation as was Jack.

Before he entered the fellowship hall, Ryan paused to admire the rolling meadow and the surrounding pines bejeweled with heavy dew that also dampened his boots. The morning sun christened the whole countryside with a golden aura that brought heaven to mind. Ryan closed his eyes and inhaled the crisp air. Fall was one of his favorite seasons. He and Shelly had even gotten married in November so they could enjoy a ski trip in Colorado for their honeymoon.

Ryan's eyes popped open. He shook his head and determined

to focus on the job before him. "Breakfast," he stated and stomped toward the task.

But a horn's frenzied blowing halted Ryan in his tracks. He swiveled to face the parking lot. A Ford truck he recognized all-too-well halted mere feet from his pickup, and his brother Jack bolted out.

As the Bullard, Texas, chief of police, Jack usually remained unruffled, but his current expression surpassed frantic.

Ryan rushed forward to meet him. "What's the matter?" he croaked. "Charli . . . Bonnie?" he hedged, knowing in his gut this wasn't about Jack's family, but dreading the thought that it might be about his.

"No," Jack said, his intense eyes filling with anguish. "It's Sean, Ryan."

"S-Sean?" Ryan dropped the grocery bag. "Is he . . ." He couldn't say the word "dead," but it trampled his mind like some portent of doom.

"No—not that we know of, anyway." Jack gripped Ryan's shoulder and continued, "It looks like he's been kidnapped."

"Kidnapped?" Ryan croaked, and the cold air that once invigorated, threatened to suffocate.

"Yes. I'm so sorry, Ryan."

"H-how! Where was he?"

"In his bed." Jack shrugged. "When Shelly got up and checked on him, he was gone. Someone used a glass cutter to cut the window. They reached in, unlatched the lock, and crawled through the window. The front door was ajar, which indicates they left that way."

A wave of nausea only added to the spin in Ryan's head. "The alarm system was down!" he rasped and rested his head in his hands.

"Yes, that's what Shelly said," Jack replied, his voice full of compassion. "When Shelly called 9–1–1, our dispatcher recognized her name. She knew Shelly was my sister-in-law and called me. I've already been over to Shelly's. I left a detective working to come find you."

"Why didn't Shelly *call* me?" His face heating, Ryan raised his head and doubled his fist. "Tim Aldridge is probably already over there! Why didn't she call *me*?" he repeated and pounded his chest. "I'm Sean's father!"

"Shelly said she tried to call you on your cell after she called 911, but you didn't answer."

Ryan reached into his shirt pocket, removed his cell phone. Sure enough, the screen displayed three missed calls. It also declared the phone was on silent. Groaning, Ryan changed the setting. "You know I switched servers and got a new number. I've been putting my phone on silent at night so no calls for the other person who had this number wake me up. I promise, whoever Doug O'Malley is, he never sleeps. I forgot to change the setting," he explained and wondered how he could even think about something as mundane as a cell phone when his son was missing.

Every horror story splayed across TV in the last few months slammed into his mind. Child after child missing, never to be heard from again. The very thought made Ryan want to tear out his hair.

"I've got to go over there!" he shouted and ran to his truck.

"No!" Jack's hard fingers ate into his arm. "I'll take you!" he demanded. "You're in no shape to drive."

The trip to Shelly's country home blurred like a journey through a bad dream. Hunched forward, Ryan vacillated between dismay and disbelief. The disbelief escalated when he baled out of Jack's truck and spotted Sean's bicycle propped against the railed porch.

There must have been some mistake, he thought. *Everything looks too normal. How could this have happened near such a small town? They've probably found Sean in the backyard, hiding in his tree house.*

Then he remembered the hole cut in the window, and all his hopes crumbled. His dismay escalating to terror, Ryan took the porch steps two at a time. As he knocked on the door, Jack's boots thumped the planking behind him. He'd barely completed two knocks when a grim-faced officer opened it. Ryan knew Payton well enough to figure that his troubled gaze sliding to Jack probably held all manner of unspoken messages.

Ryan stepped inside, spotted Shelly, and stopped caring what Payton might be communicating. Shelly looked up at Ryan from her perch on the sofa's edge. Her reddened eyes and pale face reflected the agony tearing Ryan's soul.

Ryan rushed across the immaculate living room with no other thought than holding Shelly. But when he was within five feet of his goal, Tim Aldridge stepped between them.

"Here, sweetheart," Tim crooned, "ice water, just like you asked." He settled next to Shelly, draped his arm around her shoulders, and pulled her close. She eagerly gulped the water and then lowered her head to his shoulder.

Tim glanced up and spotted Ryan. "Oh, hi," he stated, his blue eyes troubled. "They said you'd be here soon."

"Yeah," Ryan replied. He doubled his fists and turned to face his brother, who jerked his head toward the hallway.

After a final glance toward Shelly, Ryan followed his brother. Halfway down the hall, Jack hung a left and entered Sean's room. Ryan rushed toward the opened window and scanned the area, now dusted with dark powder.

"Did they find any prints?" he asked.

"*Nada,*" Jack replied. "You know how it is. We don't find prints more often than we do."

"Who dusted?"

"Payton."

"Are you sure he was thorough?" The desperation in Ryan's soul oozed from his words.

Jack's strong hand on his shoulder did little to ease his anxiety. Ryan whipped around and grabbed Jack's arm. "You've got to dust again!"

"Ryan . . . it's *Payton*," Jack insisted and shook his head. "He never misses a thing."

Ryan rammed his fingers into his hair and tugged until his scalp protested. His gaze landed on Sean's baseball glove, lying on the nightstand. He stepped forward, picked it up, and ran his fingers over the laces. The new leather smell reminded him of Friday night, when he'd resented the glove because it linked Sean to Tim Aldridge. Now Ryan could only cherish it. He plopped onto the side of Sean's bed while the brutal reality of his son's abduction burned a hole in his soul.

"Ryan? Ryan!" Jack's firm voice floated from far away, but it was so persistent, Ryan finally glanced up.

Jack hovered over him, his face as compassionate as it was grim. "The reason I called you in here . . . we need to know if you can think of anyone, I mean *anyone,* who might want to kidnap Sean. And is there anything—*anything at all*—in here that might give us a clue? Shelly's too shocked to do more than cry. She keeps blaming herself—saying something about a sleep aid." He squinted and waved aside the confusing comment. "She's not able to focus long enough to pinpoint whether or not there's a clue right under our noses."

"I-I don't know either." Ryan scanned the room. "You know I almost never come into Sean's room here. I just pick him up and . . . and he has his own room at my place."

"I know, but—"

Ryan stood and laid aside Sean's glove. "What about outside? Were there any clues out there?"

"Only a foot print."

"How big?"

"The size of Shelly's. Could have been Shelly's. She did manage to say she's been working on the flower bed outside the window."

Ryan walked the room's perimeter, searching for anything that might strike him as odd. But all that was out of place was his son's train, lying near the toy box. "I just can't believe someone broke in exactly when the alarm system was down," he worried. "It's almost like, whoever it was—they *knew* . . ."

"That's exactly what we're thinking," Jack said. "Do you have any idea? Did you mention that the system was down to anyone, or—"

"No!" Ryan erupted. "Absolutely not! I only found out Friday night myself!"

"Dena," Shelly's husky voice floated into the room.

Ryan whipped around to spot her leaning against the doorframe like a pale lily wilting in a rain storm.

"Dena?" Jack repeated. "Isn't that—"

"Sean's birth mother," Ryan croaked, his body going rigid.

Jack stepped toward Shelly. "Isn't she—"

"Unstable—yes," Ryan finished, his mind whirling with the possibilities. They'd feared she might one day regain her equilibrium and try to create problems, despite the fact that she'd signed a written agreement to remain out of Sean's life until he was an adult. Shelly's parents had also promised to play buffer and help protect Sean from Dena.

Ryan balled his fist and asked, "Have you seen her lately?"

"Yes. She was at Mom and Dad's Friday night when I got there. I was shocked when I walked in and saw her."

"Why didn't they call and tell you she was there?" Ryan demanded. "You could have waited until she left."

Shaking her head from side to side, Shelly gulped for composure.

"Stop yelling at her!" Tim Aldridge appeared behind Shelly and placed his hands on her shoulders. "She's under enough pressure as it is, without—"

"I'm not yelling!" Ryan bellowed and focused on Jack. "Do I sound like I'm yelling?"

Jack rubbed at his temple and mentioned something about pleading the fifth.

"Well, if I'm loud, it's not on purpose," Ryan defended and glowered at Tim. "I'm just upset! Wouldn't *you* be if your son was missing?"

"Sean is nearly my stepson," Tim replied. "And yes, I'm upset. I'm distraught! But I'm not yelling at Shelly!"

"He doesn't mean to be . . ." Shelly whispered. "He always gets like this when—when . . ." She peered up at her fiancé and then back at Ryan with a silent understanding that Ryan hadn't expected.

Sighing, he rubbed his face and willed himself to lower his volume. However, seeing Tim comforting Shelly nearly made him start yelling all over again.

"So did Dena *see* Sean?" Ryan asked in a gentler tone.

"Yes," Shelly answered. "He rushed in before I even noticed she was there. Then—then, she was introducing herself. And she seemed somewhat normal," she explained before more words tumbled out. "Mom told me later that Dena said she was on medication a-again. Mom was so happy; happier than I-I've seen in years. I hated to say anything about my doubts"—Shelly shrugged—"because Mom hasn't seen Dena in five years. She had even begun to think maybe she was . . . well, dead. I didn't want to even hint that Dena might have been lying or maybe had an ulterior motive, but I wondered. Now . . . now . . . now . . ." She focused on Sean's bed and then covered her face with her hands.

"I should have been more alert!" she wailed against her palms. "If I hadn't taken that sleep aid, I probably would have heard them. What if Sean cried out for me and I never even heard—"

"You can't blame yourself, Shelly," Jack soothed.

"Shelly, don't . . . don't . . ." Ryan added and stopped himself from moving closer. "There's no guarantee you'd have heard anything even if you hadn't taken the sleep aid. You know how deep you can sleep."

His gaze met Tim's, and the dentist didn't hide his irritation at Ryan's reference to their former marriage.

After a hard bite on the end of his tongue, Ryan waited until Shelly calmed again. She was stroking her face with a tissue when he said, "Did you by chance talk about your alarm system being down in front of Dena?"

Shelly helplessly gazed up at Ryan and silently begged him to make all this go away. "Dad and I talked about it on the back porch. I can't—can't remember where Dena was then!"

Ryan shared a knowing glance with Jack, and some sixth sense told him Sean hadn't been nabbed by a child trafficker. But considering Dena's background—everything from thievery to prostitution to drug abuse—Ryan feared Sean wasn't much better off with his birth mother.

"Do you have the make and model of her car?" Jack asked.

"I don't remember." Shelly buried her face against Tim's shoulder. "The car was in the driveway, but I barely paid attention to what it was. Maybe Mom or Dad could—could—"

"Can you give me their number?" Jack asked.

"I have it. Here in my cell," Tim offered while Ryan was reaching for his own phone. He'd never deleted Shelly's parents' number because they had to communicate when shuffling Sean—especially at holidays.

Ryan watched as Tim passed his phone to Jack . . . merely one more indicator that the man really was on the verge of claiming Ryan's wife and child as his own. "All you have to do is press send," Tim added, and Ryan wished the guy at least had a thread of the scoundrel in him. Tim would have been much easier to detest if he weren't as levelheaded and honorable as he appeared. But then, a scoundrel was the last kind of person Ryan would want for his son's stepfather. If Shelly's marriage to him was inevitable, at least he did seem to care for Sean. That truth strangely comforted Ryan, and he didn't try to sort through why. This wasn't the time or place to even try.

In the face of Shelly's sorrow, a new wave of grief hit Ryan; and this time, a thread of guilt accompanied it. He had no one to blame but himself. If he hadn't played the jerk, he and Shelly would have never divorced—and he would have been at the house last night. And last week, he'd have fixed the alarm system himself or arranged for a repairman the same day it went down. There would have been no lag in service. Sean would be in Sunday school by now, enjoying his friends just like he did every Sunday.

"I'm so sorry this has happened, Shelly," Ryan uttered. "You're blaming yourself, but the real blame rests with *me*."

Shelly lifted her gaze. Confusion flickered in her reddened eyes; a second of realization followed. She shook her head and lifted a hand, as if to reach out to him. "It's not your fault, Ryan."

"It's neither of your faults," Jack injected and pressed a button on the cell phone.

"If only I'd been here—" Ryan stopped and felt Tim's ire rising. He focused on his wife's fiancé. Tim's eyes had gone icy hard, although his face remained impassive.

No telling what Shelly's told him about me, Ryan thought and averted his gaze.

Shelly snuggled back into the crook of Tim's arm, and he jerked his head toward the living room. "I'm going to take her back in there. Just let us know what you find out."

"Will do." Jack nodded. "Hello, Mrs. Brunswick?"

Ryan focused on his brother and waited while Jack broke the news. An anxious mask covered his face. Finally, Jack shook his head and extended the phone to Ryan. "She's going berserk," he explained. "Maybe you can . . ."

After accepting the phone, Ryan wasted no time breaking through Maggie's reaction. While he understood her horror and the need to release her emotions, he also knew every second counted.

"Maggie! Maggie!" Ryan stated.

"R-Ryan?" she stammered. "Is that you?"

"Yes, it's me. Listen, Maggie, we don't know for sure, but we think Dena might be the one who—"

"Dena! That would be so much better than—than . . . ohhhhh, my poor baby boy!" her wail ushered in a new wave of hysterics.

Even though Sean was eight, he was still Maggie's "baby boy." In the past, Ryan had wondered if she'd call him "baby boy" until he was thirty. But now, Ryan heartily sympathized with her endearment. It seemed only yesterday that he'd held a tiny Sean in a newborn's blanket. The years had zoomed by. In what felt like a few months, Sean had gone from toddler to second-grader.

Now he was gone.

Ryan pressed his fingertips against his temple as his own phone indicated an incoming call. He dug the cell out of his pocket, checked the screen, noted his pastor's name, and extended his phone to Jack.

"He's wondering where I am," Ryan whispered. "Tell him what's going on." He turned his back on Jack and focused on the conversation at hand. "Listen, Maggie!" he commanded. "Is Daryl there?"

"Yes, oh yes. He's right—right here!"

Daryl's deep voice wobbled over the line with an uncertain greeting, and Ryan began rushing through his request before Daryl lost composure as well. "Sean's been kidnapped. We're thinking Dena, maybe. Do you know if she heard you and Shelly talking about the alarm system being down? And do you have the make and model of her car?"

"I-I don't know what she heard. We talked—talked about the alarm system on the porch. The car she was driving was my old one.

I gave it to her five years ago—right before she disappeared. It's a 2003 Toyota Corolla." The aging gentleman's voice broke.

"Yes, I remember that now," Ryan acknowledged. When they gave the car to Dena, Shelly had been irritated because her parents never could say no to her sister. They'd just paid off the car when Dena asked for it. The Brunswicks had acquiesced, hoping the vehicle would give her the transportation to get a job, which she vowed to do since she was taking her medicine. But the car only helped Dena leave the area, and she never looked back. Once again, the youngest daughter had taken advantage of her parents, and Shelly had fumed for months.

"Do you by chance have any records of the license plate number?" Ryan questioned.

"I'll look. Yes, I'm sure I must have it in my home safe. I keep all old records there. But wait! They issued a new license plate when it was put in her name. I don't think I have that one," he said, his claim holding the grief of decades.

"That's not a problem," Ryan assured. "If we have the old license number, we can cross reference to the new one. We'll also be issuing an Amber Alert, pronto. I'm sure the FBI will get involved—especially if there's any chance at all Dena could go across state lines. With them in the mix, hopefully we'll have Sean back by tomorrow."

"Tomorrow?" Daryl echoed with a hopeful tenor.

"No promises," Ryan admitted. "Only hopes."

Faint sobbing pierced Dena's dreams, marred by gyrating images splayed across her mind. This time, the images involved childbirth . . . the labor, the gut-wrenching pain, the scream of a newborn. As she swam closer to consciousness, the infant's crying took on the tenure of an older child.

She emerged from sleep like a swimmer erupting from an ocean abyss. Her eyes snapped open, and she stared at the unfamiliar ceiling in an attempt to recall her location. The child's crying grew more persistent, more shrill, more annoying, until Dena pressed at her ears and screamed, "Stop it! Stop it! Just stop it! Or I'll tape your mouth shut again!"

The crying ceased.

Dena sat straight up. Her gaze darting around the room, she searched for the boy who called her Aunt Dena, no matter how many times she told him she was his mother. Still wearing the pajamas she'd nabbed him in, he cowered on the corner pallet. He'd refused to sleep in the bed with her, and she'd refused to prepare another bed for him. So he'd made himself a pallet out of some towels he found in the cabin's bathroom. The whole time he whined about wanting his mom. Now the whines had turned into a new onslaught of sobs.

When she broke into Sean's room in the wee hours, Dena came armed with a roll of duct tape she'd filched from her father's toolshed. After creeping to Sean's bedside, she'd pressed a piece of tape over his mouth while he was sleeping. He drowsily pawed at the tape until Dena clasped his wrists and strapped them together. That's when he started kicking at her. Once she pulled him to his feet, Sean had fought all the way out the front door. Of course, his resistance was hindered by his fettered arms. Nevertheless, he'd proven a valiant rebel until Dena finally dragged him into the car and locked him in the backseat. The child safety lock had never proved more convenient.

Now she thought about the roll of tape she'd tossed on the car's floorboard and considered retrieving it. But she was too sleepy to exert the effort and opted for verbal intimidation.

"What is it you want?" Dena barked and reached for her pack of cigarettes on the nearby dresser.

"I'm hungry," Sean whimpered. "My stomach hurts." He lay on his side and hugged his midsection.

Dena's stomach grumbled as well. The bright sunshine blasting the bedroom insisted noon was near. With trembling fingers, Dena placed the cigarette between her unsteady lips and lit it. The first draw promised to abate her hunger and steady her nerves if only she indulged in several more.

"Why don't you go see what you can find in the kitchen?" she said, pointing down the hallway. "I'm sure there's some crackers or something in there. There always is."

Sniffling, Sean stood and eased toward the doorway like a child lost in a dark forest.

"There's nobody here but us," Dena said, her hoarse voice softening.

With a worried glance toward her, he finally dashed for the kitchen.

Dena rubbed her eyes and then reached for her purse sitting on the floor. She pulled out a silver flask and eagerly anticipated the first shots of the day. After a couple of throat-burning sips, she tried to make sense of her jumbled thoughts.

She hadn't planned to take Sean when she arrived at her parents'. But the compulsion to kidnap her son had grown with each minute she was in his presence. Every time Shelly stroked Sean's hair or mumbled an endearment, Dena's resolve increased. When she heard Shelly say her alarm system was down, that was Dena's final encouragement.

She glanced at the inside of her left arm where the name Rex was tattooed in blue cursive. Her latest boyfriend had taught her numerous ways to silently enter houses. He'd said Dena was an excellent student, small enough to slip through windows and tight places. For several years, they'd supported themselves and their habits by taking what they wanted when they wanted from whom they wanted. Then Rex got caught in a drug sting. When Dena ran out of money, she came back home.

Normally, Dena was an "out of sight, out of mind" kind of woman, but she missed Rex and his sister Lila, who lived in Odessa. Dena and Lila had connected in a way that she'd never connected with her own sister. For years, Dena hadn't given Shelly more than a passing thought. But seeing her last night had ignited the old resentment, bred from growing up with a "perfect" elder sister.

Shelly always had everything any woman could want . . . looks, brains, personality. The one thing Dena could do that Shelly couldn't was have children. So Shelly had taken Dena's child.

"Selfish witch," she whispered. After another draw on her cigarette, she reveled in the victory of outsmarting Shelly. *Sean belongs to me, not her*, she thought. *And she'll never get him back.*

Standing, Dena searched for last night's ash tray and found it beneath a T-shirt she'd pulled out of her overnight bag. Ironically, she recalled Shelly giving it to her one Christmas. She tossed the T-shirt on the floor. By the time the cigarette was half gone and she'd downed more whiskey, Dena began to feel as if she could make the drive that would assure she kept Sean forever. While her appetite had diminished, her stomach's subdued growl still insisted she find some food. She didn't know what food might be in the kitchen, but Dena certainly didn't want to prepare anything.

The image of Sean barging into her parents' house carrying a McDonald's cup flashed across her mind. The memory of the Sulphur Springs McDonald's followed, and she vaguely recalled a McDonald's about fifteen minutes from her parents' cabin.

After cramming the cigarette butt into the ash tray, Dena walked toward the kitchen. She spotted Sean gazing into the open refrigerator, empty except for a few jars of condiments.

"Wanta go to McDonald's?" Dena asked.

Sean jumped, slammed the refrigerator door, and whirled to face her. His distrusting gaze mingled with confusion.

"Well?" she prompted and smiled.

Sean looked down and mumbled something she couldn't understand.

Dena's mind spun. "Speak up," she snapped. "I'm tryin' to be nice, here. The least you can do is talk loud enough for me to hear you."

"Yes," he said with a nod.

"Okay, then let's go!" She motioned to the front door and then moved back toward the hallway. "But first, le' me get my keys and purse."

"But I'm in my pajamas," he said, glancing down at the flannel cloth covered in images of a space toy.

"So," Dena said. "That's all you have to wear right now. We'll buy some more clothes today. I found some money at my mom's house." She looked down at her T-shirt and sweats and didn't care that they were rumpled from a night's sleep.

Sean's eyes clouded with more uncertainties, but he finally stepped away from the refrigerator.

"Go on into the living room. I'll be there as soon as I grab my purse, okay?"

He nodded.

When Dena snatched up her handbag, her flask tipped out and plopped onto the bed. She unscrewed the lid and downed another swallow in a toast to herself. "I'm going to be a great mother," she said and smiled.

CHAPTER THREE

Shelly awoke with a start and stared around the bedroom to try to orient herself. Autumn sunshine sliced through the blinds, creating a gauzy light that hung in the shadows.

After her parents had arrived, they suggested that Shelly should lie down and rest, something Tim had been trying to convince her of for hours. Despite being certain she could never nap, Shelly had fallen into a deep sleep by three P.M. She checked the digital clock to see that she'd slept two hours.

"Sean," Shelly whispered and squeezed her puffy eyes tight as a wave of sorrow threatened to consume her. Her parents had arrived at one o'clock, still with no word on Dena—even after they'd determined the license plate number on her car.

Earlier, when Payton had left to research the license number and post the Amber Alert, Tim, Ryan, and Jack had stepped onto the porch, supposedly out of earshot. But still, Shelly heard what Jack said: "I don't want to tell Shelly this, but if Dena is the kidnapper she's had time to nearly make it to the Mexico border. If she does go into Mexico . . ." He'd left the obvious unsaid.

"What about passports?" Tim had asked. "I know Dena could have easily arranged hers, but what about Sean's?"

"Fake passports can be bought," Ryan had grimly claimed.

At that point, Shelly had covered her ears and tried to force out the reality that she might never see her son again.

Now she covered her head with the cool sheet and wished she could merge with the shadows and disappear. Anything would be better than this cavity of dread threatening to swallow her alive—and her pain, which she saw reflected in Ryan's eyes—except, his pain was laced with guilt. For the first time since Ryan made his choices, Shelly had begun to experience only the slightest tinge of pity for him. But she swept aside the emotion as severely as she tossed away the covers and flung her feet out of bed.

None of this was his fault, she thought and began to think she should stop beating herself up over the sleep aid as well. Like Ryan said, she was a deep sleeper. Chances were significant she might not have heard anything, sleep aid or no.

As Shelly made a swift trip to the restroom and exited, she realized that part of Ryan's present guilt might stem from the remorse he felt for abandoning his family in the first place. *I tried to tell you when you left,* she reasoned and relived those nights Sean had cried for his father at bedtime. The boy had lived for the weekends with Ryan, so Shelly had set aside her own feelings and made certain Sean spent ample time with his father. Ryan certainly hadn't scrimped on his child support commitments. More often than not, he even arranged for extra support, especially for needs like school supplies and medical costs.

For a second, just before she entered the kitchen, Shelly was tempted to admire Ryan's efforts . . . but realized that his overpayment might also have been driven by guilt. The insight empowered her to harden her heart anew. He was to blame for their family's split. Shelly couldn't allow herself to forget that. Even though he took his child support seriously, it was a far cry from what he vowed to Shelly when they got married . . . and promised Sean when they'd adopted him.

God had given her a wonderful man in Tim Aldridge. She had no doubt that she could trust Tim on a level that Ryan never deserved. *And Sean adores him*, she added, then remembered she might never see Sean again. The house began a slow spin, and Shelly stopped and grabbed the kitchen counter; tried to will herself not to succumb to the darkness. A low moan echoed from some forlorn soul, and Shelly soon realized the voice was her own.

Someone appeared in the kitchen . . . someone tall and strong and capable . . . someone familiar. When he offered a supportive hand, Shelly blindly grasped for his warmth for the sake of her own sanity. Wrapping her arms around him, she hung on tight until the dizziness eased and the threat of fainting diminished. Eyes closed, Shelly recognized the beat of the heart beneath her ear . . . the warmth of the hands on her back.

"Thank you so much, Tim," she sighed. "I'm afraid I must have gotten up too fast, or something."

Stiffening, Tim pulled away. At a loss, Shelly opened her eyes and gazed up for some explanation, only to realize she wasn't leaning against Tim Aldridge. It was Ryan Mansfield.

Her eyes widened. "Oh! It's you," she squeaked.

"Yeah." Mouth firm, eyes hooded, Ryan pulled from her grasp but stopped and said, "You're not going to pass out on me, are you?"

"No." Shelly shook her head and rubbed at her heating face in an attempt to hide her chagrin. "No, I'm okay now. I just need some ice water." She made an issue of frowning against the pasty taste in her mouth and said, "What are you doing here?" before she realized the words had fallen out. "And where's Tim?" She peered toward the den.

"Don't know. He was gone when I got back about an hour ago. I couldn't stay away," Ryan stated, his claim ringing with an honesty that couldn't have been feigned.

Shelly walked toward the counter to retrieve the drinking glass she'd used earlier, only to be beaten by Ryan. He scooped up the tumbler, filled it with ice and water, and handed it to her before she had time to protest.

"I brought over some chicken salad and other sandwich stuff," he said, pointing toward the dining room table, laden with more food than she and her parents could eat in three meals.

"Thanks, but you shouldn't have." She consumed half the glass of water and relished the icy path it wove to her stomach.

"I know." Ryan lifted his hand. "But like I said, I couldn't stay away—and figured you were hungry."

Fleetingly, Shelly wondered if this feast were also driven by guilt. She studied her ex-husband's face and eyes, detecting no guilt—only haggard worry.

By the time she realized he was staring back, he said, *"What?"*

"What?" she echoed.

"What's the deal? You're staring at me like I'm sprouting horns." He felt the top of his head and attempted a lame grin.

"Sorry. I was just . . . I'm sleepy, not thinking. I don't know. I was just thinking," she babbled and didn't try to explain why she'd contradicted herself. Shelly approached the table and reached for a bag of chips. Her stomach growled, and she wondered how she could succumb to such a human weakness when her child was missing. Nevertheless, her stomach rumbled again, and she realized twenty-four hours had lapsed since she'd last eaten.

Maybe that's why I nearly fainted, she thought and recalled her doctor saying that she suffered from mild hypoglycemia.

She looked down at her rumpled sweatpants and recalled slipping them on after the police left, and that she hadn't taken a shower.

Shelly fingered her unruly hair before munching a salty chip and reaching for the canister of chicken salad.

"Where's Mom and Dad?" she asked and glanced toward the living room.

"They went out back. They were talking about painting Sean's tree house when I got here."

"Oh." Shelly released the chicken salad and collapsed into one of the iron chairs. She placed her elbows on the glass-top table and rested her forehead in her hands. "Dad's been promising Sean he'd finish painting since summer. I guess he wants to have it finished when Sean comes home . . . if—if he *does* come home," she added and dreaded the thought.

"Sean's *going* to come home," Ryan responded. "He's *got* to. I'll go find him myself if I have to."

Shelly now sympathized with her friend and fellow teacher Lori Onasis, whose son drowned last summer. Even though she'd ached for her friend at the funeral, Shelly had not understood what such loss might really feel like—until now. There were no guarantees, no matter what Ryan said. As unbalanced as Dena was, she could have driven the car into a river just for spite. Shelly cringed with the thoughts of planning a funeral.

Oh dear God, she cried, *please let him come back to us unharmed!*

"At least the painting is giving them something therapeutic to do," Ryan stated. The resentment tainting his words crashed into her agony.

Shelly lifted her head and eyed Ryan again. He stood with his back to her, staring out the dining room window. He wore a dark blue sweatshirt and jeans and looked nearly as trim as he had the day they got married. He'd told her that his training to be a highway patrolman had forced him to get fit, and that he never planned to be out of shape again. He'd stuck to the commitment, and Shelly initially enjoyed the envious stares of other females . . . until she realized Ryan was enjoying them too.

"I'd have been glad to finish the job," Ryan continued. "You should have told me."

"You know Dad's usually got all that carpentry stuff under control," Shelly explained.

"He always did have it all under control, didn't he?" Ryan mumbled, crossing his arms.

Shelly stiffened. Their last few arguments before Ryan's affair involved his illogical accusations against Shelly having a fixation of sorts with her parents. Shelly had heatedly denied any such thing and even told Ryan he was crazy. Now Shelly wondered if Ryan might be about to resurrect an old subject that her counselor had dismissed as his attempt to project responsibility for his own behavior onto her and her family. The counselor had also concluded that Ryan was very jealous of Shelly's dad.

However, Shelly wondered if her father was completely innocent of that emotion himself. He'd guarded Shelly with a vengeance from the day Ryan entered her life, and only agreed to their marriage after her mother convinced him that Shelly was going to marry sooner or later anyway.

Shelly sighed and eyed the chips. Her mind was too tired . . . her emotions too ravaged to try to figure it all out. She observed Ryan again and decided not to take any bait he might throw out. She wasn't going to be lured into an argument at a time like this.

She nibbled another chip. When her stomach asked for more, Shelly opened the chicken salad and took in the fresh-made aroma.

"Sorry," Ryan said.

His words were so faint, Shelly glanced up to see if she'd imagined them. But his apologetic expression validated what she heard.

"I shouldn't have mentioned all that business with your folks. This is not the right time or place."

Shelly considered telling him there had never been a right time or place for his false assumptions, but she decided not to. Their marriage was ancient history—just as all the issues surrounding it were. None of it was worth fighting over, especially not with their son missing.

She opened the box of sliced croissants and focused on smearing a dollop of chicken salad on one of them. "Want a sandwich?" she asked, never acknowledging his apology . . . or that other nonsense he'd brought up.

When Ryan didn't respond, she glanced up to see his face had gone tight, his brown eyes intense. "No, that's okay," he said and walked toward the living room. "I'm not hungry right now."

She watched him go and shrugged. "Suit yourself," she said and chalked it up to one of Ryan's moody moments, which he'd had from the start of their relationship. Long before their marriage ended, Shelly ignored the times he'd walked out of the room without an explanation . . . and all the undercurrents that went along with the behavior.

Truck keys in hand, Ryan walked onto the front porch and closed the door. His irritation rose with every step, and he couldn't get away from Shelly soon enough. But when he stomped from the porch, the realization of what had just happened hit him. He stopped and swiveled to face the house as his irritation diminished in the face of amazement.

He and Shelly had just fallen into a milder version of the behavior they'd exhibited before Ryan's affair. After months of arguing, Ryan had become more and more explosive while Shelly grew more and more unresponsive. She finally stopped acknowledging any concerns he voiced or any attempts at apologies. Their marriage deteriorated to the point that their bedroom life was nonexistent. Given Ryan's work schedule, Shelly spent more weekends at her parents' than not; and Ryan began to wonder why she'd ever gotten married if she never planned to leave home.

Unfortunately, his new partner, Arlene Marigold, had been all too willing to listen. By the time Ryan embraced Arlene, he felt so ignored in his marriage his only concern in holding the home together rested on Sean. Then Shelly found the hotel receipt from his and Arlene's weekend together. After the eruption that left her shattered and Ryan defensive, she somehow projected all the blame for their marriage's failure upon him.

Her offer to stay together hinged on the condition that *he* would get counseling. Somehow, Shelly didn't perceive she needed it. Ryan saw the conditions as another dead end on a lifeless marriage. He filed for divorce. Ironically, she went to counseling after the divorce was final. Then, just as Ryan was planning to marry Arlene, God broke in and changed everything.

Ryan had spent the last couple of years turning the other cheek, going the extra mile, and praying for an opportunity to somehow break through to Shelly . . . to make her see that they *could* make their marriage work if they *both* took responsibility for its failure. Even though he still kicked himself for his involvement with Arlene, Ryan hoped Shelly would see his changed heart and the self-control he'd exhibited since his encounter with God. Whether she could see it or not, Ryan had recommitted to being true to her, and he'd stayed by that vow.

Now she was going to marry Tim-the-Dentist. The very thought propelled Ryan to action. He strode toward his truck and paused as he disengaged the automatic lock. Ryan jiggled his keys as a cold breeze nipped his ears and sent a rash of gooseflesh down his neck. The setting sun lengthened shadows and decreased the temperature by the minute. A sweatshirt and jeans no longer proved sufficient against autumn's chill, and did nothing to abate the frigid loneliness in his soul.

He didn't want to leave Shelly this evening. Even though his head told him she was being difficult and it was time to exit, his heart still bade him stay. Ryan turned to face the home they once shared. He figured Tim's home was probably a mansion compared to this one, and that Shelly would most likely move in with him once they married.

Or they'll buy a new house together to commemorate the new marriage, he thought and grimaced. For now, Ryan was tempted to accept defeat. The angle of Shelly's chin when he walked out proved that she was still as blind as ever. He wondered how long it would take Tim-the-Dentist to get tired of being one-upped by her family of origin.

"Maybe he's the kind of guy that it won't bother," Ryan grumbled.

He was unsure what he'd do if they did get married. He was only sure he couldn't live in the same area with Shelly and Tim. Bullard was so small, he'd probably bump into them several times a week—a setup sure to catapult him into continual heartache.

He'd kept praying that something would happen to awaken Shelly to their need for reconciliation—for Sean, if for no one else. When she latched on to him in the kitchen, Ryan's hopes had soared. Shelly had felt so good in his embrace . . . just as she did in his dreams. He'd stopped himself from sighing her name and caressing her hair just as she called him *Tim*. Ryan felt like a fool; his hope that she was finally turning to him for support withered and faded. From what Ryan understood, Shelly and Tim's wedding was scheduled for February, just three short months away. And she showed no signs of wavering.

Squeezing his eyes tight, he once again released the whole thing to God and focused on the reason he was here. His son was missing, and he had to do the best he could to get along with Shelly . . . and maybe even Tim.

Ryan rubbed his eyes, relocked the truck, shoved his keys into his pocket, and trudged back toward the porch. He'd arrived an hour ago to bring dinner and to hang out with Shelly and her folks, simply because he believed this is where he needed to be. Even though his parents had asked him to come to their place, it wasn't the same as being with Shelly.

Jack was hard on the case and had even pulled their other brother, Sonny, into the middle of it. A sought-after private eye, Sonny promised Ryan he'd find Sean or die trying. The FBI was allowing Jack and Sonny to be involved only because Jack was the police chief. They'd ordered Ryan to stay out of the investigation, due to his emotional involvement. Obeying that order was the hardest thing Ryan had ever done.

He stepped back up to the porch and determined to get along with Shelly and her parents for the evening. No matter how dysfunctional they were, no matter what happened, they needed each other tonight. Whether Shelly and her parents would ever admit it or not, he saw the need in their eyes. Despite the fact that the paperwork finalized his and Shelly's divorce, Ryan sensed a deep bond remained, which a piece of paper could not sever. They were still a family, no matter how much Shelly might love Tim.

As he reached for the front door, his phone emitted a series of short beeps. Ryan pulled the cell from his pocket and eyed a number he didn't recognize. Not wanting to be bothered, he nearly pressed the ignore button, but something inside insisted he shouldn't. While uttering his greeting, he half expected a solicitation and prepared to disconnect the call.

But the voice that floated over the line was the one voice Ryan would have given his life to hear. "Dad!" Sean exclaimed.

CHAPTER FOUR

S ean!" A hot shiver assaulted Ryan. "Sean! Where are you?"

"Dad! Aunt Dena came this morning—"

"Yes, that's what we thought," Ryan bellowed and then forced his voice to a more coaxing tone. "Listen, champ, can you tell me where you—"

"I *told* her I want to go home, but she—but she said, 'No,'" he whined. "I'm tired, Daddy. If I give the phone to her, would you please tell her to t-take me back home?"

"No—don't give the phone to Dena!" Ryan commanded and paced the porch. "Just tell me where you are."

"I'm in the boy's bathroom," Sean explained.

"Yes, but *where*?"

"At McDonald's."

A thump echoed over the line, and Sean went silent before exclaiming, "Aunt Dena! You can't come in the boy's bathroom!"

"How did you get my phone?" a muffled voice demanded before the call was disconnected.

Trembling, Ryan looked at his phone's screen to confirm he'd lost the call. Biting back an edict, he swiveled toward the door, only to encounter Shelly's haunted-eyed stare. Clutching her throat, she said, "That was Sean, wasn't it?"

"Yes," Ryan garbled out and managed a nod.

The second Ryan left the house the silence had taken on an eerie nuance that threatened Shelly's sanity. Panic had driven her to run after him to ask him to stay . . . at least until Tim returned or her parents tired of the paint job. By some glitch of logic, she'd managed to stop herself at the living room window. Instead of acting on impulse, she'd prayed for God to change Ryan's mind about leaving until he turned back and walked to the porch. Any company—even that of her difficult ex-husband—was better than the silence. Besides, they were Sean's parents. They'd always share that bond, even if they shared nothing else.

When she heard Ryan call Sean's name, Shelly had scrambled to the door, flung it open, and held her breath as she listened to her ex-husband talking with their son.

Now Ryan stared at her in a silent stupor, which reflected Shelly's own emotions. "Remember last year when I made him memorize our numbers and learn how to text, in case—"

Her eyes stinging, she nodded. "Did he tell you where—"

Ryan shook his head and croaked, "No. All he knew was that he was at a McDonald's in the men's room. He called from Dena's phone. I know it was her phone because he told her she couldn't come in the boy's bathroom and then I heard her ask him where he got her phone before the call ended."

"Dena never did mind crossing boundaries to get what she wanted." Shelly balled her fists as she recalled her sister stealing her money for drugs . . . or whatever else she happened to want. Now she'd gone from stealing money to stealing Sean.

"I figure, she let him use the restroom and then stood waiting outside the door," Ryan said.

"His voice really carries. She probably heard him talking to you through the door."

A new silence settled upon them as Shelly peered into Ryan's soul. His deep brown eyes reflected the same dread gripping her heart.

Dena had destroyed so many pivotal moments in Shelly's life, she'd almost lost count. The night she graduated high school with honors, Dena had been trying to commit suicide. Their parents had been called from the ceremony to the ER. When Shelly graduated college, Dena was being admitted for her first stay in a drug rehab clinic. Shelly told her parents not to worry about her graduation. By that point, Ryan was in her life—and he'd been so proud of her Magna Cum Laude. Then the night before she and Ryan got married, Dena got drunk and crashed their rehearsal. Shortly after that, Dena received her first diagnosis of schizophrenia. The medication seemed able to stabilize her, for a while. Then she got pregnant with Sean.

The second Shelly laid eyes on the baby, she knew she couldn't let Dena place him for adoption with just anyone. Since she and Ryan had already applied to adopt with an agency, they decided to adopt Sean instead—only with the stipulation that Dena would stay out of his life. Dena signed off all rights and never seemed to regret it. Shelly's parents had been delighted with the adoption. And only after it was final did Shelly learn they'd considered adopting Sean as well.

Somehow, having Sean had eased the resentment that had built up in Shelly through the years. When Shelly learned she couldn't have children, Sean became a symbolic gift that made up for all she'd stolen. Now, Dena had stolen Sean.

A sob welled up within Shelly. She covered her face with her hands and tried to suppress the emotion that would not be denied. Ryan's firm grip on her shoulder was all that kept Shelly from collapsing.

"We'll find them," he vowed, his voice cracking. "We've got to."

Shelly lifted her gaze. Even the haze of her sorrow couldn't hide Ryan's tears.

"If she hurts him, I'll—I'll . . ." Shelly stammered.

"I'm not worried about her hurting him intentionally," Ryan said and rubbed at his haggard eyes.

"You don't know Dena like I do!" Shelly said. "She *hates* me! She's been eaten up with jealousy almost since she was born. I wouldn't put it past her to hurt Sean—just to get at me."

"I'm more worried about a car wreck or her not being found," Ryan said, as if Shelly had never mentioned her worries.

"Dena is a *very unpredictable* person," Shelly reiterated with more force. "You haven't been around her as much as I have. I'm telling you, she could get mad at Sean and—and burn him with a cigarette or something as punishment."

Ryan's mouth went hard. "I need to call Jack." He pressed a button on his phone and placed it against his ear. "If her phone is a newer one with a GPS tracking system, the signal will be on record, and they can tell us where the call came from in a couple of hours."

"And what if it isn't a newer phone?" she questioned. "What if it's an older phone?"

A debate played across Ryan's features until, finally, he bit out the hard facts: "It could take days or weeks. And by then—"

"She'd be out of the region?"

He nodded and said, "Hello, Jack?"

As Ryan detailed the facts to his brother, Shelly's stomach rolled anew. The lightheadedness returned. She'd left the chicken salad on the table when Ryan walked out, and still had yet to take a bite. She leaned against the doorjamb, stiffened her knees, and stopped herself from reaching for Ryan, again. She had a fiancé now. Shelly didn't need to be clinging to her ex-husband.

Gripping the cell phone, Sonny Mansfield talked with Jack and paced the garage apartment they'd converted to an office after his and Tanya's marriage last summer. They'd decided to sell his small home and buy the house she was leasing. It was bigger, and the garage apartment gave Sonny a separate space for his private eye business. Tonight, he'd sequestered himself away to work on finding Sean. He and Jack had been on the phone with officials nonstop since early afternoon.

Because Jack was the chief of police, the FBI had waved their usual ban on working with a crime victim's family members. Jack had mentioned something about the FBI having to work with him on other cases after this investigation and both sides needed to keep relations positive for the future. Since the FBI knew Jack and Sonny wanted to be in the big middle of it, they acquiesced, but firmly drew the line on Ryan. He was too close emotionally to make logical decisions. As things stood, Sonny was hard-pressed not to give way to emotions, but he knew he had to stay lucid . . . for Sean.

The latest development in the case involved Sean's phone call. "All I know is it's a McDonald's," Jack said. "Could be anywhere between here and the other side of Oklahoma City or Little Rock or Houston or Ft. Worth. I don't know what town; and according to the stats they've gotten, it's not a newer phone with a GPS tracking system, and it might take days or weeks to trace the location. By then, Dena probably won't even be in that same region."

"Think, think, think," Sonny commanded himself while tapping his forehead with his fingertips. "Something's bugging me about this," he said. "Like there's something in the back of my mind trying to dig its way out."

"Could be a long dig," Jack drawled.

"Ha, ha, ha." Sonny stopped pacing. Yanking out his desk chair, he plopped down. "McDonald's . . . McDonald's . . . McDonald's . . ." He closed his eyes and tried to pull up the memory that swam close to the surface of his consciousness.

When the memory flitted away again, Sonny opened his eyes and said, "I guess Ryan gave you Dena's number from his caller ID?"

"Got it," Jack said. "Ryan and I have both tried to call it and we get no answer—only a prefab voice mail. Last time I called, there was an announcement that the person at that number wasn't available. That probably means she's turned off the phone."

"Did someone text an offer to reduce charges if she'll just return Sean?"

"Done within an hour of getting Sean's call," Jack confirmed. "No response. But we're going to keep trying."

"Man, I wish I could remember what's bugging me." Sonny smacked the desk corner. "It's something to do with McDonald's."

"So I've heard," Jack drawled. "Should I hang on or wait for you to call me back?" he asked before Bonnie's tiny voice floated from the background, "Daddy Jack, when are you coming ta read ta me?"

"I promised Bonnie I'd read a book to her before I left for the station again," Jack explained.

"Go ahead and read," Sonny said. "I'm going to eat a bite with Coty and Tanya and then head to the station myself."

"Good," Jack said. "I don't know what in the world else we can do right now, but I just feel like we need to be ready, just in case."

Sonny stood. "Right. I'll call you if I remember the McDonald's connection."

"Okay. Oh yeah, and one other thing. Mom seems to have calmed some this morning."

"Good," Sonny said. "I'm afraid she's going to worry herself into a heart attack."

"That's what Dad said," Jack confirmed. "Could you and Tanya check on them later this evening? If you take today, Charli and I can take tomorrow."

"Sure thing," Sonny agreed. Even though at this point their parents weren't fragile by any means, they did have their medical issues. The last thing their mom needed right now was to land in ICU because of another heart attack.

As he hung up, Sonny glanced toward the family photo rising from the mountains of clutter like a beacon of order out of chaos. He stroked the image of his son, as dark and petite as Sonny was tall and fair. Given Tanya's red hair and translucent skin, no one would ever mistake Coty for their biological son, but they didn't care. They were a family. The photographer had snapped the shot when Sonny and Tanya had been laughing at something Coty said. They were gazing at their son while he smiled up at them. The picture captured the joy with which God had blessed their family from the day Sonny and Tanya said, "I do."

Three years ago, Sonny would have never imagined that both he and Jack would marry women with children and both be full-time fathers. Tanya had adopted her son from Korea before she ever met Sonny. Now Coty was soon to be Sonny's legally adopted son as well, once the paperwork was finalized next month. Four-year-old Coty had so twined his way around his new daddy's heart that Sonny couldn't imagine a deranged kidnapper nabbing him. Relative or no, the very idea left Sonny's mind spinning.

He'd lost his first son when his girlfriend Karen released the baby for adoption without ever telling Sonny. Of course, Sonny couldn't have stopped her because he never even knew she was pregnant. The loss of his child had haunted him for more than a decade. Now he sensed some peace on the whole issue and, over the last month, had begun the process of finding his son. He repeatedly attempted to call his former girlfriend even though he'd learned a decade ago that the only way the birth parents could communicate with their child would be if he contacted the adoption agency first. All the parents could do was leave information on how to be reached.

Since Karen lied about the circumstances of her pregnancy and didn't designate a father at the time of adoption, the agency possessed no evidence that Sonny was the father. Therefore, Sonny wouldn't be allowed to place his name and information in his son's file unless

Karen signed an affidavit of his identity and relation to the child. Getting Karen to admit that she'd lied to the agency might prove to be an insurmountable obstacle. So far, she hadn't bothered to return his calls.

Nevertheless, Sonny still held on to a chance of meeting his son one day. But if Dena was as unbalanced as her family indicated, and if she disappeared for good, Ryan might never see Sean again. Sonny ached for Ryan even more than he ached for himself.

He walked across the aging apartment's creaking floors and caught himself humming "You've Got a Friend in Me," the theme song from *Toy Story*. Sonny thought of his life in terms of "Before Coty" and "After Coty," which he referenced as "B.C." and "A.C." He wouldn't have hummed the *Toy Story* theme B.C. if someone had held a gun to his head; but A.C.—he not only knew the movie tune but had committed the spin-off books to memory.

When his thoughts turned back to Ryan and Sean, he stopped the humming and frowned. Even absentminded humming seemed like betrayal at such a dark time in their family. Sonny snapped off the light, opened the door, and stepped onto the musty landing that led to the stairs. Despite his straining to search his mind, that elusive clue he was digging for still evaded him.

CHAPTER FIVE

The second Ryan ended the call with Jack, he rushed back into the house to check on Shelly. Her skin tone had gone from pale to pasty. When she mentioned hypoglycemia, Ryan insisted on preparing her a sandwich, despite her protests that Tim was on his way.

Tim's knock at the front door coincided with Ryan's serving Shelly a plate of food and a fresh glass of ice water. His call of "Come in" mingled with Shelly's in a coziness that echoed their years of marriage.

The dentist's expression when he entered would have left Ryan laughing out loud, if not for the impropriety of expressing the hilarity. The guy's blue eyes widened, his face reddened, and he issued Ryan a silent challenge that would have involved a dual to the death were they Renaissance men.

When Shelly motioned for Tim to sit by her on the couch, her engagement ring twinkled—a confirmation of where her loyalty lay. Tim's expression softened as Ryan's gut hardened.

"I'm so glad you're back," Shelly breathed, and Tim hurried to her side. Only then did Ryan notice the bag of food Tim carried, with the words "Olive Garden" on the side. The aroma of a hot meal filled the room and rivaled Ryan's offering of sandwiches and chips.

"I went to Tyler and got Olive Garden," he explained and pointed to the bag. "Apricot chicken, your favorite."

Shelly took a bite of Ryan's sandwich anyway, then nodded her approval. "I'll take it," she said after a swallow. "I'm starving. I haven't eaten since last night and I almost fainted twice. Remember, I told you the doctor says he thinks it's hypoglycemia."

"Yes." Tim nodded. "I was worried about your not eating. That's why I brought dinner. There's more in the car. I got enough for your parents, too."

"Thank you so much, Tim." She laid aside the plate Ryan had prepared and eagerly accepted the Styrofoam box stuffed with food. "You're the most thoughtful man I ever met," she added before briefly resting her head on his shoulder.

Not able to stomach another syllable, Ryan exited the living room and wondered if he'd been in some kind of an idealistic trance when he convinced himself he should stay the evening. *Maybe the decision stemmed more from my needs than from concern for Shelly and her folks,* he thought.

He stopped at the kitchen sink and gazed out to the backyard, where Daryl and Maggie were rinsing paintbrushes in the spray from a water hose. A few feet away, a green tree house boasted a finished paint job. He imagined his father-in-law entering the kitchen and looking at him with a silent, *What are* you *still doing here?*

A new restlessness overtook Ryan. He needed to be *doing* something. Even though the FBI had sternly warned him to stay out of the investigation, the patrolman within insisted that Ryan get in his car and scour the countryside for any signs of Dena and his son.

What would it hurt? he reasoned. *Nobody even has to know. If I spot something that needs reporting, I'll just call Jack. He can report it to the FBI as a tip and leave it at that.*

A sound at the kitchen doorway alerted Ryan that he was not alone. Fully expecting Tim, he braced himself before glancing that way. His expectations were confirmed. The dentist was dressed in the best of gentleman's casual, right down to a pair of loafers that probably cost a couple hundred bucks. Ryan hid his grimace.

"I went out to the car and got the rest." His expression guarded, Tim lifted two more Olive Garden bags. "There's extra here, if you want it." He placed the bags on the table next to Ryan's deli offering. "No, thanks. I'm fine with a sandwich, and I'm going to do good to eat that. My stomach's been in knots all day."

"I can imagine," Tim replied, his tone softening. He even added a sympathetic smile to round off the whole new attitude.

Ryan examined the dentist and wondered what all the friendly-friendly stuff was about.

"I, uh, guess I was a little hard on you earlier today," Tim admitted.

"Oh?" Ryan questioned, trying to remember what he was talking about.

"When you were in Sean's room. You were really upset, and I thought you were yelling at Shelly." Tim shrugged. "I can see why you'd be so emotional. Shelly said she didn't think you meant any harm."

"No, I didn't even realize my voice was raised." Ryan rubbed his face and warily eyed his rival. "Have you ever been married, Tim?" he asked. "Ever had kids?"

Tim shook his head. "No."

"Figures," Ryan mumbled and didn't bother to expound, or even try to figure out why he said that.

A tense silence sprang between them. Finally, Tim spoke again. "Look, I'm trying really hard to be open-minded about . . . everything."

"Such as?" Ryan lifted his eyebrows.

"Well, we're going to have to work together to get along once Sean's back home and when Shelly and I get married. I don't want there to be strife—even though it's all an awkward situation. I'm a Christian man, and it makes a difference."

"So am I," Ryan said and tried not to frown in the face of Tim's surprise. "You mean, Shelly didn't tell you?" he prompted.

"No, I thought—"

"What? That I'm some sort of a heathen?"

"No, not that. It's just—"

"When I blew it in our marriage, I'll admit, at the time I wasn't a Christian. But all that changed a couple of years ago." He eyed his wife's fiancé and couldn't imagine a more peculiar turn of events.

"Do you believe it's God's will for you to marry Shelly, Tim?" Ryan asked, and didn't quite know where the question even came from.

"Yes, of course," he said, the defensive edge back. "Shelly and I both have prayed about it at length. I've waited all these years for the perfect—for the *right* woman. I don't doubt it's God's will for a second."

For the first time, Ryan considered Tim as more than just a rival for Shelly's affection. Tim Aldridge was a man—just like Ryan. He loved the Lord—just like Ryan. And just like Ryan, he believed God wanted him to marry Shelly.

He wondered how it would affect Tim if Shelly were to miraculously decide to reconcile with Ryan.

He'd be devastated, Ryan thought and closed the door on any further considerations. The last thing he needed to do was start sympathizing with Shelly's fiancé. That was simply too weird; but this whole day had been weird. The fact that the two of them were civilly talking in what used to be Ryan's own kitchen only added an odd twist to the day's surreal events.

"I guess I'm going to be shoving off now," Ryan said and rubbed his hands together. "I've done all I can here, and I've got some driving I need to do."

Without a word, Tim stepped aside and allowed Ryan to pass. Ryan sensed Tim's silent response—a near-tangible relief—but didn't cast him another glance.

So much for hanging out here, Ryan thought.

Come on, sweet boy," Sonny called down the hallway. "It's time to go see Grandma and Granddad!"

Four-year-old Coty appeared at the end of the hallway carrying his backpack and wearing a big smile. His pumpkin-colored sweat suit enhanced the glow in his eyes, and Sonny couldn't stop himself from beaming.

Tanya had already left for work, and today was Sonny's day to drive Coty to her parents'. Since Sonny was self-employed, he was able to arrange his schedule some days so that Coty stayed home with him. But today, Sonny was going to be focusing on Ryan's case.

"Are you ready to tear out?" he prompted.

"Weady!" Coty declared and trotted into his father's arms.

Sonny scooped him up. After tickling his tummy, he planted a big kiss on his cheek. "Daddy loves you, honey," he crooned.

Coty squeezed Sonny's neck tight and said, "I love you, too, Daddy!"

After securing the backpack, Sonny trotted toward the living room, mimicking the sound of a horse's hooves, and Coty's gurgling laughter mingled with the cadence of his voice. When they turned the corner and entered the living room, they bumped into the wall and nearly knocked over a brass lamp. With a bellow, Sonny grabbed the lamp before it crashed to the floor. In the lurch, he nearly lost his grip on Coty.

"Whoa, Daddy," Coty commanded as Sonny righted the lamp and struggled to stay afoot.

Chuckling, Sonny couldn't suppress the love welling within. That love had bred a unity in their family that was so great, Sonny had nearly felt guilty a few times . . . especially in the face of Ryan's struggles. He sighed as thoughts of Ryan's current crisis barged through the laughter. Sonny had cleared his schedule today to focus on finding Sean. He patted Coty's back and hurried toward the door.

"Wait, Daddy!" Coty exclaimed, squirming for freedom. "I forgot my Barney book! Grandma is teaching me to read it!"

"Where is it?" Sonny asked and scanned the immaculate living room.

"My room! My room!" Coty declared.

"Well, hurry up!" Sonny deposited his son on the hardwood floor and gave him an encouraging pat on the bottom.

Coty raced toward the hallway, his short legs churning. As Sonny watched him depart, that elusive memory that had nagged at him when he was talking to Jack began to nibble at the corners of his mind. This time, the foggy recollection also included something about Barney. What, he couldn't imagine. Sonny pressed his fingertips against his forehead and again strained for the memory. When Coty appeared in the living room carrying his book, Sonny recalled that Sean had asked him to read a similar book to him one Christmas . . .

Sean had been three the year Shelly's parents invited Ryan's whole family to their cabin outside Sulphur Springs, Texas. The all-pine home was nestled deep in the rich woods and had served as a family getaway for years. Sonny remembered Sean cornering him and asking him to read a Barney book. Until that day, Sonny had never even heard of the purple dinosaur, and Ryan had chided him on needing to "get some culture."

So Sonny, sitting in the recliner near the fireplace, had hoisted Sean onto his lap and read the book. After finishing, Sean announced his next plans—and began coercing Sonny into taking him into Sulphur Springs to get a hamburger at " 'Donald's," his version of McDonald's. Even though Shelly protested that Sean should eat the Christmas Eve meal, replete with turkey, stuffing, and green beans, Ryan had convinced her to let him and Sonny take the boy to get what he wanted.

"It's only Christmas Eve once a year," Ryan had reasoned. "It won't hurt to let him eat what he wants tonight."

Shelly finally agreed, and Sean insisted they ride in "Unc Sonny's" truck. Ryan and Sonny had indulged him that request as well. On the way, Ryan mentioned that he'd been trying to get Shelly to come to the cabin for a weekend getaway . . . just the two of them . . . but she was so busy with her teaching and church involvement, she barely had time to breathe.

"Her mom gave us a key to the family cabin when we got married and said it was here any time we wanted to use it," Ryan had claimed. "We haven't used it once."

Now Sonny realized that Shelly and Ryan had been having marital problems even then. But Sonny shoved all such thoughts from his mind as Coty tugged on his jeans leg. "Come on, Daddy!" he demanded. "We need ta go!"

"Okay, okay," Sonny agreed and hurried into the bright morning on the heels of his son.

When he turned from locking the door, he thought, *There's a McDonald's not far from the Brunswick's cabin. It's a* family *cabin. If Ryan and Shelly have a key, does Dena?*

Dena awoke and gazed at the massive, rock fireplace that dominated the room's east wall. Her pounding head thwarted her attempts to remember where she was. Pulling her thick tongue from the roof of her mouth, she attempted to swallow against the foul taste. She covered her eyes to blot out the painful light and tried to make sense of the myriad of shattered memories cluttering her mind. Finally, one shard grabbed her attention as none other.

"Sean!" She forced herself upward and swung her feet to the floor.

Rubbing her face, Dena gazed around the room. The weak sunlight indicated early morning. That meant Sean must still be in bed.

Yesterday, after leaving a message for Lila in Odessa, Dena had planned to head west. But when she caught Sean with her cell phone, fury had blotted out her plans. By the time they arrived at the department store to purchase his clothing, she'd chastised him to the point of tears. Still livid from his behavior, Dena followed a whim rather than stick to her plans. Spotting a wine sale, she grabbed several bottles, with no care for the consequences.

On the way to the checkout, she'd also thrown some snacks in the buggy because she'd discarded Sean's McDonald's meal for stealing her phone and calling Ryan. Still, he'd wailed for more Mc-Donald's. The crumpled bag now lying on the floor substantiated the vague memory of a repeat trip to the restaurant to order him another meal—this time, at the drive-through. Anything, just to shut up his crying!

Once back at the cabin, Dena hid her cell phone under the couch cushion where she sat with her wine. While Sean busied himself with some art supplies from the corner desk, Dena tried to ease her black mood with the alcohol. When she awoke in the night, she assumed Sean must be asleep on his pallet, so she drank herself to sleep once more.

Standing, she stumbled for the bathroom and fought a wave of nausea and dizziness. By the time she stepped into the bathroom, the nausea had subsided and her jumbled thoughts were leading to one realization: she and Sean needed to get on with their trip. They'd stayed in one place long enough. She'd check her messages.

Even if Lila hadn't responded, Dena would begin the drive toward Odessa anyway.

Thankfully, she had enough money to last them awhile. Dena had found her parents' private stash in the closet's fireproof safe. She'd banked on her father keeping several thousand for emergencies. As always, the lock's combination remained the same as when she lived at home. Taking the money had been as easy this time as it had been the last.

When she exited the bathroom, Dena headed into the bedroom where she and Sean had slept the first night. Fully expecting to see him asleep on his towels, she stared at the empty pallet until her stunned thoughts suggested he might be in the bed. Slowly, she pivoted toward the bed to see nothing but a wad of sheets.

"Sean?" she croaked and waited.

The distant singing of some annoying bird was the only reply.

"Sean!" Dena hollered and lunged into the kitchen. A half-eaten package of cheese crackers and an empty bottle of juice evidenced his earlier presence—but no other sign of Sean remained. Dena lurched toward the dining area, back into the living room, and through the empty house again until she came full circle into the kitchen.

Panting, she pressed her fists against her temples while the room spun. "He's—he's gone!" she rasped.

CHAPTER SIX

A relentless pounding followed by a bell's persistent ring jolted Ryan out of a deep sleep. He jumped and raised himself up on his elbow. A quick glance at his surroundings confirmed he was still sprawled on the couch where he'd crashed early this morning after eating half a bag of Doritos. The chip bag now lay on the floor, beneath the coffee table. His mouth still tasted like nacho cheese and he still wished he had a glass of Coke—just as he did before he propped himself up on the pillows at five A.M. and prayed himself to sleep. He glanced at his watch and confirmed he'd been asleep three whole hours.

The pounding started again. The bell followed. And Ryan eyed the front door. *Not the typical M.O. for the postman*, he thought. And his groggy mind couldn't imagine what could be so urgent.

Then Ryan remembered Sean. He remembered driving the countryside all night, searching for a trace of any clue. He remembered the desperation . . . the loneliness . . . Shelly's last, haunted *Goodbye* before he left. By the time he'd cranked his truck's engine, Ryan had almost convinced himself that Shelly really wanted him to stay. But he'd dashed aside the assumption. Obviously, she'd had Tim. She didn't need Ryan last night—probably not ever again.

"Ryan! Open the door, for cryin' out loud!" Sonny's demand pierced Ryan's thoughts, and he jumped to his feet with only one thought, *Sean! They must have found Sean!*

He stumbled to the door, barely sidestepping the duffle bag stuffed with tennis gear. In his former life, Shelly's constant fussing about his tennis paraphernalia had annoyed him. Now Ryan would give it all up if only she'd let him come home.

Ryan opened the door. "Did they find Sean?" he asked before Sonny had a chance to speak.

"No, not yet." Sonny pressed past Ryan and entered the duplex.

Rubbing his eyes, Ryan snapped the door shut and decided against falling into a disappointed heap.

"I've been trying to call you for ten minutes," Sonny groused. "Is your phone on silent or what?"

Ryan reached for the cell, lying askew on the coffee table. "I decided not to turn off the ringer last night. But I do change it every night, and it looks like I was so out of it when I crashed, I must have changed it anyway." He switched the ringer to loud and said, "So what gives?"

"I *might* have a lead on where Sean is," Sonny said, his eyes wide.

Ryan leaned forward. "Where?"

"Do the Brunswicks still own that family cabin outside Sulphur Springs?"

"As far as I know. What about it?"

"There's a McDonald's nearby. Remember a few years ago when you and Shelly were together—"

"And Daryl and Maggie invited us all up there for Christmas," Ryan finished as Sonny nodded, "and Sean wanted to go to McDonald's . . ."

"Exactly! Didn't you and Shelly have a key when you were married?" he asked.

"Yeah."

"Does Dena have a key as well?"

"Who knows! What does it matter? If she wants in, she can get an axe from the shed and knock out a window." Ryan scurried to get his sneakers, lying near the Doritos bag. "Just give me two minutes!" He snatched up a shoe and rammed his foot inside. "After I get my shoes on, I'm making a pit stop, and then we'll go. It's only an hour-and-a-half away. I can take you right to it."

"Wait!" Sonny held up his hand. "I was going to get Jack and go. You're supposed to stay out of this."

"Try to stop me!" Ryan demanded. "If Sean's there, I might have a better chance of getting him away from Dena anyway. She always liked me. I was the one who talked her into letting us adopt Sean in the first place."

Sonny winced. "I don't know, Ryan. The FBI will *not* be happy campers if I let you get in the big middle of it all. I just came over here to see what you thought about the possibility—"

"Look," Ryan commanded, "Sean is my son!" He rammed his fingertips against his chest. "I've been out combing the countryside all night. I'm already involved, whether the FBI knows it or allows it or not!"

"Well, if you go, I won't be able to call them with the lead because—"

"Fine!" Ryan lifted both hands. "Don't call them! It's probably better for them not to go now anyway. If Dena *is* there and they surround the cabin, then who knows what she'd do. I might be able to go in and sweet talk her and be done with it!"

Sonny rubbed his face and shook his head. "I don't know how you always manage to get me into these fixes."

"What fix? There's no fix! It makes the most sense, and you know it."

"Yeah, but I'm putting my own involvement on the line. If they find out, I'm toast."

"They won't find out," Ryan said. "Besides, it's a long shot anyway. It will give me something to do. If she's not there, there's no loss. If she is there, I'll get Sean. If it makes the FBI mad," he shrugged, "I figure it's better to ask forgiveness than permission." Ryan hurried toward the hallway and wondered if Shelly might want to go with them.

"You know they can have you arrested if you get in the way," Sonny called after him.

"Yeah!" Ryan decided he wasn't even going to think in those terms . . . or tell Sonny he planned to call Shelly. *If I can't pry Sean away from Dena, maybe* she *can,* he thought, but then remembered Shelly's claiming that Dena hated her. Ryan entered his bathroom, shut the door, and decided to let Shelly decide whether or not she wanted to go with them.

If Sonny hollers, so what, he thought and eyed himself in the mirror. Ryan looked like he'd been on a bad camping trip—more stubble than a grizzly, more haggard than a drunk. He toyed with the idea of shaving but decided he didn't have time.

"Oh well," he reasoned. "Shelly and I were married for years. She's seen me at my worst anyway."

Shelly's cell phone rang, and she dove for it on the dining room table. She'd just stepped away from her uneaten bagel breakfast to add hot water to her tepid tea. After a fitful night's sleep, she'd awakened at her usual time of six A.M. and alternated walking the floors with sporadically cleaning house. She jumped with every noise and prayed with every breath. Now the phone was ringing . . . *just* after she'd begged God to *please* let someone call with some news of her son.

A quick glance at the phone's screen indicated Ryan's number. She eagerly pressed the answer button and rasped, "Hello, Ryan? Did you find out something?"

"No, but we may have a lead. Sonny remembered something. Short story is . . . there's a McDonald's in Sulphur Springs, not far from that cabin your parents own on the lake. Remember a few Christmases ago when Sean wanted a Happy Meal on Christmas Eve and Sonny and I took him to get one?"

"Yes, yes, I remember," Shelly said and wadded the paper napkin lying near the saucer.

"We're following a hunch . . . thinking Dena might have gone to the cabin with Sean."

Shelly dropped the napkin and gasped. "Mom told me she gave Dena a key to the cabin. I couldn't believe it! I told her Dena would probably just move in and sponge off her and Dad, but she didn't seem to care. She said Dena was doing so much better, and she wanted her to feel part of the family, just like me. So she gave it to her!"

The line was silent.

"Ryan?" Shelly prompted.

"I'm here," he said. "Do you think your parents will *ever learn*, Shelly? They've spent their life savings trying to help her. They even remortgaged their house to pay her legal fees, and she does nothing but continue to take advantage of them. Now she's nabbed Sean, and it looks like she's headed to the family cabin with him! *Why* did your mother give her that key?"

"I don't know," Shelly bellowed. "I agree with you. Like I said, I tried to tell Mom, but she insisted she'd done the right thing!"

Ryan went silent again. This time, Shelly checked the screen to see if she was still connected.

"Sorry I raised my voice," he finally said. "It's just so frustrating."

"Hey, I was yelling too," Shelly replied with a mild smile. "I guess we *can* agree on something, right?"

"Yeah. Your sister is a leech and your parents help her reattach and suck the blood out of them every time she shows back up."

"You always did have a way with words," Shelly acknowledged, "and that just about perfectly paints the picture."

"The reason I was calling—Sonny and I are going to the cabin. Do you want to go?"

"Yes!" Shelly agreed. "I called the principal last night and told him I wasn't going to be able to teach today. The Amber Alert had hit the media, and he already knew. He told me to take off all week if I need to. I just couldn't work," Shelly choked out. "I can barely focus long enough to eat."

"I know, I know," Ryan replied. "I was out driving most the night—looking for any clue. I didn't go to sleep until five, and that was on the couch."

Shelly checked her watch. "It's just after eight," she acknowledged.

"Yeah . . . I got a whopper of a night's sleep," Ryan drawled.

Shelly started to express her sympathy but stopped. While she and Ryan had somehow fallen into amiable conversation, it was easily attributable to their mutual relief over a lead to Sean. His past intentions of wanting to reconcile came to mind, but Shelly remembered telling him it would snow in July before she'd ever reconcile with him. There was no reason to encourage him with sympathy or even the chance of a friendship.

Sean was missing. She'd gladly cooperate with Ryan to bring about his return, but that was as far as it went. She and Tim were getting married Valentine's Day. Shelly at least had the decency not to give Ryan any false hopes for any other options.

Sean blindly scrambled through the woods in search of the old barn his grandpa and grandma had fixed up last Christmas. They'd lit up the place like the North Pole. The huge Christmas tree had been the size of a mountain. The wood-burning stove had made it as warm as apple cider, and Sean had been so happy because his mom was happy. Her eyes had lit up like the tree. Even the presents under the tree hadn't been as special to Sean as seeing his mom so happy.

He never understood why his dad had to leave and why they couldn't get along like when his teacher tells him and his classmates to get along. But whatever the reason, his mom never looked completely happy—except maybe when she was with Dr. Tim.

Now Sean hoped the barn would give him a place to hide until his mom and dad could find him. Last night he cried and prayed until he'd fallen asleep. He knew that God would bring his parents to find him. He just knew.

"Please, God. Please," he whispered again. As he lunged through the final feet of thicket, a dried branch smacked him in the mouth. Sean grimaced and didn't make a noise. His skin was already itchy from that awful tape Aunt Dena had put on his mouth. The tree limb added a sting to the itch and fueled his mission to battle the bushes until he burst into the clearing. The big, gray barn stood taller than his school, and Sean figured he could hide in the corner a long, long time—at least until supper. By then, his mom and dad would be there.

"Sean!" Aunt Dena's shrill voice echoing from the backyard sent him into a jump and a tiny yelp.

Sean clamped his hand over his mouth and tried to stop the shaking. Desperately, he clawed at the barn's door until it swung open with a creak so loud Sean wanted to cover his ears. He peered inside the dark, dark barn and wondered what might live inside. The musty, cool air no longer smelled like apple cider, but rather like something stinky.

"Sean! Where are you?" Aunt Dena's voice sounded closer.

He looked over his shoulder and spotted a glimpse of her red shirt through the weeds. He'd been in the kitchen eating breakfast when he heard her get up. That's when he thought of the barn and when he knew he had to hide.

He gazed back into the darkness and inched forward. Thin strips of light glowed through the walls here and there, and his eyes gradually adjusted to the darkness. Finally, he spotted the piles of hay in the corner and the old woodstove that had glowed last Christmas. Still, he hung on to the door and didn't go too far inside.

"Answer me, Sean! If you can hear me, you better answer me now or you're going to be in *big trouble*!"

The threats made him quiver and pushed him deeper into the darkness. He released the door. That's when something started growling at him.

A furry form sprung from behind the stove, and Sean couldn't stop the scream . . . or the retreat. He flung himself backward, crashed into the door, and fell outside. The door banged shut in the face of an angry dog whose growls escalated to barking. Sean scurried on all fours until he could regain his footing. The dog's continued barking upped his speed. Glancing over his shoulder, he spotted the animal squeezing past the door. Hair bristled, teeth bared, he threatened to race after Sean any second.

Only one thought hurled him forward, *Escape!* His legs pumped harder, his heart raced faster, his focus was all for the cabin waiting on the other side of the thicket. But when he broke free of the woods, he ran headlong into Aunt Dena.

"Where have you been?" she screamed, her blue eyes as wild as the dog's.

"I-I-I," Sean stammered and inched away.

She grabbed his arms and shook him until he was certain his head would roll off his body. The whole time, she yelled, "You were trying to get away from me, weren't you? Even after all I did for you—even after I bought you McDonald's twice—you still tried to run away!"

She released Sean and lifted her hand. He stumbled backward, raising his arms to his face.

"I didn't want to do this," she hollered as her hand sliced the air, "but you need to understand who's in charge here!"

As Dena's blow connected with Sean's arms, the barking dog neared from behind. Striking out for survival, Sean hit at Dena's midsection and then shoved past her. Dena's grunt merged into furious screams while the dog's snarls increased. Sean thought maybe the animal got her. But when he whipped open the cabin's back door and darted inside, he spotted Dena close behind. Not sure what she might do to him next, he slammed the door and locked it.

CHAPTER SEVEN

The drive to Sulphur Springs was as silent as it was anxious. Ryan's gut churned with the possibilities of what they might find at the cabin . . . along with the realization that he and Shelly were actually working together to find their son. Currently, she sat between him and Sonny in Sonny's Chevy truck. After their initial greetings, none of them had said much. Even Sonny, usually as witty as he was chatty, remained somber.

Ryan cut Shelly a sideways glance, noting her expression hadn't changed. She sat erect, her face pale and anxious, her gaze fixed ahead. She clutched a small handbag, fingers curled around the top like it was her lifesaver. Intermittently, the sun peeked from behind the rows of trees lining the road and pierced the diamond on her finger. The flash and flicker of the bluish stone served as a constant reminder that the closer February grew, the further the chance of reconciliation slipped from Ryan's grasp.

He tore his attention from the ring and focused on the wooded roadside. Ryan thought of Sean—of the last time he'd been with his son. He'd promised to take Sean fishing and camping. A desperate fear swept Ryan's soul, and he wondered what he'd do if Sean never returned. He thought of the lonely years stretching ahead into a blank canvas of nothingness . . . no wife, no son, only his career and an empty house.

A dark cloud of despair threatened to consume Ryan . . . until a soft voice from the center of his soul whispered, *You've still got the Lord. He'll never leave you or forsake you, no matter what.* Ryan closed his eyes and savored those words as he remembered the radical encounter that had changed his life forever.

The divorce had been final two months when Ryan and Arlene agreed to attend church with her grandmother. Even though Ryan hadn't wanted to go, Arlene had insisted that she always went with her grandmother at Easter. After trying to squirm out of the commitment for days, Ryan finally relented. He'd grown up watching his church-going mom live a rigid life, driven by guilt over every minor infraction—and he had no intention of getting sucked into such an existence as an adult.

Furthermore, the very thought of going to church had stirred up a storm of shame-streaked doubts over the affair with Arlene, a storm his mom had started once she learned the nature of their relationship. As long as Ryan didn't think about God, his doubts vanished, especially in the face of Arlene's smile. Nevertheless, it was that smile that had coerced him into attending church on Easter morning. But he'd warned Arlene he might never go again.

During his marriage to Shelly, he'd only attended church at Christmas, just to keep her happy. Since Arlene didn't regularly go to services, he'd hoped marriage to her wouldn't involve church. She'd assured him it wouldn't. At the time, Ryan had viewed her assurance as yet another perk of being married to Arlene.

Despite his resistance, from the second Ryan walked into the sanctuary, there had been something remarkably different about the church. It stirred him in a way his childhood church never did.

After being greeted by a kind usher, he settled near Arlene and her grandmother on a padded pew. Arlene had smiled up at him. She seductively stroked his palm with the tips of her fingers while her blue eyes had insisted her mind was not on church. But that distraction only lasted until the service started.

Then Ryan's attention was riveted to a cross draped in purple, claiming center stage. The cantata centered on the resurrection, but the cross spoke of a sacrifice that grew more personal with every lyrical beat. The smell of Easter lilies became hauntingly sweet as the minister delivered a short message focused on a loving God who wants to heal the broken, repair relationships, and bring about a personal resurrection in the lives of those He touches.

The minister ended the service with an invitation for those who wanted to encounter this God—a Savior miles removed from the hard-nosed dictator shoved at Ryan during childhood. A cry to know this Lord echoed from Ryan's spirit and propelled him to walk toward the cross. At the front of the sanctuary, he was met by a man his age who prayed with him and promised a follow-up contact.

When he arrived back at Arlene's side, the girl-next-door features that had once ensnared him somehow lost their appeal. Her worried expression was only foiled by Grandma Marigold's satisfied smile. On the way out of the service, Ryan heard Arlene's nervous chatter but couldn't comprehend a word. Every Bible verse about God's love he'd memorized as a child tumbled through his mind in a resonance of praise. Along with the memories came a deep sadness that the church that had taught him these verses somehow missed the meaning. The fiery presence that burned within Ryan was directing him to follow the teachings of Christ . . . the teachings that insisted his current relationship with Arlene was not right and that reconciliation with his wife was more right than he'd ever imagined.

Bombarded by the rush of these new thoughts, Ryan had remained silent until he pulled into Grandma Marigold's drive. The frame home, nestled on a corner lot, had beckoned him indoors while Grandma Marigold promised the best Easter dinner Ryan had ever eaten. He'd hesitated, nearly declined, but the worry playing on Arlene's face bade him keep his promise.

Ryan barely touched the meal, barely said a word, barely comprehended the familial dialogue that had swollen to full volume with the addition of half a dozen from the Marigold clan. Finally, he'd managed to escape into the backyard, to a wooden swing hanging from a tree. The Easter lilies blooming in the nearby flower bed soon became a poignant reminder of the service he'd just attended, the commitment he'd just made.

All he could think of was Shelly, what she was doing, who she was with, and how he'd managed to throw away their family. Even though everything hadn't been perfect, there were no guarantees anything would be perfect with Arlene either.

And it was at that moment that Ryan accepted what he had to do—but making the decision to break up with Arlene was way easier than implementing it.

"Here's the turn," Sonny's voice barged into Ryan's reverie.

His mind snapped to the present while his nerves jolted to full alert. Ryan glanced toward his brother before examining the narrow lane Sonny pointed toward.

Slowing the truck, Sonny turned right and pulled to a stop. "What now?" he asked.

Ryan eyed the woods that the lane divided. A sign near a fence stated, No Trespassing. Private Property. Ryan had helped his father-in-law erect the sign when they first bought the property years ago.

"I say we check out the house," Shelly said, leaning forward. "Isn't that what we came to do?"

"Yeah," Ryan said, "but if we just drive up and if Dena's there and we scare her—"

"She might run," Sonny interjected.

"Then we'll have to call the FBI," Ryan said.

"And if she gets away, we'll all get thrown in jail for not calling the FBI in the first place."

"Oh." Shelly wrinkled her brow and gazed at Ryan. "So, we could get arrested for trying to find Sean? You didn't tell me . . ."

"I didn't stress it," Ryan said. "But if you remember, yesterday I mentioned that the FBI asked me to stay out of it, and that's the reason I had to divert all information to Jack or let Sonny be the one to report. We've just got to be careful or we can get in the way. Believe me, Sonny and I aren't going to make any mistakes that will get us arrested. We were just trying to explain why we're sitting here, trying to decide what to do."

Shelly's face relaxed.

Ryan briefly rested his hand on her shoulder. "I won't let you get in a place where you'll get arrested. I'll put *myself* on the line before I let that happen."

Her dark eyes narrowed a fraction. Her gaze sharpened. And she peered into Ryan's eyes as if he were under a microscope. Ryan didn't flinch, didn't look away, and didn't hide his earnest commitment to her ultimate good.

She started to speak, but Sonny's words sliced through her intent. "Look, the lane branches off there. Shelly, do you know where that road leads?" He pointed toward a path that was just wide enough for one vehicle.

Shelly gazed toward the area and shifted away from Ryan's touch. Taking the hint, he lifted his hand from her sweater and decided to limit all touching to only what was necessary. He'd spent more time with Shelly in the last couple of days than he had since the divorce. They were actually talking again. There was no sense upping her defenses. Besides, his goal was to find Sean. The last thing he needed to do was stir up problems with Shelly in the process.

"I think it's just a glorified trail Dad cut out so he could take his truck to cut firewood," Shelly explained.

"If I drive long enough, is there a place to turn around?"

"Yeah, I think," she said. "Seems like there's a clearing about fifty yards into the woods."

"Does it go away from the house, or circle back toward it?" Ryan asked.

"I think it goes away . . ." Shelly said, her tone as uncertain as the glance she cut Ryan. "I don't know," she finally added on a helpless sigh. "I never paid much attention to that. I'm not here enough." She peered into the woods while chewing on her thumbnail, something Ryan had never seen Shelly do before. When she ripped that nail off, she went to her index finger. Her fiercely trembling fingers upped Ryan's concern, and he wondered if perhaps he shouldn't have included her in this trip.

"Okay, I'm going to make a call." Sonny's decisive voice pierced the tension. "Ryan, there's a compass in my glove box. Let's get it out and use it. If it looks like we're heading back toward the cabin, we'll stop. I'd rather go to the clearing and turn the truck around so we can be ready for an easy exit, but we don't want to take the chance of Dena hearing the truck either."

"Roger that," Ryan said and turned the knob on the glove box that opened up a Pandora's box of clutter. "Holy cow!" Ryan exclaimed. "Are you sure I won't get bitten?"

"Cut it out," Sonny's words were accompanied by Shelly's nervous snicker. "And just dig around until you find the compass. It should be near the top."

Ryan shoved aside a layer of papers that toppled to the floor and found a small compass tangled in a wad of shoestrings.

"Oh, good grief!" Sonny groused. "I *told* Tanya Coty high-jacked my shoelaces, but she wouldn't believe me. Now I've got proof! I couldn't imagine what he'd done with them."

Shelly paused her fingernail chewing. "Sean used to do stuff like that," she said. "One time, I found all my spaghetti broken into little bitty pieces in a bowl in the bathroom," her voice broke over the last word.

"I remember that," Ryan said, his words reflecting his increasing concern. "You were exasperated and I was laughing, which made you more exasperated." As the memory unfolded, it became a reminiscence of the family they'd once been, and Ryan forced his own composure.

"Well, it was just that—your parents were coming for dinner and I was already running late and I didn't have time to go get more and . . . and . . . and now . . . now . . ." She gulped for air and hunched forward. "I just wish he was back. I'd let him break all the spaghetti from now on." Her words merged to coughing and sobbing.

Ryan exchanged a glance with his brother, whose eyes reflected Ryan's rising apprehension. Shelly might not be able to control her emotions to the needed level, which only enforced the FBI's admonishment for the parents to stay out of the investigation. As a law-enforcement professional, Ryan had put similar constraints on family members many times. His mounting doubts over involving Shelly left him wondering if his own stress was clouding his better judgment. Sonny had certainly resisted the option of her coming with them, but had finally relented.

Maybe I should have listened to Sonny, Ryan worried.

He handed the compass to Sonny and then gently stroked Shelly's back. Not knowing what else to do, Ryan decided to try to further soothe her. Holding her hand, he said, "It's okay. Just take some deep breaths. It will pass. You're just on edge."

In the middle of a heave, she gasped, "I'm so—so—so—sorry. I know I've got—got to get a grip."

"It might be best for you to stay in the truck," Sonny said, his voice cautious.

"No!" Shelly insisted and vehemently shook her head. As if the admonishment had affected her like a slap, she lifted her face, rubbed her eyes, and released a few more whimpers. "If Dena's in there with Sean, I'll be the best one to go in."

"But you said Dena *hates* you," Ryan insisted.

"She—she does," Shelly admitted, "but she loves—loves me, too. That's why she let us adopt Sean." She coughed and swallowed hard. "I'll have to be the one to approach her." Swiping at her damp cheeks, Shelly turned her watery focus to Ryan, and a flash of something he struggled to define flickered between them. Not love. Ryan hadn't felt a scrap of love from Shelly for years. Nevertheless, there was still the connection of two souls, once merged in a family union, once the joined parents of a child they both loved more than their own lives.

Caught in the moment, Ryan couldn't reply to Shelly's insistence about Dena. His exhausted mind, racing with adrenaline, formed no coherent response even though his gut insisted Shelly's confronting Dena might not be the best option.

Finally, Sonny's voice barged through Shelly's assertion. "We'll see how it goes," he said, his tone inviting no argument, "but if you even *act* like you're going to crack again, Shelly, you've *got* to stay in the truck." Sonny's knuckles went white on the wheel.

She turned to face him, and Ryan expected a contest of wills. Instead, Shelly nodded and stiffened her back against the seat. "You're right," she affirmed. Looking straight ahead, she wadded the hem of her oversized sweater. "We're talking about Sean's future, here. If I don't think I can take it, I'll stay out of the way."

Lifting his brows, Ryan exchanged another stare with his brother, whose eyes incited him to go along with the next statement. "Same for you, okay?"

Ryan cut a glance toward Shelly before saying, "Yeah, whatever you say," but both he and Sonny silently agreed it was all for Shelly.

"Let's go."

After removing the shoestrings from the compass, Sonny positioned it on the dashboard. "Looks like this road we're on is going due east," he said.

"And the road we'll turn on is heading south," Ryan affirmed.

Sonny put the truck into gear, gassed the engine, and steered the vehicle into the woods.

CHAPTER EIGHT

Hunkering down, Ryan scurried to the back of the cabin while Sonny slinked toward the front. After confirming the absence of a vehicle, they watched the cabin for a full fifteen minutes before deciding to approach. Even if all clues insisted that Sean and Dena had been here, they were no longer. Nevertheless, Ryan couldn't be careful enough.

Despite his attempts to make as little noise as possible, the fallen leaves still crunched against his shoes and Ryan winced with every step. Once at the cabin, he knelt below the window and then eased up to inspect the kitchen area. The midmorning sun piercing the windows revealed no one present, only a scattering of food wrappers and soiled paper utensils. He moved to the other window, gazed into a shadowed bedroom. Once again, the place was empty. Only rumpled bedclothes indicated that someone had slept there.

His hands unsteady, Ryan reached for his cell phone with the intent of texting Sonny. But by the time he flipped open the qwerty board, Sonny had already sent him a text: *No one present in the front. You see anyone?*

Ryan pecked out a negative response and then added, *I'm going to use Shelly's key and go in. Looks like someone's been here recently.*

Sonny's immediate reply was filled with as much urgency as Ryan sensed: *Be careful!*

Ryan flipped the phone shut, dropped it into his shirt pocket, and fished the key out of his jeans. It entered the lock without a hitch, and Ryan turned the knob, grimacing when it squeaked. The door's creaking left him gritting his teeth. He leaned into the musty kitchen and listened, only to encounter silence.

Before he took the first step inside, Ryan recalled the drug sting he'd been involved in eighteen months ago. The drug lord had turned out to be a woman who knew how to wield a handgun with the best of them. She'd nicked Ryan's ear with the volley from her Smith & Wesson, aimed at his head.

Shelly's warning reverberated through his mind: *Don't put anything past Dena.* Nevertheless, Ryan knew he couldn't hover on the steps all day. Tempted to pull the gun he'd concealed beneath his pants leg, Ryan decided that might be over the top.

He took the first step, then another. When no sound of hurried whispers or closing doors met his ears, Ryan decided the cabin must be empty. Still cautious, he crept through the cluttered kitchen and dining room, toward the living room. A quick tour of the three bedrooms and the tiny bathroom revealed no one currently present, but plenty of evidence of recent occupation. The bathroom's soapy smell, accompanied by the damp streak in the tub, validated that the occupation had been as recent as today.

"Maybe just a few hours ago," Ryan mumbled. His cell phone vibrated. Ryan removed it from his pocket and read Sonny's text, *Okay in there?*

Ryan closed the phone and strode to the front door. Opening it, he scanned the yard and spotted Sonny standing from his crouch near the porch. "Nobody's here right now," Ryan said, "but some-body's *been* here."

"Think it was Dena?"

"Who else?" Ryan replied. "The place is a cluttered-up mess. Shelly used to always gripe about the messes she made. I'm think-ing your hunch paid off. I'm going back in to see if anything here belongs to Sean, just to give us solid evidence. Would you go get Shelly? It'll do her good to help."

"Sure," Sonny said and sprinted toward the woods.

"Tell Shelly we need to hurry, in case Dena returns."

"Right!" Sonny called over his shoulder.

Shelly had agreed to stay in the truck when Ryan and Sonny de-cided to secretively approach the cabin. However, she suspected their reasons for her to stay were a guise to leave her behind. With a huff, she rubbed at her aching neck.

"Maybe it's for the best," she whispered as the surrounding trees blurred. Her lips trembled. Shelly pressed them together, and balled her fists until her nails bit her palms.

"Stop it," she insisted. "You've got to keep your cool."

From the time Shelly understood that Dena really did have Sean, she'd been overcome by a mixture of odd relief, anger, and despair. The relief came in at least knowing who Sean was with. The anger, from understanding that Dena had once again selfishly taken what she wanted. The despair, in understanding that Dena really could disappear and Shelly would never see Sean again. The despair had driven her to gnaw at her fingernails and produced the current tears.

She sniffled, closed her eyes, and prayed. *Dear God, please let Sonny and Ryan find Sean. Let him be at the cabin. Don't let Dena get away with this. And please,* please *help me to keep control here.*

She thought about Ryan, about the fierce concern in his eyes when he said, *I won't let you get in a place where you'll get arrested. I'll put* myself *on the line before I let that happen.*

Shelly never remembered his being so ready to sacrifice for her during their marriage. Despite her peering deeper into his eyes, she couldn't find satisfaction in knowing if he really meant what he said, or if he was just saying what sounded good for the moment.

If you'd only been half as attentive to me as you were to Sean, Shelly thought. There'd been no question of Ryan's adoration of Sean from the moment he held his new son. Shelly often wondered what it would take to get him to adore her with as much fervor.

She'd not had the guts to voice her opinions on that subject until just before the divorce was final. Then Ryan had shocked her by saying he felt the same way. *Somehow, neither of us gave the depth of love to each other that we were able to give to Sean,* she thought. *No wonder he's so well-adjusted.* Even though the divorce had been hard on him, Sean had seemed to bounce back with an amazing vigor that even his schoolteacher had noted.

But of course, he spends nearly as much time with Ryan as he does with me, Shelly thought and wondered if that would all change when she and Tim married. Given the growth of Sean and Tim's relationship, Sean became more and more attached to Tim every day. *With a full-time dad at home, Sean might not want to go with Ryan as much,* she thought. Frowning, Shelly wondered how that would affect Ryan.

But Sean's gone! she thought. *And if we don't find him, he won't be spending time with anybody but Dena!* Shelly opened her eyes and stifled the sob pressing against her throat.

The click of the automatic lock sent her into a spastic jump. Even though she spotted Sonny trotting up the pathway, she couldn't harness the compulsive scream. Shelly placed her hand on her chest and tried to calm her breathing.

I'm too jumpy, she admonished herself. *I've got to do better if I'm going to be any good for Sean.*

Not waiting until Sonny arrived, Shelly scooted across the truck seat, opened the door, and slid to the ground. "What did you guys see?" she asked seconds before Sonny stopped at her side.

"Someone's been in the cabin." He jerked his head in the direction he'd come. "Our bets are on Dena. Ryan's taking another look to see if he can spot any definite clues—like something of Sean's."

"I should help," Shelly asserted before closing the truck's door and stepping toward the path.

"That's what Ryan said. He sent me to get you." The vehicle's automatic locks clicked from behind. Shelly focused on the path ahead and began a swift trot in the direction Sonny had come.

"We want to do a quick search and then get out," Sonny said, falling in beside her.

"I can do quick," Shelly answered.

"Once you and Ryan are through, I'm going to take you into Sulphur Springs and drop you off for a while. Then I'll call Jack and have him send in the FBI. My hunch is, they'll put somebody on the cabin to watch it 24/7, to see if Dena returns."

"Good," she said. Her breath created miniature clouds as she ran beside Sonny, and her lungs demanded more oxygen with every footfall. Shelly had jogged two miles a day since her college track years, but keeping up with Sonny was closer to a sprint.

Finally, they burst from the woods' path and entered a clearing that stretched to the cabin. Shelly picked up her pace and ran ahead of Sonny. After taking the steps two at a time, she burst through the front door and lunged into the living room.

Ryan looked up from the corner desk, his face ashen, his eyes stricken.

"Wh-what happened?" Shelly wheezed, noticing a piece of paper on the desktop. "S-something's happened. You look like—like—you just heard . . ." She didn't let herself even think of all the dreadful things he may have heard.

Shifting his attention to the paper, Ryan remained silent.

Shelly's gut tightened. "Ryan!" she exclaimed, rushing to his side. "Wh-what is it?"

Without a word, he pointed at the paper. "Don't touch it," he admonished. "We have to leave everything like it was when we got here."

Hovering over the desk, Shelly hungrily focused upon the images, clearly drawn by a young child. Only a few seconds lapsed before the full impact of the message left Shelly's face even colder. Then she understood why Ryan had been pale. The picture featured a woman and a man that resembled Ryan and Shelly, in hair color only. Bold letters in crayon labeled the woman as "Mom." "Dad" was scrawled above the man. Between the two a jagged line resembled a tear. On the paper's far right corner sat a crying boy with the label "Me."

Her shoulders stiff, Shelly fully absorbed the impact. She'd genuinely thought Sean was learning to accept their divorce. But this picture hadn't come from a child who had gotten full closure. He obviously felt disconnected from his parents, since he literally was. And that made the parental disconnection all the more heartbreaking for him.

Even though she knew continuing to gaze at the drawing would twist her heart into a tighter knot, she couldn't stop herself. The images sharpened in focus, and she ached more than she had since the divorce.

"Have you and Sean been here since our divorce?" Ryan asked.

"Yes, last Christmas, remember," Shelly explained. "It's turning into a family tradition."

"Then there's no guarantee that he drew the photo in the last day."

"Except that Mom and I thoroughly cleaned this place when we left." Shelly glanced around the room cluttered with magazines, a throw, and even a wadded McDonald's bag in the corner. "There was no trash at all. You said you found this lying where it is?"

"Yeah, exactly. I haven't touched it because we can't leave any prints or alter anything. The FBI would not be happy, ya know?"

"Right," Shelly agreed. "I can't imagine either one of us over-looking something like this." Her gaze trailed across the cluttered desktop. "The crayons are out too. You can tell he's been drawing." She examined the array of colored pencils and paper. The bottom drawer, now ajar, revealed other art supplies.

"I stocked this with supplies last Christmas," she explained, spotting another piece of artwork lying near the edge. "And I made certain to put everything away before we left." When she realized the drawing was more refined than the first, she reached for it.

"Don't touch it," Ryan admonished.

Shelly yanked back her hand. "Sorry. Old habits die hard," she said, eyeing the second piece of artwork. "Looks like the one we were looking at is a first draft on this one."

"Yes," Ryan said, his voice low and thick.

Shelly glanced up at him before she considered the consequences. His misty brown eyes were full of regrets and a plea. "I'm sorry, Shelly," he said, his gaze falling to the drawings, "for everything."

Her fingers flinched against her palms. "Yeah, I know," she replied and wondered where Ryan might be taking this. Even though the images Sean had drawn were heartbreaking, Shelly couldn't imagine reconciling with Ryan. She'd have to trust him again for that to happen, and *that* would take a miracle Shelly couldn't comprehend. As for Sean, she'd have to continue working with him, maybe even have him start counseling again—especially after what Dena had done.

Desperately needing a buffer, she searched the room for Sonny but found he'd disappeared.

"If we can just find Sean, Shelly, I *promise* you . . . I promise . . ."

Her legs trembling, Shelly turned her back to Ryan. She hunched her shoulders, walked to the window, and hoped he didn't follow.

Her mind whirled with the impact of Ryan's agony. And for the first time, Shelly's doubts about his sincerity began to crumble. But whether he was sincere *now* or not, their past held more devastation than Shelly ever wanted to endure again. Furthermore, there were no guarantees he wouldn't repeat.

"This is not the time for what-might-have-beens," she said, trying to keep her voice from shaking. "We just need to keep our focus on finding Sean."

Silence hung in the room like a miasma of misery that seeped into Shelly's brain and insisted she gaze at Sean's drawing again. Despite the ache in her soul, Shelly closed her eyes, crossed her arms, and refused.

"You're right," Ryan finally said.

"Look what I found in the bedroom!" Sonny's exclamation shattered the strain, and Shelly had never been so glad to see his zany grin. His hands swathed in thin plastic gloves, he held up a T-shirt with an appliqué cat on the front. Under the feline was the name "Dena."

Shelly recognized the shirt all too well. "I made that shirt for Dena's birthday!" she exclaimed.

Hurrying forward, she reached for the shirt's hem, but stopped herself. "Lift the back hem and you'll see my signature along the bottom."

Sonny complied and exposed Shelly's name.

"Bingo," Ryan said from close behind.

"It was in the bedroom floor, halfway under the bed," Sonny explained.

"Dena couldn't clean up after herself if her life depended on it." Shelly suppressed a new wave of anger. "I don't think there's any doubt they've been here."

"And if they were here, they can't be all that far away," Ryan interjected.

"You guys need to get scarce, so I can call Jack," Sonny said. "What if I just drop you off at a restaurant or something in town and then I'll come back here and watch the cabin until the FBI shows up. I can let them in and we'll take it from there. Okay?"

"Sure," Ryan said.

"That's fine," Shelly agreed before even considering that she and Ryan were being thrown into dining alone, something they hadn't done since long before their marriage ended.

CHAPTER NINE

Sonny called a final farewell to Shelly and Ryan before they entered the restaurant. Narrowing his eyes, he watched Ryan open the door for Shelly and wondered if she even had a clue how much his brother was suffering, not only over the disappearance of Sean but also over the loss of their family.

Shelly always had been a practical sort when it came to some issues. She seemed to be in that mode today with Ryan. Her only concern was for Sean. While Sonny could certainly understand her frame of mind, he couldn't fathom her lack of emotion in the face of Ryan's pain. She seemed to have made up her mind regarding marrying Tim, and Sonny wondered if anything could shake her from that goal. Sonny had certainly given up trying to talk with her after his attempt to sway her at that singles retreat they both attended last year.

"I guess it's just in God's hands," he said and decided not to think about anything but finding Sean. He rammed his truck into reverse and whipped out of the parking lot while pressing Jack's speed dial number on his cell phone.

When his brother answered, Sonny wasted no time detailing his findings.

"I'll call the FBI now," Jack said. "I'm sure they'll send in a team ASAP."

"That's what I banked on," Sonny replied. "Until they do, I'll watch the cabin and just let you know if Dena shows back up."

"Works!" Jack said. "Listen, I've been trying to reach Ryan. Has he called you today?"

"Uhhh," Sonny hesitated and concentrated on merging into traffic from the service road while trying to remember if Ryan actually *called* him. Finally, he deduced that he hadn't.

"No, he hasn't called me today," Sonny admitted. "A lot of times, he turns off his cell at night and then forgets to turn it back on in the morning."

"Yeah. He did that yesterday morning," Jack said. "I had to go hunt him down at church to tell him Sean was missing."

"Well, if you hear from him, tell him to call me," Jack said.

"Why? Whazup?" Sonny prodded.

"I just wanted to check on him. Have you turned into his answering service?" he teased.

"Maybe," Sonny retorted.

"Have you *seen* him?" Jack pressed.

Sonny swallowed a groan and finally decided to come clean. He and his brothers had never lied to one another, and he wasn't going to start today. "Yeah I have seen him, if you must know," he admitted. "But I was telling the truth about his calling me today—he *hasn't*!"

Jack's silence spoke all manner of deductions, and Sonny knew he was trapped.

"Did he go to Sulphur Springs with you?" Jack asked, an incredulous note in his voice.

Sonny sighed and eyed the truck's heater setting; the cab was suddenly becoming too hot.

"Sonny! You *know* he's supposed to be staying out of the investigation! Have you *lost your mind*?"

"I tried to tell him," Sonny countered. "But he was coming to Sulphur Springs anyway—whether he came with me or not. At least this way I could keep an eye on him."

"Where is he now? Is he at the cabin?"

"No. He and Shelly are at a restaurant—"

"Shelly came too?"

"Yeah," Sonny said, feeling like a sixth-grader caught cutting class.

"Good grief, Sonny!" Jack began and continued a diatribe against the ills of Sonny's bending the rules.

Just when Sonny was on the verge of interrupting him out of self-defense, his call-waiting alert beeped. Sonny pulled the phone away from his ear long enough to determine the caller. The number seemed familiar, but he didn't know why. Whether friend or foe, Sonny used the caller as an excuse to end the conversation.

"Listen, I've got another call coming in. We'll talk later."

"Tell Ryan to lie low and get back home ASAP!" Jack admonished.

"I will. He is. Don't worry, okay? We're not as inept as you seem to think we are."

"Who said anything about calling you inept?" Jack shot back. "I just know the FBI wants Ryan and Shelly to stay out of it, and they aren't!"

"Okay, okay," Sonny chimed, the call alert beeping again. "I gotta go. Call me later, okay?" Sonny pressed the send button and figured he'd be hearing from Jack again after he reported to the FBI.

"Hello, this is Sonny Mansfield," he said into the phone, only to hear nothing. He pulled the phone away from his ear to confirm he'd missed the call. A voice mail icon popped on the screen, along with the electronic alert that signified the caller had left a message.

Within seconds, he'd pressed the auto dial for voice mail and listened to the call.

"Hello, Sonny? This is Karen . . . I was returning your call about . . . about Blake, uh, our son. I do have information for you. Please call me back on this number I called you on. It's my cell phone . . ." she finished and recited the number that had displayed on his screen.

Ryan hesitated before attempting to pull out Shelly's seat, and was relieved of the decision when the host did the honors. He settled across from her and accepted the menu.

"You're our first lunch customer of the day," the host stated with a broad grin. "We always give a complimentary appetizer to our first customer."

"Thanks," Shelly said.

"Wonderful!" Ryan rubbed at his gritty eyes and marveled that his stomach would actually growl. However, he hadn't eaten more than half a bag of Doritos since his makeshift lunch yesterday.

"I'm hungry, but eating out at my favorite restaurant almost seems like a betrayal," he admitted.

"I know," Shelly agreed. "But I didn't eat breakfast, and I'm getting a little shaky."

"We need to keep our strength up for when they find Sean. If we're fainting from hunger, we won't be any support for him."

"Right," Shelly agreed with a forced grin. "What are you going to get?"

"I'm thinking one of these burgs."

"What I figured," she said.

And Ryan nearly said "You know me well" but stopped himself. That would have been something he said when they were married, and Ryan was trying to keep a respectful distance . . . especially after the episode at the cabin. He had no plans to repeat that sort of conversation. Despite his desperation, pressuring Shelly only upped her defenses.

Feigning interest in the list of appetizers, he tried to recall the last time he and Shelly ate out together. Their eighth anniversary came to mind. She'd dressed in a tailored pantsuit made of raw silk. The rose-colored fabric had lent a flush to her cheeks, an image that contrasted with her current pallid appearance. But even with her hair in a simple ponytail and her eyes hollow, Ryan thought she was as beautiful as she'd been on that last anniversary. Even though both of them had been growing discontent in their marriage, they'd somehow managed to set it all aside and enjoy the evening that ended in their bedroom.

Ryan glared at the appetizers and forced himself to focus on the Southwest Egg Rolls. "How do you feel about egg rolls these days?" he questioned.

"Fine. You mean for our appetizer?" she asked, lifting her brows.

"Yeah."

"Works for me. I'm thinking about a soup and salad, so that will be perfect."

Ryan snapped the menu shut like he was mad at it and stared past Shelly.

"Is . . . something wrong?" she questioned.

He avoided eye contact. "No—nothing," he said. "Just got a lot on my mind."

"Yeah. My mind is spinning, and it makes me so tired. I can't seem to focus." She rested her elbows on the table and rubbed her temples.

Her cell phone bleeped from her purse, and Shelly jerked up her head. "Oh no, I bet that's Dad and Mom texting," she said. "I told them I'd call them this morning, and I forgot."

Ryan stiffened. He hadn't told Shelly not to tell her parents what they were doing. Nevertheless, he'd assumed that she understood she couldn't tell anyone, due to the secretive nature.

While she extracted the phone from her purse, flipped open the qwerty board, and began pressing buttons, Ryan debated whether or not to tell her to keep their locale a secret. He didn't know if Shelly would understand and dreaded an argument.

"It's Dad," she supplied. "I'll tell him what we found at the cabin."

"Shelly, don't," Ryan said, leaning closer.

She stopped and eyed him.

"I'm sorry, but you don't need to involve them," he stressed, keeping his voice even and kind. "We can't tell anyone what we're up to right now. We've got to stay as incognito as possible. The fewer people who know, the better. If the FBI finds out—"

"But my parents won't tell them."

"If the FBI wants information from them, they know how to extract it. If your parents don't know what we're doing, then they won't have anything to hide."

The speculative gleam in Shelly's eyes turned to doubt.

Holding his breath, Ryan waited for her to argue. He recalled one of their last dates as a married couple. They'd gone to a community theater to see *A Christmas Carol*, and Shelly had dismissed herself two-thirds of the way through to take a call from her parents. She'd missed the final scenes of the play to hear about her folks' Christmas shopping upheaval.

Presently, Ryan wondered if Shelly was capable of not telling her parents everything all the time. Nevertheless, Ryan couldn't resent their interest. He wasn't close to being a grandfather, but he knew he'd be a texting fool if his niece or nephew had been snatched.

"Why not just tell them you're okay and that you're depending on their prayers," he offered and hoped his smile would add a note of positive encouragement. "You could also mention that we're together and that I said I really appreciate their support."

Doubt disappeared in the path of an incredulous glimmer in

her eyes. "I understand," she finally said. "I'm not used to the legal world. I'll go with what you think." Then, she began texting.

Ryan leaned back and sighed.

When the waiter appeared, Shelly closed the cell phone and said, "Dad said hello and that he can't sleep for praying."

Ryan shifted farther from the table while the waiter served their ice water. "I prayed myself into a coma in the wee hours. Surely *something's* got to give."

He waited for Shelly to place her order and then he recited his. Once the waiter exited, Ryan downed half the glass of ice water and wished for his Coke. His gaze trailed to Shelly's engagement ring, and he blurted, "That diamond could strangle a bull," before he realized the thought had left his mouth. "Where'd he find one so big?" he added with what he hoped was a softer tone.

Shelly removed her silverware from the rolled-up napkin. "Tiffany's, New York," she said, her voice as rigid as her fingers. "We flew up there together."

How nice, Ryan thought, but didn't voice his sarcasm. Trying to sound more magnanimous, he said, "Tim seems like a really nice guy. If Sean's got to have a stepfather, I guess he's a good choice."

Shelly lowered her hands, raised her gaze to Ryan's, and didn't bother to hide her astonishment.

"What?" Ryan said.

"Are you *serious*?"

"Well, yeah." He shrugged and offered a toast with his water. "Here's to Tim," he said and chalked it up to temporary insanity.

She narrowed her eyes. "He's a very good, stable man, and I don't appreciate your mocking him."

"Who says I'm mocking him? I was just trying to be nice. Good grief!" Ryan snapped.

"Well, sorry," Shelly huffed. "I guess I just assumed . . ."

Strained silence cloaked them. As much as Ryan wanted to be

with Shelly, he needed a break. Standing, he grumbled, "I'm going to find the restroom."

Shelly watched Ryan stride from the table and wondered if they could have one decent discussion without it ending in friction. She'd avoided more than brief, necessary conversations with Ryan ever since the divorce; and most of those centered upon Sean.

Resting her elbows on the table, Shelly covered her face and stifled a groan. It was bad enough that Sean was missing, but having to hang out with Ryan on top of it was almost more than she could bear. Apparently, he'd gotten out of the desperate, begging mode and swung into trying to be supportive of her and Tim's marriage.

Maybe he's giving up hope on us and accepting the inevitable, Shelly mused. But the thought failed to encourage her, especially when she considered that Ryan might actually attend her wedding.

"He *wouldn't!*" she gasped, her head snapping up. "Would he?" Balling her fists in her lap, Shelly imagined Ryan lifting his punch cup in a toast to the bride and groom and cringed. Tim would *not* be happy.

She stared out the window, across the parking lot to a young woman hurrying to meet a man. Holding a toddler, the woman gladly accepted a brief kiss from the man while the child readily leaned into his arms. The family reminded Shelly of the days when Sean was a baby. She'd taken off from teaching second grade until Sean went to pre-K. During those years, Shelly met Ryan for lunch every chance they got. Many times, they'd go to the park and enjoy a picnic.

For the first time since the divorce, a tinge of regret slithered through Shelly's heart. She'd been so devastated over Ryan's affair, she felt nothing but relief when he moved out for good. Once the divorce was final, Shelly had experienced a great sense of freedom. A divorced friend had told her that the regrets would come one day, but Shelly hadn't believed her.

She no longer doubted her friend. Thoughts of Sean's heart-wrenching drawing at the cabin only intensified her feelings. Nevertheless, Shelly refused to linger over the regrets. Ryan was responsible for their family's destruction; and she wasn't going to wallow in false guilt for his choices. The past was in the past. There was nothing she could do. The future with Tim looked bright. That is, if they could find Sean.

She retrieved her purse from near her feet and extracted her billfold. Shelly opened it to her cherished photos. Her eyes misting, she stroked Sean's recent school picture. He looked so "grown up" in his navy blue sweater vest. Arms crossed, he smiled into the camera, revealing a missing front tooth.

Shelly chuckled when she remembered his first experience with the Tooth Fairy. He'd awakened to catch Shelly in the act of exchanging money for the tooth under his pillow. That had ended all questions about the fairy's identity.

Remembering the other photos tucked behind the first-grade picture, Shelly removed the short stack and gazed at each school photo while laying the former one on the table. The last picture surprised her. It was from the final sitting she and Sean had taken with Ryan. The professional shot had been snapped outdoors. Ryan knelt near Shelly, sitting on the grass. One of Ryan's legs was up in bench fashion, and Sean sat there. Ryan's left arm was wrapped around Sean while his right hand protectively rested on Shelly's shoulder.

We looked so happy, she thought and figured the photo must have been taken right before Ryan began his affair. *He might have already been with her*, she fumed and fought the threatening resentment. Her counselor had told her that completing the forgiveness involved *re*forgiving every time the incident sprang into her mind. Otherwise, she'd be trapped in resentment her whole life. And *that* could hinder her other relationships, including her new marriage.

I've forgiven him, she thought and prayed that the Lord would continue to empower her to work with Ryan in a calm fashion until they found Sean.

"Looks like I'm just in time," Ryan said, and Shelly scrambled to hide the picture under the top of the stack. Glancing up, she spotted the waiter carrying a tray laden with their egg rolls.

Her stomach growled. "I'm going to eat every bite of mine," she said through a smile she hoped was natural.

"That's fine," Ryan said, rubbing his hands together. "But if you touch mine, you might get bitten." The dark circles under his eyes belied the lilt in his voice.

Still trying to smile, Shelly discreetly reached for the photos with the intent of inserting them back into her billfold.

But Ryan touched the top picture and said, "Do you mind if I see this, Shelly?"

Shelly cringed with the thought that he'd remove the picture of Sean and find their family photo beneath it. No telling what he'd think . . . or say. She had avoided prolonged eye contact with Ryan for ages now, but his question so caught her off guard, she failed to break focus.

Looking Ryan Mansfield square in the eyes long-term had an effect on a woman—one Shelly didn't ever want to experience again. She'd been mesmerized on their first date and had vowed to marry him by the second month of their courtship. A certain warmth stirred in his eyes that made a woman feel as if she was the exact answer to all his dreams.

Reminding herself that the effect was an illusion and that she wasn't the only woman who'd felt that way, Shelly looked at Sean's picture and wondered what Ryan wanted it for.

"Winston? Is that your first name?" Ryan asked, pointing to the waiter's badge.

"Yes, it is," he said with an assured grin.

"Winston, our son is missing," Ryan explained as the waiter set down their order. "I wanted to show you a photo to see if you'd seen him anytime in the last twenty-four hours."

Shelly lifted the entire stack of pictures and removed the top one. "That's a good idea," she affirmed and handed the photo to the waiter as she shifted the family picture out of Ryan's sight.

The waiter positioned Shelly's iced tea in front of her and then accepted the picture. "I have a daughter," he said, his eyes full of compassion. "I can't imagine what you must be going through."

Shelly swallowed a lump in her throat and gazed at the egg rolls, strategically arranged for the best appeal. But they suddenly *lost* appeal. On the heels of her emotions, the smell sent her stomach into a lurch.

Shoving the pictures into her billfold, Shelly seized control of her feelings. *This is my opportunity for nourishment*, she thought. *I have to eat*, she admonished herself, then gazed into the waiter's tanned face, hoping for any sign that he recognized Sean.

"I'm sorry." He shook his head and handed the photo back to Shelly. "I haven't seen him."

Stifling the disappointment, Shelly set aside her billfold.

"Do you have any pictures of Dena?" Ryan asked.

Her hands unsteady, she fumbled with the billfold's clasp again. "Maybe. That's a good idea," she said, reading Ryan's intent.

"Dena is my sister," Shelly said, pulling out several more photos. "We're pretty sure she's got our son. Actually, she's his birth mother."

"Oh, I see," Winston said. "I guess that's not as bad, then, is it?"

"It could be," Ryan stated. "She's very unstable."

The waiter paused. "You two are doing remarkably well, considering," he said, his deep voice full of respect.

"We're just holding it together the best we can," Ryan said. "I think we've both already had our nervous breakdowns, and now we're operating in the numb mode."

The picture she pulled from her billfold was the one Shelly had hoped she still had. The shot was of Dena, Shelly, Ryan, and their folks in front of her parents' pool at a July Fourth cookout not long after Shelly and Ryan's marriage. Dressed in shorts and lightweight shirts, the family appeared to be the epitome of the American dream. Few would believe that Dena was more prone to hallucinations than dreams.

She handed the image to the waiter. "Dena's the redhead," she explained, but figured he could easily deduce that the younger woman was Shelly's sister.

Sadly, Winston shook his head. "No, I haven't seen her—not at all."

"Would it be too much to ask you to take the pictures to your coworkers, and—"

"Sure! Not a problem." Winston offered an encouraging smile. "Maybe the manager would even let you put up a sign in the window."

Shelly gasped and held Ryan's cautious stare. "I don't know," he hedged and didn't expound.

"There's a Kinko's in the shopping strip, about half a mile that way." Winston pointed north, and Shelly was thankful she'd worn jeans and walking shoes.

"Maybe it wouldn't hurt to give some flyers to individuals," Ryan said, hope brightening his features.

Shelly nodded and didn't push on hanging the posters in windows.

"Let me see if anyone here has seen them," Winston said. "I'll rush your order. When I bring it out, I'll let you know what they say." He slid his ticket book into his waiter's apron and turned from the table.

"Thanks," Shelly said after him and then gazed at Ryan.

"I didn't want to say anything in front of the waiter," he explained, "but hanging posters in business windows will leave a trail that would incriminate us and maybe even bring all manner of wrath upon us, especially if Dena's still in the area. All she has to do is spot one of those posters, and she'll fly."

"Good point," Shelly said, impressed with Ryan's reasoning.

"I don't think it hurts for us to have some flyers on hand to discreetly ask people if they have seen Sean, though." He glanced toward the front door as a string of customers neared their table.

"All right," Shelly nodded and lowered her voice. "Should we tell Sonny what we're doing in case he comes back for us?"

"Sure. I'll text him," Ryan agreed and pulled out his cell phone. After narrowing his eyes, he said, "Sometimes it's better to ask forgiveness than permission. I'll text him later—after we see how it all goes."

"Whatever you think. I don't want to interfere, but it drives me crazy to just sit and do nothing. At least this way, we're *doing* something."

Smiling into her eyes, Ryan reached across the table and wrapped his fingers around hers for a brief squeeze. "We'll find Sean, Shelly. One way or another, we're going to find him. I'll give my life if that's what it takes."

Breaking eye contact, Shelly removed her hand from his and said, "Thanks. Tim feels the same way."

CHAPTER TEN

Sonny pulled into the cabin's driveway and parked where he'd been before. He rolled down his electric window and upped the head covering on his Dallas Mavericks hoodie as the chill seeped into the cab. Even though the woods blocked the cabin's view, he could listen for the FBI's arrival. Jack had already called, confirming the FBI was on the way. After the search validated Sonny's findings, they would put a man on stakeout for a few days. If Dena didn't resurface, they'd move on to other leads. Sonny understood they didn't have the staff to watch the cabin indefinitely. Ryan should also understand. He hoped Shelly would as well, but had his doubts.

On a sigh, he removed his cell phone from the cup holder, pressed a few buttons, and eyed the missed call from Karen. His thumb trembled over the send button, and he wondered if she would be as cooperative as she sounded in the voice mail. Karen could get horsy in a heartbeat—at least, the Karen he once knew. The fact that she actually returned his call was miracle number one. If she really did give him the location of their son, that would be miracle number two.

He unfastened his seat belt, leaned toward the glove box, and opened it. After digging through the mayhem of papers, he found a pen in the bottom. An old tire receipt proved a sufficient notepad.

Sonny pressed the send button and waited.

After the third ring, a hesitant female voice floated over the line: "Hello, this is Karen."

"Karen, Sonny Mansfield," he replied and hoped the trace of bitterness slithering through his gut wasn't manifested in his voice.

"Hello," she replied. "I left you a voice mail . . ."

"Yes, I got it. I understand you have information for me?"

"Yes. I decided to just contact the adoption agency myself to see if he'd left any information. That was the agreement—that there could only be contact if *he* initiated it, and only if his parents agreed."

"Yes, I remember," Sonny said, keeping his voice even.

"Well, he did leave information—just . . . just a few months ago," she explained, her voice thick.

"That makes sense. He's thirteen now. Lots is going on in his mind, I'm sure. Have you contacted him?" Sonny rushed.

"No."

"Ah yes, the career," he replied, recalling Karen's not wanting a child or husband to get in the way of her physics PhD. "Has it worked out? Did you get your PhD? Are you teaching at a university now?"

She didn't answer.

"Karen?" Sonny glanced at the cell screen to see if the call was dropped. When he heard her speaking, he pressed the receiver back against his ear.

"I finished my master's degree," she explained. "And did teach at a junior college for a couple of years, then . . ."

Sonny wrinkled his brow and tried to finish the story she left hanging. "Did you by chance get married?"

"Yeah," she admitted.

Forcing himself not to comment on the irony of her choices, Sonny bit the tip of his tongue until it stung.

"My husband doesn't know about Blake," she rushed. "I have two other kids. My parents still think I was *raped*."

"So you never told them?" Closing his eyes, Sonny pressed his head against the headrest. He'd long ago resigned himself to the fact that Karen could not function in the realm of gut-level honesty. Why this information surprised him was anybody's guess.

"My husband is a minister," she added.

Sonny opened his eyes, lifted his head, and said, "Just like your dad, huh?"

"Yeah." The defeat in her voice underscored her trap.

He gazed into the woods . . . as tangled as the story Karen was weaving. "He probably wouldn't have married you if he knew?"

"I . . . I don't know," she admitted.

"I told my wife," he explained. "She wants, uh . . . Blake . . . in our lives as much as I do."

"I guess she must not go to church either?"

Sonny chuckled. "Yeah, we both do." He had never attended church with Karen more than twice. Once he saw that she was part of the type of church his mother dragged him and his brothers to when they were kids, he'd declined for good. Their brand of religion was long on law and short on grace.

"I still don't think you understand," she finally said.

"I just know it feels good to live honest," he explained, and couldn't keep the sting out of his words.

"Do you want the info or not?" Karen snapped.

"Of course."

She stated the Richardson, Texas, phone number, then the address, concluding with Blake's mom's e-mail address; and Sonny scribbled as fast as she dictated.

"I checked with the agency myself," she further explained, "because it would be too much of a headache to change the files and designate you as the father."

It would also risk your exposure, he thought, *especially if your husband discovered the paperwork.*

"So the files still document that I was raped and that I couldn't confirm the identity of the father."

"Have you contacted our son's parents and explained?"

"No, and I'm not going to. I-I *can't*, Sonny!" her voice cracked. Strangely, a thread of sympathy replaced his resentment. "Don't you understand? I want to see him as much as you do. And it would be cruel if he found out I talked to his parents but didn't talk to him. Right now, I'm just not in a position . . . If my husband found out . . . The only reason I finally contacted the adoption agency and then called you back is because you wouldn't stop calling, and I didn't want my husband to accidentally stumble into one of your voice mails. At least this way, you have the information. You can do with it what you will."

"Would you at least contact the adoption agency and tell them the truth, Karen? Otherwise, when I contact the adoptive mother, they'll think I'm a rapist. Would you let your child connect with a birth father who was a rapist?"

A long silence was his only answer.

"Karen?"

"Yes, I understand what you're saying. I can't promise anything. J-just let me think about it, okay? If it's any consolation, he looks just like you!" she rushed. "The parents would be idiots not to believe you're the father, but there are always DNA tests."

"You've seen his picture?"

"Yes, it's in his file. He left it when he left his contact info."

"Can you e-mail it to me?"

"No. I left it at the agency." Her voice trembled. "He has my green eyes. Everything else is you. His profile says he's already five feet eleven inches."

"So was I when I was that age!" Sonny enthused.

Karen's silence was finally punctuated by a sniffle. "Now, please don't call me again. I can't afford . . ."

"I won't," Sonny said. Then, after some thought, he added, "If I'm able to connect with him and you ever want information about him, let me know. I'll let you know as well if my number changes."

"Okay, thanks," she rasped. "How did you get my number anyway?"

"Paula," he stated.

"My sister?"

"Yeah . . . I still had her land line from years ago and so I tried it." He shrugged. "She hasn't moved, and her number hasn't changed."

Karen released a tired sigh.

Sonny hesitated again and added, "I'm sorry everything turned out like it did. It wasn't my first choice by any means."

"I know," she agreed. "But that's what grace is for, right?"

"Yeah," he said, but doubted Karen had embraced her own words.

"Take care of yourself, okay?" he said.

"You too, Sonny. And it sounds like things are going well for you. I'm—I'm glad."

He eyed Blake's contact information. "It's better than ever," he said through a smile. "Better than ever."

The blonde behind the counter at Kinko's reminded Ryan of Arlene. Her short, chic hair, ready smile, and buxom figure could have belonged to Arlene's sister. The effect left Ryan uncomfortable, despite cold logic insisting this woman was *not* Arlene.

"I'm so sorry about your son," she said, expressing her sympathy to both Shelly and Ryan. "I've never been asked to create a project for a missing child." The poster trembled in her hand. "It's just such a dreadful thought!"

"It *is* awful," Shelly confirmed and leaned forward as the clerk laid the mock-up on the counter.

Within fifteen minutes, the adept young woman had scanned both photos, isolated Dena's image, and positioned her next to Sean in a document. The word "Missing" in bold commanded the top.

"This is *very good*," Ryan said. "Shelly's always been good at this sort of thing. I'm all thumbs when it comes to creating documents."

"That's why you have a wife, right?" the clerk said with an ingenuous grin that only drove home her Arlene appeal . . . and upped the friction.

"We're not"—Shelly pointed to herself and then Ryan—"We're divorced," she blurted.

"Oh," the clerk replied. With her lips remaining in a pucker, she cut a glance to Ryan's ring finger. Then, she focused on the document before sneaking another peek at Ryan.

He rubbed at his eyes and wondered how any woman could be interested in him when he looked like he did. His stubble had grown even more, and he was twice as tired as he had been at eight. Ryan debated if he should take his pastor's advice and start wearing a wedding ring to thwart interest. Pastor Jonas had jokingly suggested a gold band at a church dinner when a female guest started chatting up Ryan, and he had to leave to escape her. Presently, the ring idea seemed like the best one he'd heard in months. Anything would be better than the pressure from this Arlene look-alike, or any other woman in the future.

He shot another glance toward Shelly and wondered if she even comprehended the woman's resemblance to his ex-girlfriend.

Shelly's stiff-lipped appraisal of the document hinted she caught everything—right down to the clerk's investigating his lack of a wedding band.

In his younger years, Ryan had enjoyed attracting female attention. But that was the *last* thing he wanted today. Wishing the floor could swallow him, he gave the poster a final perusal and nodded. "I don't see anything that needs correcting. Do you, Shelly?"

"No," she said, her voice husky. "It's fine." When she lifted her gaze to the clerk's, all aversion had amazingly vanished. Shelly's grateful smile insisted she didn't give a flip if the woman looked like Arlene because she no longer cared what Ryan had done or what he might do in the future.

Ryan swallowed and tried not to let Shelly's indifference affect him. But, he couldn't. Furthermore, he decided he preferred her anger rather than her apathy.

At least when she's angry, that means she cares, he thought.

Shelly's cell phone emitted a romantic tune that prompted her saying, "That's Tim."

Ryan flinched, and once again he seriously considered moving out of Bullard after Shelly's wedding. He didn't really want to leave the area, because of Sean. But living in Tyler would be better than taking the chance of seeing his ex-wife goo-goo-eyed over her new husband whenever he ran into them in town.

"I'm going to take the call outside," Shelly said, a shroud of relief covering her features. "Thanks for everything." She waved toward the clerk, who shifted her attention to Ryan.

"How many copies do you want?" she prompted.

"Uh . . . a hundred, I guess," Ryan said, stating the first figure that popped into his head.

"Are you sure that's enough?" she asked, her words still full of compassion. Nevertheless, even the compassion didn't cover the spark of feminine interest.

"Sure," Ryan agreed, allowing his gaze to slide to the ajar office door behind her. "And we'll take the master, in case we want to make more copies," he said, swiveling toward the glass storefront.

"Of course," she agreed. Soon, the wheeze of a high-powered copy machine signaled it was spitting out the documents with dizzying speed.

Ryan focused on Shelly, conversing with her fiancé, and wondered just how happy Tim would be if he knew she was two hours away with her ex-husband. Even in the state of the present emergency, Ryan couldn't imagine Tim would be pleased. Keeping his expression impassive, he inched toward the front window, his attention all for Shelly. Her features pinched, she spoke into the phone as if the caller were her lifeline.

He remembered her looking at him that way the day she learned her grandmother died. Ryan had wrapped her in his arms while she sobbed. Once she gained some control, they'd snuggled into the corner of the couch in front of a warm, December fireplace. Ryan simply held her while she watched the fire and quietly wept.

They'd only been married a year then. Their relationship had still been new. Even though Ryan was already feeling slighted by her family, there were still many things that were more right than wrong.

The longer he watched Shelly, the more those old memories flooded his mind, merging into one another until tragically, the wrong outweighed the right. In the end, he and Shelly spent more time yelling at each other than snuggling on the couch. Eventually, the marriage collapsed under the weight of it all. In the midst of the collapsing, Ryan met Arlene.

He closed his eyes and wished he could erase the relationship, but he couldn't. Even though he knew in his heart God had forgiven him and had removed his sin as far as the east is from the west, Ryan had yet to convince his mind. The only thing about that whole ordeal that gave him joy was knowing it was over . . .

After the Easter Sunday that he'd recommitted his life to Christ, he'd sat on the bench in Grandma Marigold's backyard until Arlene came looking for him. The night before, he'd given her a special bottle of some new perfume the saleswoman said was all the rage. Ryan had loved the scent at purchase, but when she settled next to him, the aroma nearly suffocated him.

"What gives?" she'd prompted with no preliminary greeting. Arlene always had been rather direct, and Ryan never had been taken off guard more than then.

"Just thinking," he said with a stiff smile.

"Something's wrong. You haven't been the same since . . . since church." Her gaze faltered, and Ryan knew she knew. Without either of them saying a word, somehow she knew.

"I know," he simply stated and observed a monarch butterfly frolicking in the outbreak of crocuses.

After an aching pause, she finally said, "You went up front . . ."

"Yeah." Ryan fidgeted with nothing.

"I wasn't expecting . . ."

"Me neither."

"Does that mean . . . do you think we should get married immediately, instead of waiting a while?" she babbled. "Because, if you do, I'm fine with that. You know that, right?"

Ryan shifted his attention from the butterfly to Arlene and gazed into the candid blue eyes that begged him not to hurt her. They'd planned a fall wedding for a variety of reasons—including that he had two weeks of vacation due then. That would give them plenty of time for their Hawaiian honeymoon.

Ryan opened his mouth to explain that he was doubting their relationship, not their wedding date, but he couldn't bring himself to voice the words. A swarm of confusion bombarded his mind with the possibilities of Arlene's suggestion.

Maybe God would be okay with our just getting married, he thought. *That's got to be better than living together.*

"I don't know," he'd choked out. "I just need time to think, I guess. I'm not sure of anything right now." He attempted a light chuckle, but it came out more like a croak.

Arlene worried a button on the front of her Easter suit. She'd always been cute, but this morning the apricot-colored dress had made her peaches-and-cream complexion appear translucent, her blue eyes like that of an angel.

However, the angel vanished, and all Ryan could see was the woman he'd allowed to contribute to the breakup of his marriage.

"Your copies are finished, sir." The cheerful clerk's words severed the memory, and Ryan pivoted to face her. Astoundingly, she looked nothing like Arlene now, unless you counted her blonde hair.

I must be like the guy in Poe's Tell-Tale Heart, he thought. *My sin is making me imagine things that don't exist.*

His legs shook, and he began to wonder if he'd ever be able to break free from the guilt. Aside from the fact that he needed the flyers, Ryan now wished he'd never stepped into this Kinko's. The self-incrimination he'd felt in the garden bubbled within all over again. He glared at the woman simply because he was angry with himself.

"How much do I owe you," he said, his tone gruff.

When her smile fell and she meekly voiced the total, Ryan mumbled, "Sorry. I'm not my usual self." Nevertheless, Ryan couldn't remove himself from the clerk fast enough. As the door sighed shut behind him, he vowed he'd rather God end his life than allow himself to repeat his former mistakes.

"Okay, Tim," Shelly said, glancing up at Ryan. "I'll keep you posted. You know I will." She lowered her gaze, but not before Ryan detected a thread of guilt. "I'll be careful. I love you too," she said.

He gritted his teeth, glowered at the traffic, and knew she'd told Tim exactly what they were doing. While he waited for Shelly to finish the call, he debated what to say. Once she'd lapsed into a few seconds of silence, Ryan dared another glance her way.

"You told him, didn't you?" he queried.

Expecting her to defend the breach, Shelly gazed up with wide eyes that looked like dark pools of disbelief in a face as ashen as death.

"Sean just sent me a text message!" she said.

CHAPTER ELEVEN

Shelly watched as Ryan's expression merged from grim to desperately hopeful. He rushed to her side and hovered near her cell phone. "What did he say?" he prompted.

"Here, you read it," Shelly said, her words thick. After she shoved the phone into Ryan's hands, Sean's message replayed in her mind: *I want to come hom. I don't like her. She hit me. I hit her bak. A dog almost got me. She scremed at me. Mak her let me come hom.* Even though the message was laced with second-grade errors, the meaning was gut-wrenchingly clear.

"Did you respond?" Ryan's voice reflected Shelly's agony.

"No. I just now read it," Shelly said. "Ryan, I promise, if she hurts him, I'll—I'll—"

"Sounds like he's defending himself," he observed. "You know how feisty he can be."

"Yeah, but she's bigger than he is!"

"I know. I know." He nodded. "Here, take the flyers while I reply." He thrust the papers toward Shelly, and she accepted them without resistance. Her fingers were shaking so severely, she doubted her ability to peck out one word on the phone.

As Ryan pressed keys, Shelly drank in the image of her son. A wave of despair snatched at her breath while she wondered if she'd ever see Sean again. She recalled all the "Missing" notices of children who'd been gone so long they had to use an artist's rendition of what the child might look like now. Shelly couldn't imagine spending the next decade of her life not knowing Sean's location or whether or not he was alive.

Ryan pressed a final button and gazed at Shelly. "I just asked him where he is," he explained.

"Do you think he even knows?"

"We'll see."

This time, when Shelly looked at the posters, her focus landed on Dena. A rush of indignation sent a wave of cold sweat from Shelly's ankles to hairline. The surrounding buildings tilted, and she wished for a bench. When Ryan offered a steadying arm across her shoulders, Shelly leaned into his strength and didn't care what he thought or what Tim might say. These were desperate times, and she needed someone to keep her from collapsing into a heap on the cold concrete.

Ryan's hold tightened. Shelly clutched the posters to her chest, closed her eyes, and welcomed Ryan's warmth and solidity while begging God for Sean's return.

On the heels of her prayer came a new array of emotions involving Dena. Up until now, she had always felt a latent sympathy for her disturbed sister, even after all Dena had done to disrupt her life. But in the wake of Sean's panicked text, all sympathy for Dena vanished. And Shelly knew that if she ever got Sean back, she would never again allow Dena to dupe her into believing she was "getting better." Dena had once and for all destroyed Shelly's trust.

The cell phone beeped. Ryan loosened his hold. Shelly inched away and gazed into his face as he pressed a series of buttons. Finally, Ryan exclaimed, "He says he sees the big ball tower I took him to last summer. That's Reunion Tower—"

"In Dallas," they said in unison.

Ryan's phone rang in sequence with their words. Reaching beneath his jacket, he pulled the cell from his shirt pocket. "It's Jack," he explained after a glance at the screen.

Shelly relieved him of her cell and greedily absorbed Sean's response. A nerve-racked smile couldn't be denied when she realized her son had spelled tower "tire."

"It doesn't matter where I am," Ryan said into his cell. "We just got a message from Sean. He's in Dallas within sight of Reunion Tower." After a pause, he continued, "I know, Jack. I promise— we're staying out of the way. *Please* just give this info to the FBI. Maybe an officer will spot the car." After biting out a farewell, he snapped the phone shut and shook his head.

"We've just been told off," he explained.

Shelly raised her brows in silent request for more information.

"Somehow, Jack figured out we're in Sulphur Springs. He read me the riot act and told us to get our rears back home."

"So are we going back home now?" Shelly asked, not daring to voice her first desire.

Ryan silently observed her while indecision scurried across his face.

Shelly was toying with the idea of renting a car and driving to Dallas, but wondered if Ryan would agree. While the chances of spotting Sean were slim, if he continued texting them they might be able to track him until they actually found him.

"What do you think?" Ryan finally prompted. "Jack was pretty adamant about our going home. If we don't, and if by chance we somehow get in the way, we really could be arrested. Actually, they probably have grounds to arrest us now, but—"

"But we're not going to get in the way, are we?" Shelly rushed.

"I'd like to think we won't. But just in case we do—we're history. Are you willing to take that chance?"

"Are you?"

"I am for *me*," Ryan said, pressing his fingers against his chest. "I just don't know about *you*."

"Let *me* worry about me," Shelly said and squared her shoulders as if she were feeling far stronger than she was. "I'll take responsibility for what happens to me."

"So . . . if you wake up in jail, you won't blame me for something that was partly your fault?" Ryan asked, his words loaded with another meaning Shelly struggled to glean.

At last, the implications came into clear focus like a glacier piercing the fog. Ryan was insinuating that Shelly might blame him for getting thrown in jail just as she'd blamed him for the breakup of their marriage. The honest concern in his eyes invoked the belief that the man still fully believed that she had contributed to the end of their marriage as much as he had. How in the world he could convince himself that his having an affair was equally destructive to anything Shelly might have done was beyond all realms of logic. Nevertheless, his expression was so convincing, she might have believed him herself if she hadn't been present during the whole marriage.

"I've never blamed you for anything that you didn't do, Ryan," she defended.

Narrowing his eyes, he leaned forward only a centimeter and scrutinized her like a scientist examining a slide under a microscope.

Taken aback, Shelly looked down and grappled for something to say while all manner of responses bombarded her. Finally, she voiced the thoughts that would not be suppressed, "Even if I wasn't the perfect wife, I *begged* you to go to counseling and try to reconcile, but you wouldn't! Why can't you just accept the fallout of your own decisions and get on with your life and stop all this—"

"You begged me to go to counseling, Shelly. *Me—just* me! You refused to go! Remember? You refused to admit that we *both* had problems. And then *after* the divorce, *you* decided to get some counseling." He raised his hand and let it drop to his side. "Why couldn't you go with me before?"

"I went to try to heal after the divorce," she ground out. "Do you know how many women wouldn't have even considered reconciling under any circumstances—whether you went to counseling or not?"

"Does that make your refusal to go right?"

Shelly held her breath and tried to stop her head from spinning.

"I just wish you could somehow get to the point of seeing that we *both* had problems!" Ryan added. "That's what finally made me walk out." He pivoted and gazed toward the buildings on the other side of the freeway. "The fact that you refused to admit any blame."

Shelly's phone emitted a familiar tune. A glimpse at the screen confirmed her father's calling.

Ryan shot her a glance. "Unless you've changed your distinctive ring, that's your dad, right?"

Shelly eyed the phone. "He's worried."

"I would be, too, if I were him." He rubbed his face. "Just don't tell him what we're doing!" he insisted. "I'm going back into Kinko's to use their phone book so I can look up a taxi to take me to a car rental place. *I'm* going to Dallas. If you want to come, fine. If not, I'm going to call Sonny anyway and tell him what I'm up to. I'm sure he'll make arrangements to get you back home."

"Even if I *did* have some problems, that still doesn't validate the affair!" Shelly said, the ring stopping on her final words.

"I never said anything you did validated anything I did," Ryan shot over his shoulder. "It's hopeless. Let's just drop it! We've *got* to find Sean!" he added before whipping open the door and entering the business.

* * *

The ride to Dallas remained silent. Despite Shelly's repeated attempts to get Sean to respond to more text messages, he never did. Ryan could only speculate about the reason: *Dena probably caught him in the act again.* What she might have done to him as punishment left a knot in Ryan's gut the size of a cantaloupe.

While he didn't believe for half a second that they'd catch up with Dena and Sean in Dallas, Ryan hoped that Sean would somehow manage to communicate with them again and they'd be closer to finding him if they were already on the road. By the time they began the trek to downtown Dallas, Ryan could only hope his reasoning proved valid.

He glanced at Shelly. Gripping the cell phone as if she willed it to beep with a message from Sean, she peered out the passenger window.

He'd seen her wipe a tear or two during their journey, but presently she seemed to have regained control. Ryan had stiffened his resolve to not give in to showing emotion, for now anyway. He kept telling himself he needed to be strong for Shelly. She *had* actually allowed him to comfort her after she got the first text message from Sean—she'd nearly clung to him. Ryan figured Tim would have flipped if he'd seen them.

He almost smiled, but couldn't quite pull it off. Regardless of her clinging or not, Ryan was beginning to believe that reconciling with Shelly was a lost cause. *Whatever*, he thought. *God is in control. If you want it to happen, Lord, then I guess it's just in Your hands. I've given it my best shot. You know I've done everything I believed You were telling me to do. All I can say is, I've tried. If she marries Tim, it's not because I haven't tried.*

He flipped on the vent to a low setting and hoped it wasn't too cool for Shelly. The afternoon sun had finally warmed his side of the vehicle to the point of needing a few minutes of ventilation. Ryan had already shed his jacket, and the sweatshirt he was wearing had finally gotten too heavy.

"Texas autumns always have been whacked," he complained under his breath.

Shelly shifted in her seat and cut him a glance. "What?"

"Oh, I was just griping about the weather," he responded. "It's colder than Jack Frost in the morning and then it's nearly seventy by two."

"Yeah," Shelly said. "I was getting a little stuffy myself. I'm exhausted," she added.

"Me too. The adrenaline rush alone is about to wear me out."

"So what do we do now?"

"I have no idea," he admitted and shot her a rueful glance. "Any suggestions?"

"You're the professional." She shrugged.

"I guess we go to Reunion Tower and cruise the area. There's the long shot that they're not on the run anymore and are staying with someone near the tower, or have a hotel room that gives a view of the tower."

"So we just comb the area?"

"Sure." Ryan nodded. "Why not? We still have the flyers. We can pass them out there."

"Sounds good to me," Shelly said. "But if Dena found out Sean was texting us, I can guarantee she won't still be there."

"Problem is, we don't know *anything*," Ryan said, "and there is the chance that even if Dena has left the area someone may have seen her or overheard her mention where they are heading."

CHAPTER TWELVE

Ryan dropped the overnight bag on the hotel room's bed and plopped next to it. He and Shelly had pounded the pavement until the approach of sunset. Once they crawled back into the car, they both were so exhausted, driving back home would have been dangerous. As the sun slipped closer to the horizon, Ryan had suggested they book a hotel room. Shelly had initially protested that she didn't have any toiletries or a fresh change of clothing. Ryan had remedied that problem with a trip to Walmart. In an hour, they'd both bought everything they needed, including overnight bags, toiletries, undergarments, and a new change of clothing.

He pulled two Walmart bags from inside the small piece of luggage and sorted through his new belongings. Ryan hung up the jeans and sweater and tossed the socks and underwear atop the dresser. The toiletries and new pajamas landed on the sink counter, and Ryan didn't bother to right the toppled shampoo bottle. He was too tired.

From the bottom of the overnight bag, he removed a third bag, so small Shelly hadn't noticed it peeking from the edge of his jacket's pocket when they left the store. Ryan pulled out a blue jewelry box and popped it open. The simple, gold band gleaming against indigo velvet beckoned Ryan just as it had in the store.

After Pastor Jonas's suggestion a few months ago, he'd periodically toyed with the idea of buying a wedding band. His mother hadn't stopped fuming about "how aggressive these women have gotten" since the girls started calling him in high school. As a young man concerned only for his own gratification, he hadn't viewed the issue as a problem. But as a maturing adult who took his walk with God more seriously by the day, Ryan's goal was to live a life of honor. Since he'd made his commitment to the Lord, he'd still been tempted to toss honor to the wind more than once but had managed to stay true. The church support group he and Jack were involved in had helped. Nevertheless, the longer he thought about the gal in Kinko's, the more he thought he should take Pastor Jonas's suggestion.

But some women like Arlene don't care if a man's wearing a ring, he scoffed, and then asked forgiveness for his attitude. Ryan hadn't exactly tried to discourage Arlene's advances, so he had no validation for scorning her.

But that was before I met the Lord, he reasoned and slipped on the band. The ring fit as perfectly now as it had in the store. He'd bought it when Shelly had scurried toward the ladies' wear. Not figuring she wanted him tagging along, Ryan grabbed jeans and a sweater for himself and then wandered to the jewelry. The second he spotted the simple wedding band, he was certain he should buy it.

Standing, he went for the nightstand, pulled out the drawer, and found the book he'd counted on being there. While the Gideon Bible wasn't his own, it was still the Word of God. No matter how tired he was, Ryan fully planned to continue his reading regime tonight. He'd skipped it last night, but didn't want to make a habit of skipping . . . even in the face of the current crisis.

"Especially *in the face of the crisis,*" he decided and flipped to Psalms, where he was sure to find solace for his troubled soul.

But despite his attempts to focus on the verses, his tired mind chose to concentrate on Sean. No matter how hard he tried, Ryan couldn't keep from wondering where his son was and how Dena was treating him. Sean's text to Shelly mentioned Dena had hit him. Ryan didn't want to think about the abuse she might heap upon Sean, or whether or not she might get involved with a man who'd do the same. From the day he was born, he and Shelly had committed to treat Sean fairly and to protect him from evil. Ryan's stomach burned, and he wondered if he was growing the world's fastest ulcer.

Slamming the Bible shut, he stood and stalked toward the bathroom. After brushing his teeth and donning his new pajamas, he downed one of the melatonin sleep aids he'd purchased at Walmart. Ryan clicked off the light and padded back toward the bed. When he booked the rooms for him and Shelly, the only availabilities were suites next to each other with a connecting door. As Ryan passed the door, he heard a noise that wrenched his heart and stopped him.

The inconsolable sobs of a grieving mother couldn't be denied. Ryan doubled his fists and swallowed against the lump in his throat. That only resulted in his eyes stinging. As Shelly's mourning continued, a rash of cold sweat covered Ryan's body. He whipped open his door and eyed the knobless door that could only be opened by Shelly.

Ryan stopped knocking when Shelly's crying abated. He gripped the frame, rested his head against the door, and debated whether to knock again. When another sob erupted, Ryan debated no more. This time, his knock was accompanied by his calling her name.

"Shelly . . . it's going to be okay. Please, please . . ." *Please what?* he thought but had no answer.

Once the door swung open, Ryan needed no answer. Shelly stood on the other side, hunched over as if she'd gotten word that Sean was dead.

Ryan's face went cold. "Shelly? Is there new news about Sean?" He glanced toward his cell phone, lying on the nightstand. Unless he'd missed a call, no one had informed him of any changes.

"N-n-n-noooo," she replied, rapidly shaking her head. "I j-j-just can't hold it in anymore." Shelly gulped for air. "It's just a-all—all too much! *Oh, Ryan!* What if he doesn't *ever* come back?"

Ryan stiffened and told himself to remain strong for Shelly. Nevertheless, when he laid his hand on her shoulder and uttered a string of comforting noises, a tear slid down his cheek. Ryan blinked hard. He hadn't allowed himself to panic, and he couldn't now.

Shelly lifted her head and gazed at him as she did the day she found out her grandmother had passed away. Ryan had wrapped his arms around her then; that seemed just as fitting now. He pulled her into his embrace before he second-guessed the gesture. Not only did she not resist, she clung to Ryan as if he were her only lifeline.

He held her steady while her body shook with a new round of tears. Ryan's own tears flowed unchecked and dripped into her hair. He closed his eyes and released the iron grip on his emotions. Together, they grieved for the safety of a child that had been conceived in their hearts; and in the release, they consoled each other as no one else could.

Her ringing cell phone shattered their moment, and Shelly stiffened. "That's—that's Tim." Coughing over a new round of sobs, Shelly stumbled toward the desk and fumbled with the phone before dropping it.

Ryan hurried forward, retrieved the phone, and extended it toward Shelly.

"No!" she vehemently shook her head and scurried toward the bathroom. "You talk to him. Tell him—tell him—"

"Tell him *what*?" Ryan asked as Shelly shut the door. He pressed the send button and placed the phone against his ear. "Hello?"

Tim's initial silence left Ryan wondering if the call was dropped. "Hello," he repeated.

"Who is this?" Tim demanded.

"Ryan Mansfield," he barked.

After another stretch of silence, Tim finally said, "I called to talk to Shelly."

"I figured as much," Ryan retorted, his gut hardening.

"Where is she? Are you with her?"

"She went to the bathroom." He scowled and bit back an edict.

"Are you in her *room*?"

"Yeah," Ryan challenged and nearly added, *What's it to you*? But his reasonable side insisted he take a breath and try to remain calm. "She was crying," he explained. "I was just—" Ryan stopped and thought, *Why do I owe this guy an explanation?*

"Listen, if you lay one hand on her—"

"No, you listen!" Ryan huffed. "The last thing either of us is thinking about is getting physical. *Our son is missing!* Get off the paranoia, will you?"

Tim didn't speak.

Shelly exited the bathroom and gaped at Ryan while twisting a wad of tissue.

"Here." Ryan shoved the phone at her. "You talk to him. He's not happy."

"I-I know," she whispered. "We already talked, and—" Shelly pressed the tissue against her eyes and shook her head.

Ryan searched for the phone's mute button, pressed it, and said, "Did he yell at you? Is that part of the reason you started crying?"

She covered her face. "I just couldn't take his being so—so upset on top of everything else," she explained against her hands.

Ryan glared at the phone and considered several things he could say to Tim Aldridge, but the call-ended message appeared on the screen. "He hung up," Ryan said.

Shelly reached for the phone. "I shouldn't have made you talk to him. I-I don't know what I was thinking. I'm just confused and— and, well . . . that was the last thing I should have done." She plopped the phone on the desk and dropped into the chair. "I just didn't want to fight. I guess I should have just let it go to voice mail. He's really jealous right now, and—"

"Is he usually so possessive?" Ryan queried.

"He has a streak," she affirmed, "but this time, he just lost it. He's very threatened by you—especially with us here like this."

"Doesn't he trust you?"

"It's not me he doesn't trust." She shook her head and left the rest unsaid.

"Surely he doesn't think I'd force myself on you."

"I don't know what he's thinking. I'm not sure he *is* thinking. I don't even know if *I'm* thinking."

The phone rang and Ryan frowned as he recognized the romantic tune. "That's him again," he growled.

She eyed the screen and nodded.

"You don't have to take the call, Shelly. He can just deal with it. If he's so inconsiderate that he'd unleash on you when your son is missing, then . . . then . . . I'm not sure I even know why you're marrying him."

"He wasn't just upset about us—us being here," she explained as if she were trying to defend a friend. "I put him on hold and then I forgot him, uh, twice today when I was talking to Dad."

"Oh," Ryan said and understood from experience why Tim might be exasperated. Nevertheless, he still didn't think any of that warranted the dentist's overbearing attitude or his unjustified accusations—especially not as he faced Shelly's shattered expression.

Ryan gritted his teeth while the phone continued its peal. After a parting glare at the noisy beast, he walked from the room. It stopped by the time he crossed the threshold. A glance over his shoulder confirmed that Shelly hadn't answered the phone. He raised his brows and thought, *Good for her.*

On an impulse, Ryan turned back to face his former wife. "If you don't stand up to him now, you're going to have one miserable marriage," he said and rested his hands on his hips.

Shelly's head rose as red crept up her cheeks. "Since when did you become the resident expert on marriage?" she asked, and Ryan knew he'd overstepped his boundaries in the worst way.

"I'm not. I'm just saying." He lifted his chin to cover his own discomfort and the self-disgust for not being able to come up with something less lame.

Tim's distinctive ring started anew. This time Shelly immediately pressed a button, ending the annoying tone. "I guess I'll text him."

Ryan hovered near the doorway. "Sorry. I shouldn't have put my foot in your business."

"Yeah," she sighed. "I shouldn't have snapped at you. I guess you're just trying to help, huh?"

"More or less, I guess," Ryan said, an ironic nuance to his words. "Why in the world I'd help my ex-wife with her future marriage is anybody's guess."

Shelly's big-eyed observation would have been humorous under normal circumstances. But these weren't normal circumstances, and Ryan could find nothing humorous about mourning for a missing child with a disgruntled fiancé yelling at the woman he loved.

The longer he gazed at Shelly, the more urgently his heart begged him to go back into the room, wrap his arms around her, and hold her until she went to sleep. But Ryan's mind reminded his heart that they were no longer married, and that Shelly's earlier clinging to him had been spawned by desperation and nothing more.

He forced himself to reach for the door and prepared to shut it. "I guess we'll meet downstairs for breakfast in the morning. Does 'bout eight work for you?" he said, wondering how he could even voice a thought on something so mundane.

Her mute nod was her only answer.

In case you don't realize it, Ryan thought, his heart pounding, *I still love you. I love you more now than I ever have.*

As if she'd read his mind, Shelly looked away.

Ryan hesitated, debated whether he should verbalize the words that burned in his soul like the hot coals of a perpetual passion. Finally, he decided this wasn't the time or place to declare his love . . . or to have it rejected again.

When her cell phone began Tim's tone once more, Ryan shut the door. Apparently Lover-boy wasn't going to quit until Shelly answered. If Tim Aldridge was worth anything at all, he'd have apology on the brain. But Ryan didn't want to witness those two making up.

I didn't want to tie you to the bed, but you didn't give me a choice," Dena emphasized as she knotted the nylon rope on Sean's wrist. She'd spotted the rope on a shelf before they left the cabin. Dena had never thought of tying Sean up until she saw the rope, and then she immediately realized it was the perfect solution. After she secured the other end around the headboard's post, Dena straightened and stared down at her son.

His tousled hair and hollow eyes gave him the desperate appearance of a helpless, scared thing, and a ripple of motherly instinct stirred Dena's heart.

"I'm sorry," she whispered and reached to stroke his hair.

Sean flinched away and glared in silent defiance.

Dena narrowed her eyes but didn't slap him . . . this time.

The whimpers that had characterized his first night had gradually been replaced by angry outbursts and open disobedience. After the barn episode, he'd locked the back door on her and then almost locked her out of the front door as well. If not for the aging dead-bolt, he'd have succeeded. Then somehow, the little monkey had even gotten to her cell phone again and sent a text to Shelly. All this convinced Dena that she could not allow him to have free run of the hotel room.

With a huff, Dena turned for her purse and fished out her half-empty flask. She recalled the bottle of whiskey she kept stashed under the driver's seat and tried to remember if it was still there. If not, she'd have to make a trip to a liquor store soon.

"You know I'm doing all this for your own good, right?" she asked over her shoulder.

Still, Sean remained silent.

"You need to be with me. I'm your mother—not Shelly."

"You're not my mom," he croaked.

Gritting her teeth, Dena unscrewed the flask's lid, downed a swallow, and waited for the alcohol to calm her nerves so she could go to sleep. They'd had burgers and fries at the Whataburger drive-in. The heavy meal along with the early hangover had left her ex-hausted. Add to that having to fix a flat west of Ft. Worth, and Dena was ready to lose herself in slumber.

Even though Dena still hadn't heard back from Lila, she planned to make a double effort to contact her in the morning. Lila would help her. She always did. Dena hoped Lila might even use her Mexico contacts to arrange for her and Sean to live across the border for a while. Once they disappeared into that old country, nobody would find them.

CHAPTER THIRTEEN

Early the next morning, Sonny Mansfield sat at his computer, staring at the screen. He'd worked into the night, trying to compose the e-mail for Blake's adoptive parents. Not happy with his efforts, he resumed the task this morning before breakfast.

The clang of pots and pans, the sizzle of bacon, the smell of hot coffee all beckoned Sonny to abandon the task and indulge his growling gut. But so far, the letter still held his attention. He stared at the words he'd penned and once again grappled with the same line. After telling the Wickmans' who he was and referencing the attached photos from the past and present, he'd begun to detail the circumstances of Blake's birth.

Sonny explained that Blake's birth mother still wasn't in a position to broach contact due to the fact that "Her church isn't a forgiving church." He breathed and scrutinized the line as he'd done the night before. Shaking his head, Sonny hit the backspace button and erased the words. After a good minute of finger drumming, he positioned his hands above the keyboard again and tried to come up with the words that would best describe Karen's situation without stating the actual problem.

Another five minutes slipped by, Sonny rewrote the same line he'd already deleted: "Blake's birth mother isn't in a position to contact him because she's afraid her family and her church will find out, and her church isn't a forgiving church. This is also the reason she hid the truth about the circumstances of Blake's birth. She didn't want her parents or her church to know that she made willful choices that led to his conception. I guess she just couldn't take their rejection," he added.

"Knock, knock," Tanya called from the bedroom doorway.

Sonny looked up and returned his wife's smile before his gaze slid to the steaming cup of brew she held.

"I brought your coffee," she said.

"Thank *you*," he enthused. "The smell was about to drive me batty."

Tanya entered the room, set the cup on a coaster near the desk's edge, and gazed at the screen. "This *letter* is driving you batty, isn't it?"

"More or less," Sonny said before sipping the hot coffee. He and Tanya took turns cooking breakfast every other morning. Sonny enjoyed the mornings she made the coffee. Somehow, hers always tasted better than his.

"I woke up last night around one, and you were still working on it."

"Actually, I had been to bed and got back up after midnight and tried again."

"What's the problem?" she asked. Resting her hand on the back of Sonny's chair, she leaned in for a perusal of the words.

"I just don't know how to say what I need to say without making Karen and her church look like a bunch of hypocrites."

"Yeah, that last paragraph is pretty direct, isn't it?"

"Problem is, it's all the absolute, unadulterated *truth*."

Tanya chuckled. "The thing I like about you, Sonny, is that you're about the most honest person I've ever met. You just lay it out there."

"Is there any other way?" he questioned.

"I guess not. Except . . ."

"What?" Sonny focused on his wife. Tanya's blue eyes, red hair, and freckles gave her the youthful appearance of a college kid. Only her scrubs hinted that she held a position in the medical field.

"I was just wondering, why say anything about Karen? Can't you just say that she's not in a position to make contact?"

"But Karen said she was raped. So that means they'd think I'm a rapist," Sonny reasoned.

"Ugh!"

"Why would Blake's parents want to let their son see a birth father who's a rapist?"

"Good point," Tanya agreed. "But maybe you could just make delicate references without point-blank calling Karen a liar."

"If the shoe fits," he snapped and wished the bile in his heart wasn't so blatant in his tone.

"Odd . . ." Tanya mused with an impish grin.

"What?" Sonny challenged, but he sensed he probably didn't want to hear what she had to say. That little grin of hers usually preceded a pointed remark that was too applicable for comfort.

"That you'd be so unforgiving of her and her unforgiving church."

Touché, he thought and rubbed at his heavy eyes. Given the distraction over the e-mail and the worry about Ryan and Shelly beating the pavement in Dallas, Sonny had slept so little last night, his tired mind couldn't conjure a reply. All he could think about was how much he wanted to finish the message and crawl back into bed. But he couldn't. He had to help find Sean.

"What? No retort?" Tanya teased.

"Nah." Yawning, he stood, stretched, and figured he ought to hit the shower and get out of his pajamas. It was his turn to take Coty to Tanya's folks for the day.

Tanya moved closer for a hug, and Sonny wrapped his arms around her. "I'm sorry," she crooned. "I guess I was too hard on you."

"You were just being as honest as I was. It wouldn't have been so bad if you weren't so right. I guess I should just gloss it somehow. Say something like, 'For reasons I really am not at liberty to divulge, the mother felt the need to cover the circumstances of our mutual relationship and Blake's birth. I never knew I was a father until after the adoption was complete. Blake's birth mother gave me your contact information and still asks to remain anonymous.' How's that?" he prompted, astounded that he'd actually stumbled into a string of words that sounded like they might work.

"Perfect," Tanya affirmed. Pulling away, she planted a kiss on Sonny's cheek.

Never too sleepy to take advantage of an opportunity, Sonny repaid her show of affection with a kiss on the lips that lengthened with the tightening hug.

Only the mild *wuff* of air at the doorway suggested they had company. Suspecting the audience involved more than one spectator, Sonny broke away at the same time Tanya did. The two of them gazed toward the entryway, and spotted their cocker spaniel along with their son. Smiling, their four-year-old trotted toward his parents and wrapped his arms around their knees.

"I wanta kiss and hug too!" he said.

Sonny scooped up Coty and included him in a family hug that prompted him to place wet kisses on his parents' cheeks.

Another *wuff* near Sonny's knees attested that the other family member wanted in on the action. Tanya's dog sat on his hind legs and flapped his front paws in the air like the beggar he was.

"Come here, Happy," Tanya said. "It's time for you to go outside for the day." She lifted the dog, scratched his ears, and turned for the doorway. "I'll take Coty to Mom and Dad's today. You finish your e-mail, then focus on finding Sean, okay?"

Prepared to argue that it was *his* turn to take Coty, Sonny decided it wouldn't do any good when Tanya shot him "that look." He'd learned that arguing at this point was only a waste of energy.

"Okay," he said, and didn't reveal just how thankful he was that she was going to help out. Coty rubbed Sonny's cheek and said, "You need to shave, Daddy."

"I know," Sonny agreed and stroked his chin. "I'm looking like a grizzly bear." He playfully growled and rubbed his face against Coty's.

The child squealed and squirmed as much as he laughed.

Tanya turned before she was out of the room and added, "I don't think it would hurt a thing if you went back to bed for a while. You look like you haven't slept in a week."

"Feel like it too," Sonny admitted. "Truth is, I don't think I've slept more than a few winks the last two nights. This deal with Sean is about to wear me out. And Jack and I are worried about Mom too."

"Me too," Tanya admitted, and the dark circles under her eyes proved her worries were as real as Sonny's. "But we're no good to your parents, Ryan, Shelly, *or* Sean if we kill ourselves worrying." She shifted Happy to her other arm.

"Whatever you say. You're the doctor," Sonny said, referencing her position as a nurse practitioner.

"Well, close enough," Tanya affirmed. "Come on, Coty!" she called as she turned back toward the hallway. "You can help me put Happy out, and then we'll eat breakfast. I'm going to take you to Grandma and Granddad's today."

"Yea!" he exclaimed and slid to the floor.

Sonny affectionately patted Coty's bottom before the child

zoomed out of reach. Then he reclaimed his chair and finished the e-mail.

What do you mean, I can't come?" Dena screamed.

Sean jumped and opened his eyes. In a drowsy daze, he stared at his aunt, who paced the hotel room and looked as mad as that barn dog. Her wiry red hair and thin lips reminded him of a Halloween witch.

His wrists felt like somebody had rubbed them with sandpaper. All his covers were on the floor, and he couldn't get them. The rope still held him to the bedpost so tightly he could barely shift to his back.

"You've got to let me come, Lila!" Dena demanded. "I need help. You said if I ever needed help you would—"

Sean closed his eyes and wished he could close his ears. Aunt Dena's voice clawed at his mind like his grandpa's garden rake. On top of that, he had to go to the restroom and didn't know how long he could hold it. He swallowed against his dry mouth and hated the flavor. He hadn't brushed his teeth since Saturday night because Aunt Dena didn't make him. Now Sean knew why his mother always made him, and he didn't think he'd ever get aggravated about it again.

"Listen here, you little . . ." Dena started saying words Sean had never heard before. He was sure they must be bad. "I'm coming whether you like it or not. And you're going to help me whether you like it or not."

After a pause, she laughed like she really didn't mean it. "Yeah, right! Like I believe that! You aren't going to call the police! You've got too much to hide yourself! But if you don't cooperate with me, *I'll* tell the police you helped me get Sean and you'll go to prison like your brother!" She picked up her brush and threw it across the room. It whizzed over Sean's head, and he flinched as it crashed into the wall near his bed.

While Dena yelled some more, Sean tried hard not to go in his pants. He hadn't wet the bed in a long, long time, but the hairbrush had scared him so bad, he was afraid all that might change . . . and soon.

"Do you understand me?" Dena shrieked out a final demand.

Silence followed her question. Her face red, she pulled the cell phone away from her ear and stared at the screen. "She hung up on me!" Dena bellowed and slammed the phone onto her bed. "I oughta run my car right through her living room! That'll stop her from ever hanging up on me again!"

Dena whirled to face Sean. "Get up!"

When he didn't budge, she eyed the rope like she'd never seen it. Finally, she bent over him and loosened the knot around his wrists.

"Go to the bathroom or whatever you need to do. We're going to Lila's!" She reached for her flat, shiny bottle, and Sean scurried to the bathroom.

CHAPTER FOURTEEN

Shelly nibbled her bagel, gazed out the hotel lobby's window, and wondered if Ryan was going to make it down. He'd mentioned meeting her for breakfast at eight last night before he closed the door on her call with Tim. She checked her watch and noted it was nearly eight thirty. Ryan wasn't usually late.

Probably overslept, Shelly thought and yawned.

She would have overslept, except she had asked Tim to provide a wake-up call at six thirty. He had apologized last night on the phone and even begrudgingly asked Shelly to extend the apology to Ryan. Nevertheless, he'd still seemed tense this morning when he called. Shelly usually squirmed when he fell into his possessive mode. Last night, she'd collapsed. Dealing with the pressure of his disapproval had been the catalyst that sent her into an emotional meltdown.

When she thought about how she'd clung to Ryan, Shelly studied her coffee and wondered if there was any way she could dismiss the behavior if her ex-husband mentioned it. At her house when she'd welcomed his embrace, she'd been so woozy she thought he was Tim. Last night, there was no way she could use that excuse.

She'd known whom she was hugging from the start, and he knew she knew. Despite this morning's embarrassment, Shelly had *needed* Ryan last night. Not even Tim could have shared her grief on the level Ryan had.

The reality left her confused and a bit defensive. She prayed Ryan didn't sense just how much she'd wanted him to hold her. Because no matter what weakness had driven the need, it didn't change the reality of the morning. Her engagement ring was as real last night as it was this morning. She touched the stone.

Tim's a good man, she told herself. *Not perfect, but good.*

A telltale bell dinged, and Shelly looked up. The open dining area allowed her to see into the whole lobby, including the elevators. As Shelly expected, Ryan stepped out, wearing the new jeans and sweater he'd bought last night. The overnight bag, slung on his shoulder, gave him the appearance of a carefree businessman heading for a day on the golf course. His square jaw, prominent brows, and chiseled nose suggested he was a Greek blueblood who *owned* the golf course. The impact affected her pulse, just as it had the first time she met him. This time, Shelly squelched the reaction; the first time, she hadn't.

She'd been pushing the speed limit on Highway 69 because she was nearly late for school—a definite faux pas for a student teacher. When she rolled down her window, the officer who stared back asked for no arguments. Appearing to already have his mind made up about the ticket he was going to write, his eyes softened a tad when he asked for her driver's license and insurance card. Once he returned, he held a white slip of paper that wound up being a warning.

After attempting a glower and admonishing her about the evils of driving too fast on a damp road, an endearing smile graced his features. That's when Shelly got over the jitters enough to realize her highway patrolman looked more like the cover boy for *GQ* magazine and that she recalled seeing him around town. When he inquired if she had been at the Chamber of Commerce chili cook-off the week before, she'd affirmed her presence. From there, they fell into light conversation that led to Ryan asking for her phone number.

The next evening, Ryan had called. Two days later, she'd run into him in Brookshires—the only grocery store in Bullard. After chatting her up, Ryan had cautiously asked if she'd like to join him for coffee and dessert. Rattled, Shelly initially declined but found herself eating a slice of cheesecake at a downtown diner within thirty minutes. Even though he had no interest in spiritual matters, Shelly had been too mesmerized to worry about it. Six months later Shelly married the man whose looks and charm left her breathless.

But as the first couple of years unfolded, Shelly began to view his charisma and uncommon good looks as a curse on their marriage. More than once, she'd caught a woman shamelessly flirting with him while Ryan seemed oblivious to the affect he was having on her. And for the first time in her life Shelly had identified with that old, classic song, "When You're In Love with a Beautiful Woman," except she was in love with a "beautiful man." During the next few years, Shelly's doubts about Ryan's abilities to withstand the temptations increased, until finally she discovered her doubts were founded. Ryan had succumbed to one of his admirers.

As Ryan rounded the three-foot wall that surrounded the dining area, her attempts to squelch the leap in her pulse failed. Shelly was stricken anew with how handsome he was. Even though their marriage was over, Shelly couldn't avoid the fact that Ryan Mansfield still had it—his share, and that of a few other men.

And strangely, for the first time since his affair, she couldn't find the resentment she'd once nursed. *My counselor would be thrilled*, she thought.

"Good morning," he said with a broad grin.

"Morning," Shelly said and slid her gaze from his. No sense taking even the slightest risk of falling under Ryan's old spell. Once they found Sean, she was going to marry Tim. He didn't have Ryan's looks or blatant masculinity, but he was safe. He would *never* break his vows. Furthermore, his ardent expressions of love and devotion seemed more authentic than Ryan's ever had. Using her thumb, Shelly stroked her engagement ring's golden band and smiled.

"Have you already eaten?" Ryan asked.

"If you can call it that," Shelly replied. "I've nipped at a bagel and drank part of a cup of coffee."

"You always were a big eater." Aside from the Sean-shadow in his eyes, his smile seemed genuine, more relaxed.

"Yeah," Shelly agreed and decided not to try to understand the source of his easy attitude. She wasn't sure she'd ever understood Ryan anyway. *Maybe that was part of the problem in our marriage.* The thought barged into her mind from nowhere, and Shelly couldn't stop the frown.

"What is it?" Ryan questioned.

Silently, Shelly eyed him and grappled for a reply.

"Is it Sean, or—"

"N-no, of course not," Shelly rushed. "I was just," she shrugged, "thinking, I guess." The last few words faded, and she gulped her coffee.

He squinted while a puzzled expression flitted across his features. "Okay," he said, plopping his bag in the nearby chair. "Whatever. I'm going to grab a bite, then we can decide what's next."

Ryan rubbed his hands together and eyed the breakfast spread. A flash of gold on his left ring finger snared Shelly's attention. Her focus followed the ring all the way to his hip, where he rested his hand.

"I'm going to force myself to eat. You need to do the same," Ryan admonished.

"Okay," Shelly agreed and wondered when Ryan had started wearing his old wedding band. But the longer she observed the ring, the more she was convinced this was not the one she'd given him, but a simpler one without the diamonds their matching bands had.

A warm wash of confusion started in Shelly's gut and crashed her mind. Fleetingly, she wondered if the man had secretively gotten married without telling her. *But that wouldn't make sense,* she thought, and rubbed her temple. *Only yesterday, he was still hinting about reconciliation, and he hadn't been wearing the ring.* She strained to remember if he had it on last night, but couldn't recall. She'd been too busy crying and clinging to him. She wondered what he must think about that whole ordeal and even if their marathon hug fueled his attitude now.

No telling what he thinks, she stewed as a wave of regret heated her cheeks. *He might even be encouraged, thinking we're close to reconciling.* Shelly lowered her head and made a bigger deal of rubbing her temple.

"Shelly, are you okay?" Ryan asked again. "Are you sure there's *not* something you aren't telling me?"

"Yeah, I'm sure. I just . . ." She waved aside his concern and hoped he didn't press. "Go get your breakfast. It's nothing. I'm just—just not myself."

"Of course not," he agreed, his tone suggesting a deep compassion that Shelly hadn't expected.

Her eyes stung, and she gazed across the lobby beyond the glass walls, toward the busy street. Last week, she would have never believed she'd be eating breakfast with her ex-husband at a Dallas hotel . . . or that he'd be wearing some wedding band for who knew what reason.

"Okay, then. I'll just go get my breakfast," Ryan said, but his words seemed to come from a distant planet.

She mumbled some response and watched him amble toward the breakfast bar. He'd gained a few pounds since she first met him, but Shelly thought he looked better for it. Ryan had been lean yet muscular when they wed. His commitment to exercise had kept him fit, but age had still won a pound or two. She wondered if he still had trouble keeping his socks together before they hit the dirty clothes, and if he still left his toothbrush on the bathroom counter instead of putting it in the holder.

Doesn't matter, she thought, and decided the stress of Sean's disappearance must be making her sappy.

She watched Ryan butter a piece of toast and wondered how she'd feel if he *did* decide to get married again some day. *It doesn't matter,* she repeated. *I'll be deliriously happy with Tim by then. What Ryan does with his life is his choice. Right now, I just need to worry about finding Sean and getting on with my life.*

Oh, dear God, she added and gazed out the window once more, *please let us find Sean. I'll give my life for his, if that's what it takes.*

"Shelly!" Ryan's urgent voice broke into her reverie. She jumped and spotted him rushing back from the breakfast bar, cell phone to his ear. "We've got to go!" He grabbed his overnight bag and then reached for hers.

"I'm on the phone with Jack," he continued, his features tight. "There's been a report of someone spotting Sean in a liquor store west of Abilene!"

"Look, Ryan," Jack continued, "I didn't call to tell you this so you could go chasing after him. I really think it's best for you to just stay put—or better yet, *come back home!*"

Ryan hurried toward the lobby clerk. He tossed his room key on the counter and then awaited his receipt. "I know what you think," he said. "But a herd of elephants couldn't stop me, and don't even *think* about stopping Shelly. Even if they are still moving, the closer we are to them when Sean is found, the sooner we get him back.

Besides, are you going to tell me that if Bonnie was nabbed you wouldn't chase after her?"

Jack's silence was answer enough. "Just keep me posted on where you are, and stay out of the way," he chided. "This could affect my dealings with the FBI in the future. They're conceding to allow me and Sonny to be involved because of the future—future cases and stuff—where they want my cooperation, you know? But if my brother blows their search because of something I told him, then they might not be so chummy later on. Understand?"

"Absolutely," Ryan agreed before ending the call.

He waited while his ex-wife extended her debit card to the clerk. Her hands shook as badly as Ryan's knees. He had attempted to pay for her room, but she'd insisted on covering her own expenses, including the trip to Walmart. Ryan wondered if the debit card with her name on it might be linked to Tim's account, but he didn't pry.

It's not my business, he thought and gazed toward the street.

After an intense prayer session last night, Ryan had somehow gotten a release on his pursuit of Shelly. He'd lain awake a full hour, waiting on the sleep aid to overtake his racing brain. He'd prayed for Sean until he was on the verge of crying all over again. Then Ryan had turned his thoughts to Shelly.

Yesterday, he'd offered a token prayer of release. Last night, before he slipped into the arms of slumber, Ryan had solidified it. He'd decided that continuing to pine after Shelly when she was clearly committed to Tim was insane. Even after the way Tim treated her, even after her and Ryan's unbelievable hug, she'd taken her fiancé's call before going to bed.

Ryan vowed he'd focus on finding Sean today. Once his son was safe, he'd stop yearning for a woman to reconcile who had no intentions of ever reconciling. Ryan had made his mistakes. He'd broken her heart, killed her love. And now it was time to accept that in her mind there was no undoing what he'd done. Even though he'd hoped for a miracle, God wouldn't force a miracle on someone who refused to accept it; and Shelly Mansfield appeared to want no part of Ryan's miracle.

Sean pressed himself against the passenger door and gripped the handrest. Once they turned off the big road and onto the narrow road, Aunt Dena drove faster and faster and kept drinking out of that little silver bottle. The smell made Sean want to vomit— especially after no breakfast. Aunt Dena had barely given him time to go to the bathroom and get a drink of water. She wouldn't even let him get out of the car to buy a snack when she got gas. Now his stomach had gone from growling to feeling sick.

A burning knot in his chest insisted he somehow get Dena to stop the car. The trees whipped by so quickly that Sean felt more scared than he had on the roller coaster at Six Flags. Plus, the awful smell made him think she must be drinking something like beer. After one of Sean's friends was nearly killed in a car wreck with his drunk older brother, his dad had started telling him to *never* ride with anyone who was drinking and driving—not his friends' parents or brothers or sisters. *Nobody!* Dad had even let Sean sniff some beer so he'd know when someone smelled like it.

His father's warning floated into the child's mind just like he'd said it yesterday. *Even if you're at a friend's house and the friend's mom or dad is drinking beer and they want to take you somewhere fun—like the water park—don't get in the car! If you have to, call me and I'll come get you! Understand?*

But this time, Sean didn't have a choice. Aunt Dena had made him get in the car. Sean's palms went cold and damp and he rubbed them against his jeans. Even though he didn't have a choice in riding with her, maybe he could get her to stop.

"Is that beer you're drinking?" he asked.

Dena gave him a hard stare. Her blue eyes reminded him of the ocean with a lot of trouble mixed in. "Shut up!" she blasted.

"If it's beer, you're not supposed to drink and drive. It's—it's dangerous! My dad says it makes people have wrecks. My friend almost got killed, even."

"Shut up!" she hollered and slapped at him. The nasty liquid splashed across the front seat. The car lunged. Sean hit the door and then the seat belt ate into his stomach.

Dena screamed. The silver bottle flew from her hand, slammed the dashboard, and zoomed over the seat. She fought with the steering wheel while the car rocked from side to side.

Sean closed his eyes, covered his ears, and hunkered lower. His heart felt like it was coming out of his throat, and he prayed he wouldn't die. The car began a terrible spin. Then a sudden stop flung Sean forward while the sounds of shattering glass and crumpling metal mingled with Dena's wild cursing.

CHAPTER FIFTEEN

Sonny's eyes lazed open, and he tried to remember what day it was and why he was in bed when the sun was so bright. He closed his eyes to shut out the piercing light, forcing its way through the blinds, and grimaced against his dry mouth. Gradually, he recalled finishing the e-mail to Blake's parents and then crawling back into bed. He lifted his head and spotted the half-full coffee cup sitting on the edge of the desk. Not only had he not finished the coffee, he'd never bothered to get breakfast. Furthermore, he held no memory of Tanya's leaving.

He rolled to his side and gazed at the digital clock on the nightstand. It displayed 10:30 in bold red, and that meant Sonny had been asleep three hours.

"Man!" he exclaimed. Tossing aside the covers, he swung his feet out of bed and rubbed his face. "This isn't like me," he groused and stumbled to the computer. He grabbed his cup and had it halfway to his lips before stopping. Frowning at the cold liquid, he debated whether to make another pot of coffee or check his e-mail. The icon at the bottom of his screen announcing he had a message made the choice for him.

He plopped the cup back on the desk, dropped into the chair, and held his breath before bringing up his e-mail. Sonny wanted to assume that Blake's parents had already written back, but didn't dare allow himself to hope. When he sent the e-mail, he'd prayed for a response within a week. If he got one within hours, that would be miraculous.

He clicked on the task bar prompt that brought up his e-mail program and witnessed the miracle. His heavy eyes bugged when he spotted an e-mail second on the list of incoming mail that bore his subject line, "From Blake's Birth Father."

"Already . . ." he whispered, and his fingers quivered against the mouse.

Closing his eyes, Sonny gritted his teeth and prayed the note was positive. If Blake's family rejected his attempts to contact his son, Sonny's quest would be finished. He'd have to somehow get some final peace on this whole episode of his life.

Dear God, please let them say they want contact, he prayed, not bothering to analyze the futility of praying for God to influence the contents of an e-mail that had already been sent.

He clicked on the message and waited while his heart flipped in his chest. The first line alone left him riveted to the screen.

Dear Sonny,

> *This is Donna Wickman, Blake's adoptive mother. Your message today was an answer to prayer. You have no idea how I've prayed that we would hear from Blake's birth mother. I never dreamed we might hear from his birth father, but under the circumstances, I think you might be the best option at the moment.*

When I first read your e-mail, I was skeptical. But when I
saw the photos of you as a kid, I was astounded at how much
you look like Blake. You look like twins. See his photo attached.
I did immediately call the adoption agency, and they confirmed
your story.

"Okaaaaay. Karen *did* follow through," Sonny drawled as he clicked on the attached photo. The picture that popped up dashed aside all thoughts of her and her issues. Gaping, Sonny absorbed the image that could easily have been his own photo from childhood. An onslaught of paternal affection left Sonny reeling. He squeezed his eyes tight.

This is no time to get emotional. There's more to read, he lambasted himself and refocused on the letter.

When we adopted Blake, we both knew God had answered
our prayers. We'd been childless for twenty years and had
been on an adoption list for two years. When we heard that a
birth mother had chosen us as parents, we were ecstatic. Blake
brought so much joy to our lives. I never imagined that the teen
years would bring so much turmoil. I just assumed that since
he never mentioned his birth parents, he was fine with having
been adopted and didn't pine for his parents.

Occasionally, we had the usual upheavals that most parents
have with kids. But it was when he was eleven, nearly twelve,
that we began to recognize that his angry outbursts were getting
worse and might be linked to suppressed anger issues. We took
him to a counselor, who learned that he was angry over having
been placed for adoption. We found out he kept having the re-
curring nightmare of being dropped in a Dumpster—essentially,
thrown away. We tried to convince him that wasn't the case and
tried to reason with him. But the anger continued to boil.

Oddly, it seemed he was angrier with his father than his mother. We never told him that Karen had claimed she was raped. We were afraid that would make matters even worse. Now that I know the truth, I'm thrilled we chose not to tell him.

Finally, the counselor did suggest that we try to get in contact with the birth mother. We knew that the adoption was, for the most part, closed. We did get to meet Karen during the adoption process. But after that, all contact was supposed to be over, unless we initiated it. We were a little nervous about initiating it and didn't at first.

But then my husband suddenly died with spinal meningitis earlier this year. That only made matters worse with Blake. I was desperate . . . and still am. I don't like the friends he's running with, and I'm terrified that if something doesn't change he'll get sucked into drugs and alcohol and the Lord only knows what else. But he's so gifted in sports—especially basketball— he could have a very bright future if only he could get some peace. . . .

Sonny skimmed the concluding lines. By the time he read the last word, tears trickled from the corners of his eyes. He stiffened and tried to keep up a tough persona. But when he clicked on Blake's photo again and gazed into troubled eyes that asked for someone to understand, Sonny's resolve melted. The tears fell unchecked in testimony of his relief . . . and his burden.

Shelly gazed across miles of central Texas terrain. Even though the flat prairie that stretched to the horizon starkly contrasted with the rolling hills of east Texas, the scenery was lost on Shelly. All she could think of was Sean—who had spotted him, and exactly where, and whether or not Dena was heading to the border or just to an acquaintance near Abilene.

She clutched a road atlas that she'd bought when Ryan stopped for gas. According to the map, there were numerous towns west of Abilene that Dena could be targeting. Odessa, Midland, and Lubbock were the larger ones. But dozens of smaller towns presented reasonable options. Shelly leaned her head against the passenger window, shut her eyes, and tried to recall anything Dena might have said about staying in Abilene . . . or any other town.

Of course, she's been gone for five years, Shelly thought. *No telling where she's been living . . . or with whom.*

"Okay over there?" Ryan's soft question sounded as hesitant as it was curious.

"Fine. Just thinking." Shelly lifted her gaze toward her exhusband. Once again, she was stricken with just how attractive the man was . . . and wished she'd quit being *stricken*. She'd spent the first eighteen months after their divorce oblivious to his appeal. Now an onslaught of honesty made Shelly admit the truth: in the last six months she'd been sporadically aware of just how alluring Ryan could be—both inside and out. Then, ever since he stopped her car a few nights ago, didn't issue a warning, Shelly's thoughts had turned more and more to what he did right in their marriage . . . and to what a good father he was to Sean.

Of course, his pulling her over for speeding had been what started their relationship in the first place. *Maybe I'm just reliving that whole event in some twisted sort of way*, she thought and wished she'd stop.

He shot her a glance, raised his brows, and refocused on the road. "'Bout what?"

"I'm trying to remember anything that Dena might have said about Abilene or any town nearby. I just hope she's heading for a place in Texas, and not . . ." She left the rest unsaid and checked her watch. They'd been on the road a couple of hours and wouldn't hit Abilene for about thirty minutes.

"She's probably already left the country," Shelly stated, her voice as flat as her deflating emotions. "It's almost futile for us to chase after her like this."

"Chalk up one for faith," Ryan's mockery was softened with a chuckle.

Shelly thought about glaring at him, but decided to make light of the jibe. "Yeah, you know me. Always Miss Positive." She doubled her fist and gently thrust it into the air.

"Really, I'm starting to get as depressed as you sound," Ryan admitted. "I told Jack we wanted to be nearby in case they find him, but the chances of us being in the vicinity are so slim."

"But we can't just sit at home and stare and wait. I promise, I think I'd lose my mind."

"Me too," Ryan agreed. "So here we are . . . driving across Texas while Jack is threatening me with my life if I get in the way. I promise you . . . the last time I talked to him, I think he *was* on the verge of tracking us down and arresting us."

Shelly recalled the brief conversation Ryan had with his brother when they were only one hour into the journey. Ryan remained stoic during the whole exchange. When Shelly asked if there was news of Sean, Ryan said, "No," and there wasn't any other explanation. Now she knew that Jack Mansfield was beyond just "not happy" with his brother and her.

And, at this point, Shelly cared for nothing more than the return and safety of her son. If Jack got so mad his eyes glowed and his hair fell out, so let it be—his disapproval meant nothing in the face of holding Sean in her arms again.

"So what's the plan?" Shelly questioned.

"You mean when we get to Abilene?"

"Yes, exactly."

"I thought we'd cruise to the gas station where they spotted him. If there are no officers there, we'll snoop around, maybe do our own questioning, just see if we might be able to talk to someone the FBI missed."

"Okay," Shelly agreed.

"Might not hurt for us to pray together before we go in, though. If we get caught at this point, Jack will boil us in oil."

"So we pray for God to help us be sneaky?"

"Yeah, exactly." Ryan smiled.

Shelly returned the grin and tried to recall if she and Tim shared in the light banter that she and Ryan had enjoyed early in their marriage. They'd tease each other mercilessly and loved every second. While Tim certainly had a sense of humor when faced with something hilarious, he lacked Ryan's lighthearted embrace of life.

If only everything had stayed the way it was those first couple of years, she thought and recalled the family photos yesterday that had ushered in the regrets. Shelly swallowed an unexpected lump in her throat and tasted the regrets again.

She observed Ryan out of the corner of her eyes. He gripped the steering wheel with both hands, revealing that gold wedding band that still intrigued her. After seconds of deliberation, Shelly decided to appease her curiosity and just ask him about it.

What's the worst that can happen? she thought and went through a short mental list that ranged from his calmly telling her it was none of her business to his getting mad. But none of these potential reactions proved powerful enough to stop Shelly.

"I noticed you're wearing a wedding band . . ." she said and couldn't stifle the interest that dripped from every word.

CHAPTER SIXTEEN

Ryan hid the shock with a mastery that surprised even him. Shelly's bringing up the gold band had been the *last* thing he expected. He'd begun to think he was a virtual invisible man in her world. Even though she focused on him occasionally, she seemed to look right through him, as if he really wasn't there—at least not in a way that impacted *her* life. A mischievous voice suggested he should toy with her curiosity.

But a quick glimpse at her served as sufficient warning against the urge. Her interest was mixed with a hint of vulnerability that Ryan couldn't understand. And given the distraction of driving and the worry over Sean, he didn't have the mental space to figure it all out either. Finally, he decided to just give her a straight answer.

"It helps to ward off interest some," he said.

"You mean like the woman at Kinko's yesterday?" she snapped.

"Uh, yeah," Ryan said and never dreamed Shelly cared enough to get snippy. "A lot of women don't make a move if they think a guy is married."

"Some don't care, though!"

Ryan's fingers flexed against the steering wheel as Arlene's memory floated into the car and settled between them like a troubling ghost. "Yes, but a good number do," he replied, astounded at how calm his voice sounded.

A long stretch of silence ushered in Shelly's next question, "So, you don't want to remarry?"

"Hhmmph." Ryan didn't bother to hide the irony in his humorless laugh.

"I mean . . . to—to another woman," she explained.

Another glance revealed her cheeks had gone pink, and Ryan held no clue how to interpret any of these developments. He finally decided to stick to his plan of simple honesty. "No," he said.

"Not ever?"

"Uh . . . at least not right now," he said. "Maybe in the distant future, but only if I'm certain beyond doubt that God releases me . . . and if Angel Gabriel skywrites." He threw in a chortle that she didn't join. "I just want to concentrate on getting Sean raised and, well, on my relationship with God." He shrugged. "I guess maybe this ring is like a purity ring the teens are wearing now."

"It's a little late for *that*, isn't it?" she scoffed.

Ryan flinched and didn't answer while he gassed the engine and maneuvered around a lumbering dump truck. When he finally did come up with a reply, he astounded even himself. "It's never too late with God, Shelly. He's in the business of redeeming everything . . . and everyone who'll let Him." *Even marriages gone wrong*, he thought.

Ryan didn't gaze at her again until he heard a faint sniffle. A quick look her way revealed she stared out the passenger window. With her hair in a ponytail, her profile was clearly visible, so were the rivulets of tears. Her fingers unsteady, she dashed at the moisture and balled her fist in her lap.

Dumbfounded, Ryan stared at the highway and grappled for something to say. Last night, he'd found a peace in accepting that he and Shelly would never reconcile. Now he refused to allow himself to hope that her interest in the ring or her reaction had anything to do with a potential reconciliation.

Probably just the worry over Sean, he mused. When the memory of her clinging to him in the hotel room threatened to take him under, Ryan resisted but lost the battle. During that hug, he'd closed his eyes and pretended they were still married and that they were weathering this storm together. He'd savored her warmth, cherished her presence, and drowned in the aroma of her perfume . . . the very fragrance she wore this morning.

Sighing, Ryan focused on driving and wished he'd waited to put on the wedding band. Shelly, then, would have never asked about it, she wouldn't be crying, and he certainly wouldn't be so confused.

He hadn't felt this confused since his Easter encounter with God. But while the new confusion centered on Shelly, the old confusion involved Arlene. His fresh encounter with God that Easter had promised to simplify his life, but the pathway to simplification involved navigating some stressful complications. . . .

Ryan had gone back to his and Arlene's apartment that day with a plan to do nothing but watch TV and laze around. Arlene snuggled by him on the sofa and suggested the classic movie channel. Ryan hadn't protested, even though he'd have far preferred ESPN. He draped his arm around her in response to her prompting, but the closer she got the more uncomfortable Ryan grew. Finally, he was overcome by an unexpected attack of claustrophobia mixed with the sensation of suffocation he'd experienced in her grandmother's backyard. Somehow, he'd managed to extract himself from her, move to their bedroom, and sprawl on the bed while watching ESPN.

That night, he'd stayed on his side of the bed, much to Arlene's disappointment. When he awoke, Ryan lay so close to the edge he marveled that he hadn't fallen off. Arlene had risen early for work and had left a note on the kitchen table, professing her love and devotion. But the misery in Ryan's soul blotted out the sentiment.

The next night, he slept on the couch. He'd used the excuse of falling asleep while watching TV, but somehow Arlene knew he was pulling away and that it was related to what happened at church. The third night, she'd broken down and cried over dinner. The scene was so wrenching, Ryan convinced himself that perhaps God would be fine with them staying together, if only they'd just get married.

Ryan had promised her they could get married soon, but that he could no longer sleep with her until they were married. He explained his new commitment to God, and she agreed to attend church with him the next Sunday morning. But the more Ryan prayed, the deeper he dug into the Word of God, the more he realized that marriage to Arlene was not what God wanted. He wanted Ryan to try to reconcile with his first wife. And with that realization came the resurrection of his love for Shelly. But this selfless love was like none he'd ever experienced before.

Memories of Arlene's sobbing the day they split up bombarded his mind, and Ryan ached for her even now. He detested hurting anyone; his new heart for God increased his revulsion tenfold. But, ironically, this new heart for God was also what insisted he break away from Arlene.

"I hate you!" she'd screamed when he retrieved his last suitcase. "I hate you, Ryan Mansfield. I hope I never see you again!"

His resolve as stony as his face, Ryan had walked out. Arlene transferred to another city—he didn't even know where—and she got what she wanted. They never saw each other again.

Thank God, he thought and marveled that he could have ever allowed himself to get sucked into that relationship. He recalled his childhood pastor saying, "Sin will take you places you never thought you'd go." Ryan never believed that statement more than now.

"Do you have any idea how much you hurt me?" Shelly's angry

demand barged into Ryan's thoughts like a boulder dropping from the sky.

"Excuse me?" he prompted, certain he must have misunderstood her.

"Do you have any idea how much you hurt me?" she repeated, turning her reddening face to his.

An irate horn blasting from the left jerked Ryan's attention back to the road. Glimpsing a vehicle close enough to crash, Ryan realized he was swerving into the other lane and yanked the steering wheel to the right. The overcompensation sent the vehicle into a rocking frenzy that left him grappling for control. Shelly's scream mixed with more honking before the car steadied. By that time, Ryan shook so violently driving proved impossible. He slowed, pulled to the road's wide shoulder, engaged his emergency blinkers, and stopped. Sagging against the headrest, he rubbed his face until it stung.

"I'm sorry," Shelly whimpered. "I shouldn't have brought all that up. It's just that—"

"It's not your fault," Ryan encouraged and laid his hand on her shoulder. "It's mine. I shouldn't have taken my eyes off the road." She fixed her big brown gaze on his; the anger had slipped away, leaving only raw pain in its wake.

Ryan's frantic heartbeat slowed to a hard thud as the near crash faded in the face of Shelly's unexpected honesty. Even though Ryan had always fully understood that Shelly was angry and that he'd hurt her . . . he had assumed she cared much less than her expression now suggested.

"I . . ." Ryan fought to find some way to respond, but came up with nothing.

"You were so focused on yourself and on what *you* wanted and on *your* needs, you never even considered that *I* had needs too. And judging by the look on your face, I don't think you even get it now!"

Ryan swallowed and decided the time had come to speak. He

opened his mouth and prayed what he was about to say would be the right thing. "I get it, Shelly. Believe me, I get it more than you ever know. I guess I just got to the place of thinking that you didn't really care what I did in our marriage. You were so focused on your job and your family and Sean that you didn't seem to have any time for me or even seem to listen when I tried to tell you about my needs. We hadn't been intimate in forever, and I just . . . got tired of trying, I guess, and I . . . I fell." Ryan lifted his hand. "Then, when you found out, you were just angry. I thought the affair made you mad more than anything else."

Hunching forward, Shelly placed her elbows on her knees and covered her face. "It *did* make me mad," she said, her voice muffled. "And it infuriated me even more when you blamed *me* and said *I* needed to go to counseling."

"I already told you I did *not* totally blame you!" Ryan exclaimed. "You were just too mad to hear me!"

"Well, you'd have been mad too!" Shelly challenged, turning her face to his. "Put yourself in my shoes. How would *you* feel if I'd had an affair? Would you have stayed in the marriage? . . . *Knowing* I'd been with another man? Would *you* have been willing to go to counseling after I spent who-knew-how-long *lying* to cover my tracks?"

In the face of Shelly's agony, Ryan couldn't answer. The emotionally-charged silence only upped his inability to speak.

"Would you?" she demanded.

"I-I don't—don't know," he finally croaked and had never despised the stark truth more.

Shelly's phone began Tim's nauseating, romantic tune, and she began fumbling for it. "It's Tim," she explained before eagerly answering.

While Shelly entered the conversation, Ryan tuned her out, leaned toward the driver's window, and drowned in hopelessness. His commitment last night to finally let go of Shelly grew more pivotal by the hour, and Ryan was more convinced than ever that the inevitable was going to happen. She would marry Tim, and Ryan would just have to deal with it. Even though she did bring some problems to their marriage, none of her stuff warranted what he'd done. Ryan had destroyed her love. Even if Shelly *did* forgive him, forgiveness was different from reconciliation. Reconciliation required mutual trust, and Ryan doubted Shelly could ever trust him again.

At least, not without God's help, he thought and didn't dare hope she'd allow the Lord to work a miracle in her heart.

"Oh no . . . no . . . no . . ." Shelly's moans snapped Ryan out of his reverie, and his heart swelled. Her face pale, Shelly reached for Ryan's hand and gripped it with furor. "Where is the car?" she questioned and remained silent. "Do they think the blood is Sean's?"

"Blood!" Ryan exclaimed.

"Wait, Tim! Someone's beeping in on me." Shelly removed the phone from her ear, read the screen, and then rushed, "It's Daddy. Just hang on. He's probably watching the news as well."

"What's going on?" Ryan urged.

"Hello. Daddy?" Shelly said, her desperate gaze fixed on Ryan. "Yes, yes, I know. I was just on the phone with Tim. He told me."

Ryan's phone blasted out a ring from his shirt pocket. Releasing Shelly's hand, he retrieved his cell and figured it was Jack or Sonny. His assumptions were correct.

"What's going on, Sonny?" Ryan demanded.

"They found Dena's car on a county road east of Odessa. Looks like she had a wreck and abandoned the car. There's blood. They don't know if it's Sean's or hers. They're testing it now for type. We need Sean's blood type. Do you know it?"

Ryan removed the phone from his ear and said, "Shelly . . . Sean's blood type—it's B positive, right?"

"Yes, yes," she said with a vigorous nod before continuing the conversation with her father.

"B positive," he repeated and swallowed against the nausea.

"The FBI didn't let us know anything this time, until they needed info from us. Jack thinks it's because they've figured out you're following. He said they tracked you in Dallas."

"Doesn't surprise me," Ryan said. "We showed Sean's picture to quite a few people."

"It's all over the radio and TV now, so they let us contact you. There's a big alert on statewide. You could have known an hour ago, but the FBI was sure you'd rush in and destroy the operation. Listen, Ryan, you've *got* to stay back. Where are you?"

"We're nearly to Abilene."

"Stay in Abilene! You're close enough now!"

"Okay—okay!" Ryan agreed. "Just don't leave us hanging!"

"We won't! I promise!"

The phone went silent, and Ryan checked the screen to see the called-ended message. Sighing, he rubbed his face and then observed Shelly. Her expression impassive, she stared straight ahead. Now that her own call was over, she gripped her cell phone in her lap.

"Shelly?" Ryan prompted.

A hard sob erupted from her, and she reached for Ryan at the same time he reached for her. Ryan lost all track of time as they cried together. Thoughts of Sean being hurt, bleeding—possibly dying—fueled a primal emotion that shook Ryan to the core. Images of their son crying for them, needing them, reaching for them but unable to have them, left him weaker by the second.

Shelly's phone started Tim's tune again, and she managed to utter something about Tim . . . about forgetting him. Soon, she was stammering into the receiver, "I'm—I'm sorry, Tim. After Dad called, I just hung up. The shock was so great—please don't be angry. I just . . ."

Even in the face of Ryan's being so shaken, the idea of Tim pressuring Shelly at such a time only added exasperation to his grief.

"It's okay, really," she finally whimpered. "I know. I know. Th-thanks for letting me know. I just—just wasn't thinking."

So now he's apologizing, Ryan groused.

"Maybe I do," she said, wrinkling her forehead. "Yes, he's still here," she added with a guilty glance Ryan's way.

He lifted his brows and wondered how Tim could even think about whether or not Shelly was with Ryan when Sean's life was on the line. He scrounged around for a tissue, found a rough napkin, and scrubbed at his wet cheeks until they stung.

"Everything's—everything's okay." She darted a baffled expression toward Ryan and then looked away. "I'll call you again soon," she added before hanging up.

CHAPTER SEVENTEEN

I think it's best if we find a spot to land in Abilene and stay put awhile. Sonny's saying the FBI didn't immediately call them on this latest news because they figured out you and I are on the trail. Sonny's rabid about our staying back, and I imagine Jack will decapitate me if I don't get in line."

"Th-that's okay," Shelly said, too stunned to do anything more than agree. The news about Sean coupled with what Tim had just said left Shelly spinning in a whirlwind of confusion. Finally, she decided to tuck away Tim's claims for another day. Shelly simply didn't have the emotional energy to deal with romantic upheaval in the same day she was facing the potential loss of her child.

"I understand," she added. "But where do we go?"

"I don't know right now. Maybe we should just check into another hotel and hang out."

"Oh yeah, Tim will be just *thrilled* with that," Shelly drawled.

"Tim is the *last* person I'm worried about right now," Ryan barked.

Shelly stared out the window, toward a pasture full of what

looked like winter grain. She never imagined life could get so complicated so quickly and didn't know what to say. Thoughts of her voluntarily clinging to Ryan . . . again . . . only upped her confusion. Even in the midst of her desperation over Sean, Shelly had sensed that Ryan had somehow grown into a source of support he'd never been in their marriage, someone to whom she could turn if she was too weak to hold herself up. Twice now he'd been there. He'd held her; he'd asked nothing in return. But Shelly sensed that she'd also been a support for him. Nevertheless, she'd come away both times with the distinct impression that she'd been the bigger recipient and that he would have selflessly offered himself even if the need was all hers.

If only he'd been this way in our marriage all the time, she thought and admitted there had been a few times when he'd managed to set aside himself for her best interests. The biggest event was when they received the devastating news that Shelly couldn't have children.

After a year of marriage, she and Ryan had begun trying to conceive. But when their second anniversary arrived with no baby in the future, Ryan had gladly agreed to go for testing first. Once his results were all normal, Shelly had arranged for testing by a specialist. The battery of tests left her hopeful that if there was a problem, it could be discovered and corrected. When the bad news came, Ryan had simply held her in bed that night and allowed her to sob. The next morning, he'd surprised her with breakfast in bed. The treat was a double shock because he was supposed to work that Saturday.

"You know I had vacation time stacked up," he'd said with an endearing grin. "I arranged to take a day." The fluffy eggs, perfect crepes, and unbelievable sausage had transcended anything Shelly knew he could cook. When he confessed he'd ordered takeout from a local café, Shelly had collapsed with laughter.

She cried again when Ryan also "served" her an Internet printout from a Dallas adoption agency. He promised they'd have a child, and that when she was ready they'd start the paperwork. Breakfast was a forgotten luxury as they made love with a passion unmatched.

Shelly's stomach warmed as old feelings stirred . . . feelings she never imagined she'd experience again. Truth be known, she'd been far more physically attracted to Ryan than she ever had been to Tim. But as a mature woman, Shelly also understood that a solid marriage was built upon far more than physical attraction. She also assumed that once she and Tim consummated their marriage she might feel much differently.

Out of loyalty to her fiancé, she resisted the old memory that still played on the fringes of her mind. *I guess Ryan did a lot right,* she thought and even recalled thinking they had something special during those first couple of years.

"Well, I guess we need to go ahead and drive into Abilene," Ryan said, and Shelly was jolted back to the present.

The realization that she'd been recalling those early years with Ryan in the face of the current crisis with Sean spawned a wave of guilt that snatched at her breath. Her cell phone's ringing again upped her shame. *Tim.* She'd promised Tim her future. Loyalty demanded that she not savor the past with Ryan.

How could I even go there after what Ryan's done? she thought and considered if the stress with Sean was making her lose her mind.

When the phone stopped ringing, Shelly gazed at the missed-call message and wondered why she hadn't answered. Every second that passed ushered in more bewilderment.

"Maybe we can get some lunch and sit in a restaurant until they kick us out," Ryan said. "Do you have any ideas where you'd like to eat?"

The phone's renewed ringing took on an impatient edge. This time, Shelly didn't hesitate to answer, "Hello, Tim?"

"Shelly! Is everything okay? I was worried when you didn't answer."

"Yes. I . . . just . . . I'm struggling right now," she said and wondered how Tim would react if he could read her mind.

"Listen, I'm rescheduling my day. I'm going to fly to Abilene," he said in his this-is-the-way-it's-going-to-be voice. "I'm pulling into Pounds Field now to fire up the Cessna. Once I get clearance on landing, I'll call you with the address of the airport there. You can type it in your phone's GPS. I should be there within a couple of hours—probably sooner."

This new turn of events only upped Shelly's burden and confusion. Thoughts of Tim in the vehicle with her and Ryan turned the car into a stifling box. Her face, once heated with passionate memories, now flashed cold.

"Shelly? What is it?" Ryan prompted. "Is there more news of Sean?"

All Shelly could do was shake her head. Why she extended the phone to Ryan was anybody's guess. When he said, "Hello," Shelly covered her face with her hands and tried to stop the unearthly shaking.

"Okay . . . okay," Ryan said, his tone all business. "I understand . . . No problem . . . Of course, you want to be with her. I understand," he repeated. "We've been given orders to cool our heels in Abilene anyway. It will give us something to do while we wait. Uh-huh . . . No . . . I . . . don't think so. Yes . . . Here she is."

"Shelly?" Ryan's gentle tone prompted her to lower her hands.

The chilling air urged her to wrap her jacket closer while turning her attention to Ryan. She eyed the phone he extended.

"He wants to talk to you. He's really worried about you."

Shelly accepted the phone, put it to her ear, and managed to emit a wooden, "Hello."

"Are you going to be okay?" Tim's concerned voice oozed with love and anxiety.

"I-I don't know, really," she admitted and wished the shaking would subside.

Tim's silence finally ended when he said, "I'm on my way, honey. I'll be there as soon as I can. Just hang on. Okay?"

"O-okay," Shelly replied and struggled for something else to say.

"I love you," Tim said.

"I love you too," Shelly replied out of habit before ending the call.

"He said he owns his own plane," Ryan said.

"Yeah," Shelly croaked.

"Figures," he groused.

Ryan's tone was the trigger that prompted Shelly's explosion. "Stop it!" she yelled, wadding the jacket's hem into a tight ball. "Just—just—just stop it!"

"What?"

"You're always taking shots at him!" she exclaimed, not daring to add that he should get out of her head and permanently stay out. "Just stop it!" her voice cracked. "I can't take you two at each other's throats on top of Sean's missing. If he's coming, you've got to get along!"

"Try telling *him* that," Ryan defended. "I don't think he's exactly ready to build sand castles with *me*." As he laid his hand against his chest, Shelly focused on his sweater that reminded her of a similar sweater he'd worn one Christmas. He'd given her a diamond solitaire necklace. Shelly had been so elated, she accidentally spilled her hot chocolate all over him. In the aftermath of their kiss, Ryan hadn't cared about the hot cocoa mess.

She thought about the solitaire, still in her jewelry box, and wondered why she hadn't gotten rid of it . . . or the simple engagement ring Ryan had given her.

"Oh, God help me!" she groaned and covered her face again. "This is crazy! I'm losing my *mind*!"

"Shelly?" Ryan's voice had gone soft.

"I need— I need— *To get out of this car!*" She flung open the door and stumbled from the road's shoulder toward the pasture. The cold breeze sent an icy shiver from her wet face to the center of her soul. Desperate to put some space between her and Ryan, Shelly shoved on. Only when the hard ground bit into her knees and hands did she realize she'd stumbled over who-knew-what and hit the ground.

And Ryan was hovering over her, pulling her to her feet, steering her to the car. Only when she was wrapped securely in his arms, clinging to him once more, did Shelly realize they were in the car, out of the biting wind.

"Shelly, it's okay," he crooned, stroking her hair. "I promise, we're going to find Sean. He's going to be okay. I won't cause any trouble with Tim. I promise I'll be good," he added. "Just relax. We're going to find Sean," he repeated, and the certainty in his voice balmed her tattered nerves. "He can't be far. They'll find him. They will. Just relax."

Reduced to occasional sniffles, Shelly closed her eyes and drank in the comfort. Ryan's gently stroking her hair and back righted her spinning world and brought a measure of sanity into an insane situation.

While she waited for the shaking to subside, Shelly could only hope Ryan was right about Sean . . . and that once Tim arrived, the old memories would prove to be a fluke that would disappear in the face of Tim's support.

"Let's go ahead and drive to the airport," Ryan said before pulling away.

With a nod, Shelly groped in her jacket's pocket for a tissue. "I've got a GPS on my phone. Tim's going to send me the address once he gets to the other airport. We can use my phone and get directions then." She inched away, but the farther she drew from Ryan the colder she became.

"Why don't I just call information, get the Chamber of Commerce number for Abilene, and let them give us directions?" Ryan asked, scooting over to the steering wheel. "I'll ask if they have a restaurant at the airport. If they don't, we'll go eat somewhere first. A good burger always settles my nerves." With an encouraging smile, he patted her arm and then reached for his phone.

She attempted to return the smile but her wobbly effort failed. After fastening her seat belt, Shelly focused out her window awhile, until she noticed that Ryan was exiting off I-20. She possessed no sense of when Ryan's phone call had ended.

"The chamber said he'll most likely be flying into Abilene Regional Airport and that it is super easy to find," he commented. "We take the loop to Highway 36 and then hit Airport Boulevard off 36. She said there were signs. Help me look for them, okay?"

"Sure," Shelly said, feeling more numb by the minute. Her phone's bleeping out a text notice announced a message from Tim. She picked up her phone and soon was reading the text. "He is saying it's Abilene Regional," she confirmed, "and he's arriving by one fifteen." Shelly checked her watch and noted that was just over two hours away. While her fiancé's arrival should have ushered in peace, it only upped her anxiety.

Despite her vow not to think about the verbal grenade he'd dropped in their earlier conversation, Shelly thought about it anyway. *Shelly, do you know you keep ditching my calls for your dad's. It's like I don't even matter when he's in the picture—today or ever . . . I know this isn't the time or place to talk about this, but I promise, sometimes I feel like I can never compete. I know you love your dad and mom, but I'm about to be your* husband.

Considering Tim's claim added dismay to her anxiety. His words had taken on the nuance of Ryan's, and Shelly wondered if they'd read from the same script. When Ryan had said that Shelly put her family above him, even her counselor had assumed that Ryan was using that as an excuse for his choices. Shelly had clung to this theory, but now she didn't know what to think. As much as she'd like to dismiss Tim's words as well, Shelly couldn't. But neither could she dwell on what he said—especially not now, not with Sean missing. It would all have to wait until after she held her son again and knew he'd be safe forever.

"We're here," Ryan said.

Shelly was jolted back to reality. "I didn't help you look for signs," she muttered.

"It's okay. It was a piece of cake." He shot her a kind smile that insisted he was there for her . . . all the way there . . . any time she needed him.

Shelly diverted her attention toward a sign that said, "Abilene Regional Airport."

"The chamber said they do have a restaurant," he confirmed. "We can have lunch and just wait until Tim arrives."

"Sounds fine," Shelly agreed and stared across the spacious parking lot. A field covered in some winter crop stretched from the other side of the highway to the horizon.

Sean's out there somewhere, she worried and knotted her fingers. All thoughts of Tim and Ryan and the dread of having them together faded in the face of her missing son.

Dear God, she prayed. *Please God, keep him safe. Please let the FBI find him. And please—please don't let that blood be his.*

You keep ditching my calls for your dad's, Tim accused. *It's like I don't even matter when he's in the picture—today or ever.* Tim's words floated to the surface of Shelly's consciousness and ushered her from the land of slumber. She opened her eyes, blinked, and stared around the hotel suite while the words preyed on her drowsy mind.

Yesterday, they'd picked Tim up at the airport with no problems. He'd insisted upon renting a vehicle and Shelly had ridden with him. They'd agreed to stop at the first Holiday Inn they came to. That turned out to be an upscale Holiday Inn Express on the outskirts of Abilene. Tim and Ryan had remained civil during the whole check-in process. As soon as Shelly got her room key, she vowed she needed a nap. The attempt to escape the friction of being with Tim or Ryan turned into a true need by the time she lay on her bed.

She hadn't awakened until sunset, when Ryan called her with the news that the blood type was Sean's—but her mom confirmed that it was also Dena's. So they still knew nothing. While Ryan decided to order room service for dinner, Tim had insisted upon taking Shelly out to a steakhouse that was a long way from cheap. He'd been a perfect gentleman while Shelly nibbled her shrimp and offered little toward conversation. Claiming exhaustion, she chose an early night. Shelly watched TV for a couple of hours and cried herself to sleep.

Now Tim's disturbing claim had disrupted her sleep and relentlessly clutched her mind. *You keep ditching my calls for your dad's. It's like I don't even matter when he's in the picture—today or ever.* Shelly rubbed her eyes and checked the digital clock that proclaimed midnight had just passed.

"Great!" she groused. "I've been asleep two whole hours."

When Tim's accusations barged through her mind again, she groaned, threw aside the covers, and trudged toward the restroom. Flipping on the light, she squinted and fumbled for the cup sitting near the bucket, still full of ice. After downing a cup of cold water, Shelly observed herself in the mirror and grimaced. She couldn't remember looking so fatigued.

She grabbed a washcloth, dampened it with cold water, and sponged at her heavy eyes. She'd cried so much yesterday, her eyes still appeared puffy. Pressing the cold cloth from one eye to the next, she walked back to the bed and determined to shove Tim's claims from her mind. She set the cloth on the nightstand and dropped back into bed. But the second her head touched the pillow, Tim's words plummeted her thoughts again.

"Oh God," she finally breathed, "if Tim's saying the same thing Ryan said, does that mean I really do have a problem?"

Her eyes stung, but Shelly stiffened her spine and refused to give in to more crying. Not a woman who cared much for makeup, she had purchased precious few cosmetics at the store yesterday and therefore had very little with which to cover the ravage of tears.

With a huff, she tossed aside the covers again, flipped on the lamp, and reached for the remote control. An old Alfred Hitchcock movie proved to be a good diversion. Only when the inevitable advertisements came on did Shelly's mind turn back to Tim's words, which continued to hold Ryan's tone of voice.

"But that doesn't mean the affair was my fault," Shelly finally defended, and remembered Ryan telling her he never claimed it was her fault—just that they both had issues.

She stood and began pacing the room while the movie went unwatched. The internal struggle drove her to pace until exhaustion forced her to collapse on the bed. Even though she begged sleep to invade her mind, she found no release. While her heavy body forbade her to move from the bed again, her mind continued to whirl with Tim's observations . . . and the dread that Ryan might have been right after all.

CHAPTER EIGHTEEN

The next morning, Sonny's phone started ringing the second he stepped into the police station's entrance. He fumbled the cell out of his shirt pocket and couldn't look at the screen soon enough. As he'd hoped, the number was one he recognized—Donna Wickman's. Sonny had called yesterday afternoon and left a voice mail. He'd barely slept last night in anticipation of her return call. This morning, he'd jumped every time his phone rang. Now at long last she was returning his call.

Jack appeared in the hallway and jutted his thumb toward the men's room. "I'm hitting the outhouse," he proclaimed. "I've been waiting on you. Meet me in my office."

"Will do. Gotta take this call first, though," Sonny explained. "It's important." He pressed the answer button, stepped back into the cold, and placed the phone to his ear. "Hello, this is Sonny," he said, his warm breath dancing around his face like a specter.

"Sonny, this is Donna Wickman. Blake's mom."

His eyes stung, and it wasn't because of the fine, cold mist that threatened to turn to snow later that day. Feeling like a fool, Sonny swallowed hard and finally produced a greeting: "Hi, it's good to hear your voice."

"Yours too," she replied, "and you have no idea how much I mean that."

Sonny imagined the smile of the blonde in the photos with Blake. While she wasn't beauty-queen material, Donna Wickman was an attractive woman whose love for Blake shined forth even in the photos. "As I explained in the voice mail yesterday . . . I called in response to your e-mail," he said. "I would enjoy trying to get together with you and—and Blake," he added on a reverent note. "I wondered if you might have some time in the next few weeks."

"Actually, yes. We're available this weekend."

"This weekend?" Sonny gasped.

"Is that too soon?"

"N-n-no, it's—it's perfect!" Sonny gripped the back of his neck while the trees tilted. "It's too good to be true, actually," he hurried.

Donna laughed. "I'm glad to hear your enthusiasm." She sighed, and her next words came out on a quiver. "I need it more than you know right now. The reason I didn't call back yesterday evening— you might as well know—Blake got into a fight at school. I had to go pick him up and meet with the principal. The police—"

"Police?" Sonny croaked, eyeing a nearby black-and-white topped with lights.

"Yeah, that's standard now at these larger schools. They're like security guards. They decided not to file charges," she explained. "This time, it does look like Blake was attacked and it was just self-defense. There were witnesses. I wish I could say that every time. Then, this morning, I decided to wait to talk to his counselor about your coming. She'd like to meet with you before we say anything to Blake. I know you must have a job. She can arrange for a Saturday session. Would it be possible—"

"I can come tonight if you want me to," Sonny offered. "I'm self-employed."

"Thank you so much for wanting to get involved," she said, her voice oozing with appreciation. "These past few months since my husband died have just been so hard. It's almost impossible to believe God has answered my prayers. As soon as the counselor gives the nod, we can arrange a meeting with Blake."

"Let me know when she's got an opening. I'll drive up there today or any day this week. I'm only a couple of hours from Richardson. I'm working on a case right now, but there are other professionals involved, and I can work on the road if I need to." Images of Sean flitted through his mind, and Sonny tried not to let the worry about his nephew cloud his words.

"Okay, good," she responded. "And is this the number I can always reach you on?"

"You bet," Sonny said with a smile. "It's my cell. It's on me all the time. Just make the appointment with the counselor, and I'll bend my schedule to make it work."

"Thank you," Donna repeated.

"Would it help if I brought references?" Sonny prompted, feeling like a candidate for a job interview.

Donna's chuckle brought back his smile. "Yeah, and you can throw in your name, rank, and serial number, too, while you're at it. Seriously, we'll see what the counselor says. She's really good at reading people. If anything, she might want to meet your wife."

"If at all possible, I'll bring my wife with me. She's as excited about this as I am."

"It's wonderful that she's so supportive. Many women wouldn't—"

"Tanya is the most wonderful woman I've ever met," Sonny exclaimed. "Blake will love her. I just know it."

By the time Sonny finished his call, he was attacked by a permanent grin along with a case of the shivers. He pulled up the headgear on his hoodie and slipped his hands into his pockets. But when he turned back for the police station, his smile faded. Jack had opened the door and stepped onto the grounds. His grim expression, as daunting as his chief of police uniform, reinforced that while one Mansfield brother might be finding success in connecting with a lost son, another wasn't.

"That was Donna Wickman," Sonny explained, hurrying toward Jack. "Blake's adoptive mother."

Jack nodded. "So do we have good news?" he asked, gripping Sonny's shoulder.

"Yeah." Sonny nodded. "She wants me to meet with Blake's counselor and then if the counselor approves, she wants me to meet Blake."

"Awesome!" Jack slapped Sonny's back. Even though a smile deepened his laugh lines, his eyes still remained haunted.

"Is there new word from Sean?" Sonny asked. "I mean, since I talked with you this morning?"

"No." Jack shook his head. "They're still combing the area. Nothing new. I just came to find you because the FBI is ready for the conference call. They want to know if you'll be willing to join them in Odessa. For some reason, they're thinking you might be able to sniff out Sean."

"Why? Are they desperate?" Sonny said in a lighthearted attempt to depreciate himself. But the second he released the last syllable, he wished he hadn't spoken so spontaneously.

"You know they'd never admit that," Jack said, but the doubts in his eyes hinted that he suspected the same.

All manner of possibilities stampeded Sonny's mind. From the second they had confirmed the blood was indeed Type B, Sonny had dreaded the thought of them finding Sean's lifeless body abandoned in a ditch somewhere.

"Sorry. I shouldn't have been so flippant," he said, stepping into the police station warmth ahead of Jack. "I almost feel like a traitor as it is. Here I am finding my son, and Ryan . . ." He shrugged.

"Doesn't know if he'll ever see his again?" Jack prompted.

"Yeah."

"I understand," Jack said, falling in step with Sonny. "But you can't put your life on hold either. This is a pivotal time for you. Ryan will understand—even if you can't make it to Odessa."

"Oh, I'm going to Odessa," Sonny confirmed. "Maybe Sean will miraculously appear, and it won't come to that," Jack encouraged, but his tone held little hope.

Missing something?" Tim asked. He placed his full plate on the hotel's dining table and extended a key-card toward Shelly.

"Oh! Is that mine?" Shelly fumbled in the side pocket of her purse and realized her key was missing.

"Found it on the floor behind your chair," he explained.

"I must have dropped it. Thanks." Shelly laid the card beside her plate and offered a lame smile as Tim pulled out the chair across from her in the hotel's breakfast lounge. Sipping her coffee, she wondered if Ryan planned to join them for breakfast . . . and how he was faring.

After her sporadic night of sleep, full of nightmares and worries, she'd last awakened nauseated—and presently couldn't hold a bite if she tried. "My stomach's churning," Shelly admitted as Tim eyed his plate laden with a bagel and fruit.

"It's nerves, I'm sure." Tim squeezed her hand and smiled into her eyes. His designer sweater, slacks, and loafers gave him a professional appeal that Shelly had always found attractive—not in Ryan's knock-your-socks-off way. But nevertheless, she knew many women would be glad to call Tim fiancé. A few even attended their church.

"I hope you're feeling better today," he continued. "You looked like you were on the verge of tears from the minute I got off the plane."

"I had been crying off and on," Shelly admitted and recalled the comforting hug Tim had wrapped her in. "It's all very hard and stressful. I've heard of people whose kids get nabbed, and I always thought it would be my worst nightmare. I was right. If we don't find him, I don't know what I'll do, Tim. It's like my whole life has come to a standstill."

"I know, I know," Tim soothed, wrapping her hand in his. "But we're going to find him, Shelly. We have to. We have the whole church and half of Bullard praying. God will answer our prayers!"

Tim's certainty diminished some of Shelly's dismay. "I went to sleep praying," she admitted. "I guess my faith is just taking a beating."

"Anybody's would," he assured. "But we can't lose hope."

Nodding, Shelly wondered about Ryan again. Last time she saw him, his shoulders had sagged in a dejected stance that nearly drove Shelly to offer a quick hug before he boarded the elevator. She'd restrained and pretended she didn't notice his depression.

Now she stared past Tim toward the elevators and wondered again if Ryan was coming down. The prospect upped her anxiety, and Shelly suspected the two men would be hard-pressed to remain amiable the whole day. She brainstormed ways to keep them from interacting and finally decided it would be best for her and Tim to find something to do alone and let Ryan do the same. Just sitting here looking at each other was the perfect formula for conflict.

Tim glanced over his shoulder. "Watching for Ryan?" he challenged with a hard edge to his voice.

Shelly blinked and focused on her fiancé. Few people would miss the jealousy flitting across his features. Glad the breakfast area was void of other guests, she tensed and wondered if Tim was about to go into one of his possessive moods. He certainly did not like the fact that she and Ryan had spent so much time alone, but none of that was Shelly's choice. And this morning, she was less inclined to make room for any of Tim's accusations. In the face of Sean's disappearance, this was not the time or place.

Shelly squared her shoulders and looked Tim in the eyes. "I was just wondering if Ryan was coming down and thinking it might be best for you and me to plan to do something today while we're waiting for news."

Tim's eyebrows arched. "You don't have to be so defensive about it."

Her toes curled. "Yes, I do. When you use that tone of voice—"

"Look, Shelly," he began, lifting his chin to a condescending angle, "the last thing we need to do is argue. I realize you're uptight, but you need to just stop."

"Maybe *you're* the one who needs to stop," she shot back.

"Well, what did I do?" He lifted both hands.

"You asked me about Ryan like you were accusing me of something. Listen, Tim, I can't help it that our son is missing and that my ex-husband is involved."

Leaning forward, Tim balled his fists on the table. "If he was happily married, I wouldn't have a problem. But he isn't. And until all this blew up, I didn't realize just how much he's still enamored with you. It's all over him! He'd take you back in a heartbeat, Shelly. Do you realize that?"

Shelly opened her mouth, but nothing came out. She'd never told Tim about Ryan's desire to reconcile. She simply hadn't seen the need. There was no way she ever planned to go back to Ryan, and since the sentiments were all Ryan's Shelly saw no reason for Tim to know.

"If you're feeling threatened," she said, "rest assured I'm *not* interested in going back to him, Tim!"

"I'm not so sure anymore," Tim snapped.

"I'd be crazy to—"

"Crazier things have happened. And you two were looking awfully cozy yesterday when I arrived—about as cozy as you were looking Sunday evening when I brought you Olive Garden."

"Why can't you just stop it?" Shelly insisted, her pulse pounding in her throat. "This has all been so hard on me. The last thing I need—"

His face reddening, Tim spewed, "You know, Shelly, this has all been hard on me as well. It's not just about you!"

"Well, Sean *is* my son!"

"He's already like my son, too, you know." He lifted his hands. "And—and it's like all you can focus on is Ryan and—and your mom and dad . . . while you hang up on me! Do you even understand how many times you've ended my calls for your parents? It's like I don't even matter when you're talking to them—and it didn't just start in the last few days either. All that and . . . and Sean's missing have shaken me to my core! . . . I couldn't even sleep last night—"

"I have some melatonin," Ryan's voice floated in from nearby.

Jumping, Shelly focused on her ex-husband, entering the breakfast lobby. His expression hinted that he had no clue she and Tim were arguing.

"Would you like some?" His diplomatic smile flashed an unspoken invitation to a friendly truce between him and Tim.

Tim gazed up at Ryan as he grabbed a nearby chair and set it at their table.

"No," Tim finally snapped. "I can get my own."

Ryan plopped into the chair, pointed a smile toward Shelly, then back at Tim, tapped the table's edge with his fingertips, and said, "Okay . . . I guess I'll go grab a bite to eat. Until we hear something, there's nothing else to do around here."

"I was just thinking that maybe Tim and I could go shopping,"

Shelly said, her voice flat. "I can't keep wearing the same clothes." She glanced at her corduroys.

"Yeah, I was thinking the same thing," Ryan said, stroking the front of his sweater. "But we've got different cars, right? So maybe you guys can go off together, and I'll take care of my own shopping. There's also a rec room down the hallway." He jutted his thumb over his shoulder. "I'll probably hit it sometime this morning." He patted his belly and shot another smile toward Tim. "I try to stay in shape."

Shelly squirmed. Ryan seemed unusually sociable, and she wondered what he might be up to.

Tim's eyes narrowed before he looked away, and then he refocused on Ryan with a smile of his own. "I guess I could use a round in the rec room too. Do they have a handball court?"

"I wish," Ryan said.

"Maybe we should try to play together sometime," Tim offered, and Shelly stifled a groan.

"Sounds like a plan," Ryan said and stood. "Meanwhile, I'm going to check out the breakfast bar and see about eating some steak and eggs."

"Yeah, right," Tim said over a chuckle.

Shelly watched Ryan stroll out and marveled at his timing. He'd undoubtedly decided to make the best of an awkward situation and was going to pull Tim into his scheme whether he wanted to be pulled in or not.

"I'm sorry," Tim mumbled.

Shelly stared hard at her coffee and decided it was time to draw a line. "Thanks for the apology," she said. "But what I really need to know is that you won't repeat it. This is the third or fourth time in a couple of days. I've got too much on me right now to have you coming at me too."

Tim's silence drove Shelly to lift her gaze. Her fiancé glared past her like she wasn't present. Finally, his focus shifted to her, and Shelly amazed herself by conjuring the strength not to flinch.

"Do you love me, Shelly?" he prompted, his features hard.

Shocked by his question, Shelly could do nothing more than bleat, "Of—of course."

"More than you loved Ryan?" Pain now mingled with the anger in his eyes.

Despite her determination to not think about her love for Ryan, her mind spun in a whirlwind of memories. By the time she and Ryan married, Shelly had been smitten beyond anything she'd ever felt before or since. But then, she'd been younger—and Ryan had been her first, true love. There was no comparison to that.

"I'm way more mature than I was when I met Ryan. So my love is going to be different. But I can promise you—"

"Do you still love him?"

"No!" she exclaimed. Pressing her fists against her temples, Shelly vehemently shook her head. "I don't! Don't even say that!"

"Well, the way you look at him . . ." Tim's voice trailed off, and this time the anger and pain had given way to sadness. "I'm really not trying to be difficult," he admitted. "But I guess I'm just scared I'm going to lose you. Something keeps telling me—" He shook his head.

"I really wish you'd wait until we find Sean to talk about all this," Shelly rushed and stood on legs that threatened to collapse. "You're really making things hard on me. I-I can't talk about any of this anymore. It's like you think I've done something—something immoral. But I haven't! Nothing has happened! I stopped loving Ryan Mansfield when he walked out on me. Why can't you understand that?"

Confusion and dread battled for prominence across his features. "I don't know if you really ever stopped loving him, Shelly. I really don't."

"No!" Shelly knotted her fingers and backed away. "No! I-I—"

"Hey, guys!" Ryan called from the doorway.

Shelly snapped her attention toward her ex-husband while Tim hunched his shoulders.

"No steak and eggs here. I must have been deranged to think there would be. I'm heading to Denny's instead. Y'all want to come?" His smile suggested they were all the best of best friends.

Shelly gulped and tried to stop panting.

Tim's hard expression softened before he turned a smile toward Ryan. "No," he said, standing. "We're about to go do our shopping. Come on, Shelly," he encouraged, leaving his food untouched.

Fumbling with her purse, Shelly hurried after Tim while trying to insert her room card into her bag's outer pocket. When it slipped from her grasp, Ryan bent for it. "I've got it," he said, his tone far too supportive for Shelly not to yearn for the comfort of another one of his hugs. This unexpected desire, coupled with Tim's words, left her shaken anew.

"Thanks," she rasped and accepted the key. Despite her desire to avoid eye contact, she succumbed to the pull of his focus. Ryan smiled into her eyes while a desperate confusion threatened to swallow Shelly whole.

Tim's vow that Shelly was placing her family above him blasted through her mind again; and she relived those dreadful hours when she'd wrestled against truth like Jacob wrestled with the angel of the Lord. Now, looking into Ryan's face, Shelly perceived undaunted honesty blazing from his soul . . . a level of honesty she had yet to step into herself. Shelly had been so devastated by his affair, she'd been blinded to anything she could have done to contribute to their problems. When the counselor suggested Ryan was trying to divert blame to her, that had been a perfect cover for Shelly to cling to. And while she believed the counselor meant well, she was on the verge of admitting she hadn't been right.

"Shelly?" Tim reappeared on the dining room's threshold.

She jumped like a child caught filching chocolate from her mother's stash.

His amiable mask gone, Tim glared from Shelly to Ryan and back to Shelly. "Are you coming with me or not?" he barked.

Clasping her room key, she scurried after her fiancé but wondered if she should stay and talk to Ryan.

CHAPTER NINETEEN

Shelly?" Ryan stood from the settee at the hallway's end, where he'd been awaiting her return.

With a faint jump, she pivoted to face him while gripping a black shopping bag. "Ryan!" she gasped. "I didn't see you sitting there. You scared me!"

"*Sorry.*" Keeping his stride slow and nonthreatening, he moved toward her hotel room's doorway.

"Has there been any news?" she asked.

"No." He shook his head. "Other than they've called in the big guns—that would be Sonny. He's like a coonhound when it comes to sniffing people out."

"Have you talked with him?"

"Only briefly. A couple hours ago. He had just flown into Odessa and was getting ready to go for it."

"Do you think he'll find them?"

"If anybody can, it will be Sonny," Ryan assured and laid his hand on her shoulder.

He'd been sitting by the hallway window through a glorious

sunset. While the sky turned from indigo to black, he'd waited for Shelly to return and hoped Tim didn't escort her to her door. Ryan assumed the dentist had probably bought her everything she fancied and then indulged her in the finest dining. The guy certainly didn't spare any money on her or Sean. But despite Tim's monetary generosity, he seemed to be giving her a hard time in other areas. His emotional outbursts shocked Ryan to new levels at every eruption.

He'd only caught a few syllables of their argument from this morning. Shelly's distress had been enough to make him want to grab Tim by the scruff of the neck and teach him a few lessons. Instead, he'd done what he hoped was best for Shelly and tried to smooth over the situation.

Now she was looking at him with questions cloaking her features, and Ryan knew it was time to explain his visit. "I just, uh, wanted to talk with you for a minute." He looked up one end of the hallway and then the other. Ryan had wanted to check on Shelly to make certain she was okay. After the tension Tim was causing, Ryan figured she needed a friend.

If they were at her house, Shelly probably would have asked him to come inside. Entering her hotel room was a bit more risky—especially if her fiancé found out.

Although, he thought, *I went into her room the night before last.*

When the elevator bell rang and a klatch of noisy teenagers invaded the hallway, Shelly bit her lip and worriedly observed them. She didn't have to voice what she thought. The concern was all over her face. If Tim happened to come down the hallway and saw them talking, there would probably be a blowup. But Ryan also knew that Tim's discovering Ryan in her room would be even worse. Nevertheless, Tim would only find out if Shelly let him in.

After several seconds' deliberation, she finally blurted, "Come into my room," and hurried to insert the card key into the door's slot.

"Here, let me have your bag," he said as she fumbled with the knob. She relinquished her burden and Ryan noted the name "Loraine's" in gold on shiny black.

No telling what Tim spent, Ryan thought.

Shelly swept inside and flipped on lights as Ryan closed the door. His brows arched when he realized she'd somehow landed in a two-roomed suite, replete with a den separate from the bedroom. Trying to recall the arrangements when they were booking their rooms, Ryan only remembered getting his key and heading upstairs while Shelly and Tim finished their booking. He wouldn't have even known what room she was in if he hadn't read it on her key's sleeve this morning when he picked it up for her.

He whistled. "Wow! This is nice!"

"Thanks. Tim insisted. There was only one available. That's why I'm on the top floor and he's two floors down." She reached for the oversized bag. "I'll put this in the closet for now," she said.

"Sure." Ryan released the bag and walked toward the picture window that revealed several miles of city lights. Ryan wondered where Sean was . . . if he was crying for him and Shelly. He swallowed at a knot in his throat and tried to stay strong. He hadn't come into Shelly's room to sob like he did last night before falling asleep.

"I was going to make some decaf coffee," she said. "Want some?"

"Sure," Ryan agreed and debated if she wondered where all this was leading. Ryan certainly was beginning to. Even though he'd planned to talk to her, Ryan now deliberated about how to start and exactly what to say.

Maybe I just wanted to be with her, he thought, staring out the window at nothing, *and was using talking to her about Tim as an excuse.* He sighed. Even though he'd decided their reconciling was futile, Ryan still found such comfort from being with Shelly. Despite what their relationship might or might not ever be, they were Sean's parents and there was an unspoken understanding between them that helped Ryan stay strong.

Dear God, he began praying, *please help Sonny find Sean. God, please give him a clue. Help him, Lord. Help Sean. Dear God, help Dena as well. Get into her head and make her see she needs to return Sean.*

A stream of car lights zipped up and down the highway, blurring into a golden glow. Only when Shelly said, "Here's your coffee," did Ryan realize part of the blur was due to the moisture in his eyes. He blinked and observed the steaming cup of coffee.

"I had no idea I'd been standing here long enough for the coffee to be made."

"You haven't," she said. "I bought some coffee bags when I was out with Tim last night. They're like tea bags, only full of coffee."

"Oh, I see," Ryan said and noticed the white string with a green tag hanging over the cup's edge.

"All I had to do was zap some water in the microwave."

"You always were resourceful," Ryan said through a smile.

"I try," Shelly said with a grin of her own. "I thought you'd want it black, like you always liked it?"

"Yeah, I'm still drinking it black," he said, observing her blond brew. "I see you still haven't grown up yet, huh?"

She chuckled at the old joke. Ryan had always said that when she grew up, she'd drink her coffee black, like his.

"No, I'm still too fond of my cream and sugar," she said before an extended silence crouched upon them.

Shelly moved closer to the window and hunched her shoulders. The unspoken inevitable hung between them, and Ryan wondered if either of them would get a wink of sleep tonight.

Finally, Ryan decided to say what he came to say. "I, uh, overheard you and Tim arguing this morning."

Shelly went rigid.

"I really just came by to check on you. I was worried he was being difficult. You know, too hard on you. I was worried about you, I guess," he said, not certain he was making any sense.

"What did you hear?" she questioned without ever turning around.

"Just that he was as upset over all this as you; but I could tell by your expression that there had been a good bit more said, and that it wasn't going well. So I tried to make things better for you. I-I hope I helped." Scrutinizing her back, Ryan wondered why her shoulders sagged. When she faced him, her relieved expression matched the wilt of her shoulders. All that lead him to wonder exactly what part of their argument he'd missed.

Moving to a nearby desk, Shelly dropped into the chair and set down her coffee. She propped her elbow on the desk and rested her forehead in her hand.

"Shelly?" Ryan stopped himself from moving to her side.

"I'm okay," she said, her voice unsteady. "Really."

"I didn't mean to upset you. Honestly, I was just concerned. I-I know all this has been awful for you, and I felt so bad about the way Tim was treating you. I just was worried," he repeated and wondered if he sounded like he was babbling. "And . . . and wanted to check on you," he finished on a lame note.

"Tim and I are through," she said, sounding as if someone were choking her.

"*What?*"

Her head snapped up. Ryan's gaze shifted from her pale cheeks to her engagement ring before she continued.

"It's not official, yet, but we both know it. I *have* grown to care for him a lot," she admitted. "But I don't think it's enough—not for forever anyway. And I'm not so sure what he feels for me is enough either, to tell you the truth.

"Plus, today—today didn't go well . . . *at all*. We barely spoke to each other. He's gotten *so possessive*. He . . . he . . ." She gulped. "And all I could think about was . . . was . . ." She gulped again.

Ryan set aside his coffee, stiffened his spine, and stopped himself from rushing to her side, falling to his knees, and begging her back. This news bordered on miraculous.

After a deep breath, she finally released another verbal grenade: "He has made me realize something." She lifted her gaze to Ryan and said, "I owe you an apology."

"You do?" he croaked.

Her lips trembling, Shelly nodded. "You were right, Ryan. I *did* put my family before you. And in the last couple of days I've begun to see that it *did* contribute to the problems in our marriage."

Ryan sat on the edge of the bed. Gripping his knees, he hunched forward and wondered if this was some kind of a bizarre dream he'd conjured. But his heart's thudding against his chest was far too real to be a dream.

"Ryan?" her voice echoed from afar.

"I'm—I'm okay," he said and lifted his gaze to hers. "It's just such a shock. I didn't sleep well last night. I'm exhausted." He rubbed his eyes and wished he could think of something more appropriate to say, but nothing came except, "I can't believe this."

Shelly responded by worriedly chewing on her bottom lip. "I don't really understand what's going on," she finally said. "I just know that I could hardly sleep last night for thinking about . . . Then this afternoon, when I came back to my room to rest before Tim and I went back out again, I did a lot of praying. And I finally knew that . . . that I had been fighting myself all night. God was asking me to apologize to you for my . . . *my* part in our divorce. I know I wasn't the perfect wife, Ryan. And I'm—I'm sorry." She shrugged while Ryan continued to mutely stare at her.

Now what? he thought. "It's okay, Shelly. Looking back, you were a way better spouse than I was. I think I had a lot of growing up to do."

"I did too," she said, gazing into space as if viewing the replay of their years together.

"I really don't deserve your forgiveness. I don't guess any of us deserves God's forgiveness, either, but He's forgiven me," he said, daring to forge forward. "Whether you can ever fully forgive me or not . . . if I stay single the rest of my life . . . you can rest assured I'll never have another affair. My relationship with God is way more important than any woman or any fling." The strength in his words surprised him, but Ryan knew it was not coming from within, but from above.

Shelly's eyes rounded. "Somehow, I know you mean that," she said, shaking her head. "It blows my mind that I would say that, but I just know."

"It's the truth." He stood, took one step toward her, and hesitated.

Shelly gazed at him while fear and amazement mingled upon her features.

"Ryan, I—" she croaked.

"I don't want to push you." He raised both hands. "But I *do* want to let you know that," he swallowed hard, "no matter what happens, no matter what you decide, I'll always be here for you—whether we ever remarry or not. I made a vow to you when we got married, and I intend to keep it until I die—no matter what. But if there's a chance that you'd reconsider, my offer still stands." He left the rest unsaid.

"I don't know what to say," she whispered. "This has all been so fast. I-I . . . If you'd told me a week ago that Tim and I would be breaking up and you and I would . . . would be having this conversation, I'd have never believed you. I don't know what to say," she repeated.

Ryan moved closer, knelt beside her, and placed his hand on her shoulder. "It's okay, Shelly," he whispered. "Like I said, I'm not pushing, here. You just need to know I'm in your court forever, no matter what."

She reached for his hand. "I'm not saying yes right now. But I can't say no anymore either. I guess I just need more time to think." She squeezed his fingers. "Maybe after we get Sean back and life gets back to normal . . ."

Ryan wrapped her hand in both of his and held on tight while he quivered from the inside out. When she winced, he loosened his hold. Shelly extracted her hand, removed the engagement ring, and deposited it on the desktop. Then, Ryan reached for her hand again, and Shelly complied.

"Tim told me this morning . . ." she began. "He said . . . he said some things th-that—" She shook her head. "He just said some things that really made me do some soul searching today. At the time, I denied it; but later today I began to think he might be right."

"Was it something about us?" he questioned.

"Yes," she simply answered. "Yes, it was."

CHAPTER TWENTY

Shelly awoke to her cell's incessant ringing. Groping through the darkness, she fumbled with the phone until she dropped it midst the covers. Only when she spotted Ryan's name glowing on the screen did a jolt of hope thrust her to wide awake. A glance at the digital clock indicated it was six A.M. Ryan wouldn't be calling unless there was news of Sean.

She pressed the send button and blurted, "Ryan, what is it?"

"Sean. They found him. Or rather, he found *them*," he rushed. "He called 9–1–1 this morning at four o'clock. Sonny called me at five."

"And you're just now calling me?" she shrieked.

"There's been some red tape and some delays. I knew you were asleep and I decided to let you sleep until—"

"Until he graduated from high school?" she raised her hand as her voice's pitch increased.

"No, no, no," Ryan said. "We were just trying to save you from chewing your fingernails for hours. But look, here's the deal. Somehow, it's leaked to the press. They've covered up the hospital. It looks like this has turned into a statewide media sensation."

"Has he been admitted to the hospital?" Shelly worried.

"No. Dena has. He's fine, though. The deal is—"

"What's wrong with Dena?" she asked. Even in the face of such a crisis, Shelly still hated the thought of her sister being seriously injured.

"Concussion and some bleeding on the brain, but she's supposed to be stabilizing," he replied.

Shelly winced. "Have they called Mom and Dad?"

"I'm assuming so. Sonny mentioned that they were on the way. The main thing right now is that Sonny got permission to slip Sean out of the ER. The doctor says the last thing he needs right now is to be surrounded by cameras and lights. He needs peace and quiet and his mom and dad. Sonny sneaked off with him and is headed here now. That's why I didn't call sooner. It's just a waiting game now."

Shelly flung aside the covers and stood. "We've got to be ready to meet him!" She snapped on the light and darted around the room in a crazed search for her new clothing.

"Sonny said he won't be here for a couple of hours. We have time."

"I can't wait!" Shelly exclaimed. "Let's meet him halfway. Call Sonny and tell him we'll meet him halfway. What city's about halfway?" she babbled.

"Uh . . . you were the one looking at the map yesterday."

"It's still in the car. Meet me at the car in fifteen minutes."

"Well, the plan is that Sonny's bringing him here."

"No!" Shelly demanded, her motherly instincts superseding all else. "We're going to meet him halfway."

"Do I have a choice?" Ryan prompted, a smile in his voice.

"Of course not!" Shelly blurted. "I can't just sit here and wait! I'll go mad!"

"Okay, okay then," Ryan agreed. "I'll call Sonny and tell him the plan. Meet me in the lobby in fifteen. And don't worry about packing up now. We'll come back and check out."

"Roger that!" She hung up, recalled placing the bag of new clothing in the closet, and pulled out a pair of designer jeans, a sweater, and a pair of pointy-toed pumps.

Within fifteen minutes, she stepped off the elevator and spotted Ryan darting from the breakfast area. Holding two cups of steaming coffee, he rushed to Shelly's side and shoved one into her hand. "I grabbed a couple of cereal bars too." He reached into his coat pocket and pulled out a red package. "Want one?"

"Not now," Shelly said and kept up her brisk pace all the way to the exit door. "I'm sure I'll probably be starved later, but the coffee is fine for now."

Ryan hit the exit one step ahead of her and opened it.

"I still can't believe you waited to call me!" Shelly zoomed through the door and trotted ahead of him toward the Taurus, parked within sight. By the time she arrived at the passenger side, the automatic lock clicked and Ryan opened the door for her.

"I really thought I was doing what was best for you. I didn't want to wake you," he explained as she crawled in. "I didn't mean to aggravate you."

"Well, how would you feel if I knew for a whole hour and didn't call you?" She shot him a pointed gaze.

"I'd probably be livid," he admitted and closed her door before she could reply.

After plopping her coffee in the car's cup holder, she dropped her handbag on the floor.

Ryan's door popped open, and he slid inside. "Sorry," he said. "But if you have to know, part of the reason I didn't call was because Sonny and the gang were afraid you'd *have* to come to the hospital, and they were doing their best to get Sean away from the reporters. They even arranged to fax me the medical release papers from the

ER to keep us from having to be there. They decided it would be better for him to get him out of there. So maybe we could say it was doctor's orders."

He shrugged and then offered a sheepish smile. "Forgive me?"

Breathless from the mad dash from her room, Shelly tried to tell herself that her heart's pounding was solely from physical exertion. Except, when Ryan's gaze slid to her lips and Shelly's mind joined his she could no longer claim physical exertion as the sole reason. Before he left the room last night, Ryan had wanted to kiss her. Shelly saw it all over him. Even though she'd been tempted, Shelly hadn't given in and she wouldn't, until she knew she could tell him yes. There was no reason to give him false hope. Nevertheless, the urge to press her lips against his arrived anew, and this time it was stronger than last.

She told herself it was just the jubilation of finding Sean. Lots of people kissed as an act of celebration. She was simply falling prey to the impulse to commemorate Sean's return. Despite the rationalization, Shelly's pulse hammered harder by the second, especially when she recalled how much she'd once enjoyed Ryan's kisses.

She reached for her coffee and indulged in a hot swallow that jerked her mind off the memories. "I'm so thankful you got us coffee," she said before going for another gulp. "I barely had time to brush my teeth, let alone get a drink. This is wonderful."

"Glad you think so," Ryan said before cranking the car. "But you never answered my question."

"What?"

He put the vehicle in reverse. "Do you forgive me?"

"For what?" Shelly croaked, her mind whirling with all the things she should forgive him for.

"For what we were just talking about," he explained before gassing the vehicle. "For not calling you sooner about Sean."

"Oh that. Yes—yes. Sounds like you were just following your

guess for what was best for me," she said, dismissing the whole irritation. "The main thing is Sean's coming home! Now let's just *go*!"

He fished his cell phone out of his pocket. "I've got to call Sonny," he explained while maneuvering out of the parking lot. "I told him I'd call when we left and figured out the halfway meeting point on I-20."

"Right!" Shelly reached for the map lying on the dashboard. "Find out where he is right now. I can figure out where the best spot is to meet him." She examined the map while Ryan initiated the call and steered the car from the parking lot.

Shortly after greeting Sonny, Ryan exclaimed, "Sure! We'd love to talk to him! Shelly's right here. Just a minute." He cut a glance toward her. "Wanta talk to Sean?"

"Do I?" Dropping the map, Shelly snatched the phone and pressed it against her ear. "Sean?!" she exclaimed through a broad grin.

"Mom!" Sean crowed. "I missed you so much!"

"Are you okay, honey?" Shelly asked, not able to stop her voice from cracking.

"I'm fine. But Aunt Dena's hurt really bad. We were at her friend's. She wouldn't let me call 9–1–1 on her phone. But this morning I sneaked out of my bed and found the real phone and called anyway. I was going to call Dad, but that other mean woman woke up and took the phone away."

"Did they— Did they hurt you?" Shelly asked, trembling in dread of the answer.

"No. I'm fine. Doctor says I'm fine. Aunt Dena's just hurt—real bad. It's her head. She kept telling me *she* was my mamma, but I told her *no*! She's really strange." He huffed like an exasperated adult.

Shelly smiled and wondered how her sister had birthed such a practical, well-adjusted child. "She's just confused, honey. *I'm* your mamma," she stressed and planned to eventually explain everything to Sean. But for now, he knew all he needed to know.

"Uncle Sonny's stopping at a gas station to get us a drink. I gotta go now, okay?"

"No! No, don't go!" Shelly urged. "You need to say something to Daddy first! But I also need to talk to Uncle Sonny. Give him the phone right now, okay?"

"I need to talk to Sonny too," Ryan said.

Shelly nodded before Sonny's voice came over the line. "How's Dena?" Shelly asked, genuine concern mixing with a new onslaught of ire.

"She's got some pretty serious head trauma," Sonny explained. "Your parents have been called. They're supposed to be taking a shuttle flight from Tyler."

"Oh, my word!" Shelly gripped her forehead. "I'm losing my mind. I should have called them!"

"It's okay," Sonny assured. "They've already been notified."

"Do you think Dena will make it?" Shelly nabbed her bottom lip between her teeth. Even though she'd spent many hours furious with her younger sister, Shelly would never wish her dead.

"Yeah. She's lost some blood, and they're saying she's got a concussion. The rest of my info is sketchy. I guess she and her friend were just going to let her lie up and get well on her own," he said, a sarcastic thread in his words.

"Who knows what they were thinking," Shelly said. "I quit trying to apply logic to her choices years ago. All I've known to do is try my hardest to be the best I can be for my parents and maybe make up for all Dena has put them through."

"Right," Sonny agreed, and Sean's tones floated from the background. "Hey, Sean wants to talk to his dad now."

"Sure." When she extended the phone, it trembled as violently as her hand.

After Ryan spoke with Sean, he connected with Sonny and said, "Shelly, where do you think the best spot to meet Sonny is?"

"Probably Colorado City," Shelly predicted, studying the map. "It's a small town and looks like we'll get there at the same time. Sonny might get there first, but we won't be far behind."

"Okay—okay," Ryan agreed. "Sonny, we're shooting for Colorado City. Whoever gets there first chooses the meeting place. When you get close, let us know. Shelly thinks you'll get there before we do." Ryan finished the details while Shelly gained her equilibrium.

"I think that's in order as well," Ryan said at the end of the call. "I promise, I won't tell Shelly!" He winked her way.

"What?" she prompted while Ryan hung up.

"It's our little secret." He dropped the phone back into his shirt pocket and gripped the steering wheel.

"No secrets!" Shelly playfully punched his arm.

"Sonny said Sean's wanting a Coke and some chips for breakfast, and—"

"You said it was fine?"

"Yeah, just this once." He lifted his index finger. "Don't you think?"

Sighing, Shelly nodded. "Yeah, maybe just this once," she agreed. "I have a feeling Mr. Sean's going to get everything he wants, for a while anyway."

"Not from *me*," Ryan said, laying his hand on his chest.

"Yeah, right," Shelly teased. "You'll be spoiling him like a grandpa by the weekend."

"No way!" Ryan shook his head.

"You're in denial," Shelly retorted and playfully whacked him again.

"Ouch!" Ryan gripped his arm. "Now you're abusing me!"

Laughter welled up in Shelly, and Ryan joined her. At last, he gripped her hand, kissed the back, and said, "I am *sooooo* happy, Shelly!"

"Me too," she breathed, gazing at his profile. "Me too."

Again, Shelly thought about Ryan's visit to her suite. She gazed at her left hand wrapped in his. Shelly never put her engagement ring back on this morning. Regardless of what happened with her and Ryan, she knew continuing with Tim would be a mistake. He'd been more focused on himself than anything else during this whole upheaval. Shelly did not want to enter marriage on those terms. Furthermore, she was beginning to think that the relationship with Tim might be nothing more than a balm for the loss of her marriage—again, not the terms for a good union.

To top it off, yesterday morning Tim had scandalized her with the claim that he thought she still loved Ryan. She lifted her gaze to Ryan once more, and her pulse leapt as the memory of their first kiss trickled through her mind like warm honey sweetening her soul. They'd been enjoying a spring picnic in the park when an unexpected shower sent them running under a stone bridge. There in the shadows, Ryan had taken her in his arms and rocked Shelly's world. That day, she knew she could fall in love with this new man in her life; and she had. She darted her attention to the road ahead and hoped Ryan hadn't sensed her watching him.

Despite everything that had happened, Shelly could no longer deny that Ryan Mansfield still stirred her. All day yesterday, she'd pondered Tim's claims and hadn't wanted to admit what might be the obvious. Shelly's anger had suppressed everything she felt for Ryan, leaving only resentment to rule. But when she'd expressed to him how much he hurt her, the final cords of anger and resentment began to unravel, leaving room for the old love to sprout anew. Fully realizing that she'd also made major mistakes in their marriage dissolved her resentment.

Granted, Ryan's affair was a drastic violation of their vows. Nevertheless, that wedding band he'd decided to wear coupled with the earnestness in his eyes when he promised allegiance to God and her validated his determination to living a godly life. Even though

Shelly believed he meant it now, she wondered if he'd maintain his determination year in and year out.

What happens if another woman throws herself at him? she worried.

While Shelly realized she could probably work through any left-over wounds the affair created, she seriously wondered if she could ever fully trust Ryan again; and trust was imperative for a healthy marriage.

Shelly gazed across the acres of farmland and thought, *That will definitely take a miracle. . . .*

But do you really want that miracle? a haunting voice echoed from the recesses of her soul as cold chills rushed through her. Several times in her life, she'd known for certain God was speaking to her. Now was one of them. And as the words unfolded in her heart, so their meaning penetrated her mind: she'd have to want God's miracle enough to allow Him to perform it.

I'll never fully trust him in my own strength, she thought. *Even with the changes he's made, there will still be a shadow, unless . . .*

Shelly closed her eyes tight and thought of Sean, of what was best for him. That picture he'd drawn at the cabin sprang upon her mind. As a teacher, Shelly had seen so many children suffer when their parents divorced. She never imagined after adopting Sean that she and Ryan would break up. Quite the contrary, Shelly had determined not to do to her child what so many parents had done to her students. By the time she and Ryan had adopted Sean, Shelly had heard little ones lament that "Mom and Dad don't live together anymore" enough times to haunt her for life.

But we did the same thing to Sean, she thought. *We hurt each other, and we hurt him.*

Ryan's cell phone interrupted her thoughts; and only when he disengaged his hand from hers did Shelly realize they'd held hands for quite a stretch of time. The contact that started as support had turned into the comfort of a married couple, ready to reunite with their child.

"Is that Sonny again?" she questioned.

Ryan gazed at the phone's screen. "No." He shook his head and extended the phone to her. "I think it's Tim, actually, if I recall his number right."

"Tim? Why didn't he just call me?" She glanced toward her purse before accepting the phone. Not seeing her cell in the outer pocket, she never recalled retrieving it from the nightstand. "Oh no," she groaned and confirmed the number on the screen was Tim's. "I left my phone in the room. I bet he's been trying to call me and is worried."

"You didn't call him about going after Sean?"

"No," Shelly said and extended the phone back toward Ryan. "You talk to him."

"No deal," he gently pushed her hand. "I already took two of his calls for you. Why do you keep shoving him off on me anyway?" he teased. "He's your burden—I meant, uh, fiancé."

Sighing, Shelly couldn't answer his question. She had handed Tim off to Ryan twice . . . just like she'd handed off difficult people to him in their marriage. Shelly had always depended on Ryan to deal with the uncooperative folks. In turn, Ryan told her as long as she'd manage the money, he'd handle the people problems.

I reverted back to our marriage deal, she thought and once again eyed Ryan's profile. But this time, she didn't look away when he glanced at her.

"Are you going to answer?" he asked, and the phone went silent.

"He's probably going to be huffy," she groused, fully expecting the phone to begin a new round any second. "I'm sure he's been trying to call my phone. He may have even tried to get me to answer my door. So now, he's probably thinking we're together or he wouldn't be calling you."

"On top of that, you didn't tell him about Sean. Get ready for an explosion. I'd be hopping mad," Ryan said under his voice.

"Thanks a lot!" Shelly retorted. "Since when are you on *his* side?"

"Not saying that." Ryan shook his head. "I'm just saying . . ."

The phone began to ring anew. With a sigh, Shelly answered the call.

"Shelly?" Tim questioned. "Are you with Ryan?"

"Yes."

"Well, where are you? Are you in his room?"

"Good grief, no!" His implications sent a burn to her gut, but Shelly managed to control her tone. "Sean has been found. We got a call from Ryan's brother who was on the case. He's meeting us in Colorado City, about an hour west of Abilene. He's got Sean."

"And you never bothered to *tell* me?" Tim bellowed. "I've been pacing the floor, worried sick because you aren't answering the phone or your door and you've run off with your—your ex-husband to meet your son whose been missing for days and you don't even think to *call* me!"

Shelly rubbed her face. "I haven't *run off* with anyone," she defended. "We're going to get Sean. That's all!"

"Well, thanks for thinking of me."

"I'm sorry, Tim," she said, her words stiff, "but the only person I'm thinking about right now is my son. This isn't about *you*."

Ryan's low whistle was accompanied by Tim's momentary silence.

"Think how *you* would feel, Shelly!" Tim defended.

Taking a deep breath, Shelly fully understood how she would feel. Ryan's waiting an hour to call her had put a kink in her morning. If he hadn't called her at all, she'd have been even more irate.

"Like I already said, I'm sorry," she said and meant every word. "This whole ordeal has just made me crazy. All I could think about when Ryan called was getting to see Sean. I was so caught up in—"

"Did any thought of me even enter your head?"

Shelly didn't respond. She dreaded stating the absolute truth, but despised lying as much.

"You know, Shelly," Tim finally said. "I really don't think we're going to survive this."

"Yeah, I agree. It's been quite an eye opener."

"I know it has been for *me*."

Shelly clenched her teeth and fought a retort.

"I *would* like to see Sean before I leave," Tim continued, his words thick. "I really care about that little guy, and I'm glad he's coming home."

"He's fond of you as well," Shelly admitted.

"I'd hoped maybe we all three could fly home in the Cessna, but I guess you'll be riding back with your *husband*?"

Shelly's fingernails pressed into her palm. "Yes," she answered in a mechanical voice. "It looks like that would be best."

"I want my ring back, by the way," he said, his words taking on a petty twist. "It cost a mint. Maybe I can recoup—"

"You can *have* your ring back," Shelly vented. "I wanted the smaller one anyway, if you remember correctly."

"I know, but I wanted to give you the best," Tim claimed with a superior air. "I guess my best wasn't good enough for you!" The line went silent.

Pressing her lips together, Shelly glanced at the screen to confirm the call-ended message. "He hung up on me!"

Ryan chuckled.

"What's so funny?"

"Oh, I don't know," Ryan chimed and shot her a smile that would have dazzled a corpse. "I'm just happy! As a matter of fact, this is one of the happiest days of my life!"

CHAPTER TWENTY-ONE

After Sonny purchased Sean's Coke and chips, he threw in a sausage biscuit from the convenience store's deli. The child devoured everything and then slumped in his seat and went to sleep—with a peaceful expression. One would never suspect that he'd just been through a dreadful ordeal. According to the hospital psychologist, he didn't behave as if he had undergone such a traumatic experience, nor did he appear to have any devastating damage.

"He'll probably have some nightmares, and some fears of sleeping alone. I'd recommend several months of counseling to help him get through. But the main thing right now is to reunite him with his folks. Is there a way to get him out of here before the press traumatizes him more?"

Sonny had readily volunteered to escort Sean and had received remarkable cooperation from the officials in dodging the growing group of reporters camping outside the emergency room. Now that the excitement was wearing off, his heavy eyes insisted he act like

Sean and get unconscious. He took the first exit for Colorado City and spotted an Exxon station visible from I–20.

"This is as good a meeting place as any," he reasoned, steering the rented Toyota toward the station. *Maybe I can catch a cat nap before Ryan and Shelly get here.* He secured a parking place beside the station, pulled out his cell phone, and pressed the speed dial button that connected him to Ryan.

"I'm at an Exxon just off of I–20," Sonny explained and examined the area for other landmarks. "Look for a Grandy's sign right next to the Exxon sign . . . and a Comfort Inn on the other side of the highway. You shouldn't miss it. This isn't like Grand Central Station or anything."

"Okay, good. We're probably about fifteen minutes out," Ryan replied. "How's Sean? Still holding up?"

"He's fine as frog's hair," Sonny said through a yawn. "He ate his breakfast and conked out. He's sleeping like a baby."

"Good, good!"

"I promise, he's a resilient little dude!"

"You're telling me," Ryan replied.

"He just sat in that exam room and talked to the psychologist like getting kidnapped is an everyday thing!"

"About six months ago, I lost him in the store and found him chatting up the hardware manager. They were talking about his tree house. The only person who was upset was *me*. His teacher tells us one day he'll take over the world and we'll all be thankful. He's fairly sassy when he wants to be."

Sonny laughed and reached for the lever that reclined his seat. "Maybe he takes after his uncle Sonny."

"Yeah, right," Ryan retorted. "Like he has your genes!"

"It's all influence," Sonny claimed, relaxing against the seat.

"Oh, *please*," Ryan complained.

Closing his eyes, Sonny snickered and was too exhausted to form a comeback. "Look, I'm in a red Toyota," he said through another yawn. "I'm parked beside the gas station. You can't miss me. I'll be the one asleep."

"I promise, this will be the shortest nap you'll ever take!"

"Sure," Sonny said and laid the phone on the dashboard without bothering to disconnect the call.

Before sleep overtook him, he thought about his next appointment. He and Blake's adoptive mother currently had a deal: the second Sean was found, Sonny had a standing engagement with Blake's counselor. Hopefully, she could work Sonny in this evening. The sooner Ryan and Shelly arrived, the sooner he could call for the appointment. The sooner the appointment, the sooner he would get to meet his son. As he slipped toward a light snooze, Sonny smiled.

Shelly scrambled out of the car the second Ryan pulled it to a stop beside the red Toyota. Just as Sonny said, he was parked at the back of the gas station, and he and Sean were both asleep in the front seats. Teary and trembling, Shelly arrived at Sean's side at the same time Ryan did. They simultaneously pounded the window.

Sonny jumped and focused on Ryan and Shelly.

Sean sat up and blasted his parents with a sleepy grin. "Mom! Dad!" he crowed while Sonny released the locks.

Ryan opened the door. Shelly grabbed Sean. And Ryan's strong arms pulled them close. Shelly's sobs mixed with laughter as Sean clutched at her neck and cried, "I missed you! I missed you!"

The child swiveled to grab Ryan while both parents stumbled over the words in an attempt to express joy and concern. "We missed you so much . . . Are you okay? . . . Are you *sure* no one hurt you? . . ."

Sean pulled back and held up his wrists. "She tied me to the bed!" he said, and a cold horror laced Shelly's gut. She shared a startled glance with Ryan and didn't want to imagine what else might have happened.

"And there was a dog in the barn at the cabin," Sean continued. "He almost bit me and nearly got Aunt Dena, too. I tried to lock her outside with the dog, but she got in anyway."

"Probably a wild, mamma dog," Ryan mumbled. "They can get really vicious."

Shelly drank of her son as he continued his wide-eyed spiel. "And she taped my mouth shut in my room and then there was the wreck!" Sean continued. "I told Aunt Dena to stop drinking and driving. I told her everything you told me, Dad, 'bout drinking and driving, and I told her you said I wasn't supposed to *ever* ride with anyone who was drinking and driving!"

"Good," Ryan encouraged.

"And then she tried to hit me but she hit the tree and then her head was bleeding, but she still could use her phone, so she called Lila." He stopped long enough to take a breath. "I don't like Lila either. She's *mean*!" He narrowed his eyes.

"Who's Lila?" Shelly prodded.

"It's the lady who wouldn't let me use her phone. *She* came and got us because Aunt Dena said she would call the police. And then we were at Lila's house and Aunt Dena's head was bleeding right here way more," he touched his temple, "and then Lila told her she needed a doctor and then Aunt Dena said no, and then I sneaked out of my room in the dark and called 9–1–1, just like you told me, Dad."

"Good boy," Ryan affirmed and rubbed his son's back. "Good, good boy." When Ryan looked down, Shelly glimpsed tears in his eyes, and she blinked against new stinging in her eyes.

"And then the police came," Sean continued, "and there were lights and then . . . then . . ." He stopped and grabbed both parents and squeezed all the tighter. "Now I want us to go home and be together like it used to be! Can we *please*?"

His sleepy-eyed plea, replete with tousled hair, sent a quiver to Shelly's knees. She helplessly gazed into Ryan's eyes and grappled for something to say.

Finally, Ryan said, "We're working on it, Champ," and went in for another family hug.

This time, Shelly allowed her instincts to guide. She rested her head on Ryan's chest and snuggled closer.

When Sonny mumbled, "Is there something you'd like to share with the whole class?" Shelly realized she'd forgotten they had an audience.

Ryan's gaze shifted to Sonny, and Shelly eyed the brothers as they exchanged a silent communication. Finally, Ryan flashed a giant smile that must have hurt.

At last, Sean wiggled free of his parents' arms and pointed toward the convenience store. "Can I get another Coke?" he questioned, grinning up at his folks in a way that insured he'd get what he wanted. "Mine's all hot now."

"You bet!" Ryan cheered. "You can have anything you want."

"But he already had one," Shelly worried and spotted the half-empty bottle in the car's console cup holder.

"Only part of one," Sonny supplied. "And it has gotten warm."

"Why don't we just get him a cup of ice to pour the Coke in?" Shelly suggested in the typical fashion of a responsible mother. "Or maybe some milk?"

"Maybe we should just get him a slushy!" Ryan suggested.

"Yeah, yeah, yeah!" Sean cheered, bouncing beside his father.

Shaking her head, Shelly didn't bother to argue. Instead, she beamed into Ryan's face when he draped his arm around her shoulders.

One month later, Ryan stood beside Sean's bed and watched him sleep. The last few weeks, they'd fallen into a comfortable routine that made Ryan long to take his and Shelly's relationship to the next level—through a doorway marked "I do." Every night he could, Ryan arrived around five to assist Shelly with dinner and laundry and whatever else she needed and then he'd help Sean get ready for bed. Once Sean was tucked into bed, he and Shelly usually enjoyed a cup of decaf before Ryan went back to his apartment.

He hadn't rushed Shelly, hadn't even tried to kiss her, had only held her hand or offered a brief hug, as her comfort level indicated. Ryan had decided to wait for Shelly's hints about whether it was time to move closer. So far, they'd been getting reacquainted, renewing their friendship, and relearning the art of witty conversation.

Tonight, he and Shelly had hosted his parents for a hamburger cookout. After Sean's safe return home, his mom's heart had stabilized and his dad had become unusually attentive. He'd even helped Ryan repair Shelly's alarm system. His father had been absent for most of his own sons' childhoods, and that was a driving force in Ryan's determination to be an excellent dad. He stroked Sean's hair and found it hard to believe that he'd been missing several days a mere month ago. His being found made statewide news—and he and Shelly had to battle reporters for days despite attempts to avoid them. Now that all the hoopla had diminished, their lives seemed to be settling back to status quo. But deep inside, Ryan knew nothing was status quo. Sean's disappearance had not only shaken his distant father into being supportive, it had also catapulted Shelly into considering reconciliation.

Tonight, she'd at last dropped a hint or two that she'd welcome his kissing her good night. It was nothing she'd said; more the way she looked at him and the warmth in her eyes . . . eyes that held her heart. Ryan quaked a bit as he faced the moment he'd anticipated all evening, the time when Shelly and he were alone.

His parents had left right before Sean's bath. Once the boy was in bed, Sean had insisted upon both his parents sitting in his room while Ryan read to him. When he fell asleep, Shelly mentioned brewing their usual decaf. Ryan had readily agreed. Now the smell of coffee wafting into Sean's bedroom invited Ryan to embrace the opportunity to be alone with Shelly.

Hovering over his son, he brushed his lips against his forehead and relished the smell of shampoo, the feel of soft skin. At this close vantage, Ryan once again scrutinized every inch of exposed skin in search of any scars or signs of abuse. Despite the fact that Sean promised his detailed accounts of what happened were complete, Ryan still worried. As with all the other times, he saw nothing that might give him concern. He had finally told Shelly that the ER psychologist did mention that there might be some eruptions and fallout from the whole episode later. As a professional who works with children, Shelly said she'd already considered that.

Sean stirred in his sleep and whimpered, "Dad . . . stay."

Ryan held his breath and didn't move as his heart wrenched. While Ryan helped his son get ready for bed, Sean had periodically begged his dad to spend the night, but Ryan had repeatedly informed him he had to go back to his duplex.

"Tomorrow's my day off, though. It's Saturday. I'll be back in the morning, and we'll go to Uncle Jack's ranch, okay?" Ryan had promised. Not knowing what all Shelly might have overheard, Ryan shamelessly hoped Sean's begging might be one more catalyst toward their reconciliation.

When Sean was once again motionless, and Ryan satisfied that his son was asleep, he stepped into the hallway and ambled toward the kitchen. More awkward than he ever remembered being, Ryan shoved his hands into his jeans pockets and tried to stop himself from fidgeting like a schoolboy. He reminded himself that he and Shelly had once been married, but that only upped his nervousness . . . especially when he recalled their wedding night.

Lord help me, he thought, and hoped Shelly couldn't read his mind. *She'd probably throw me out on my ear!*

Keeping his expression calm, Ryan stepped into the dining area to find Shelly pouring their coffee. Wearing a sweater and jeans, she looked like she was ready to go out on the town, except for the fact that she'd ditched her shoes and was padding around in woolly socks.

"Want some more of your mom's lemon pie?" she questioned, pointing to the pie plate near their cups.

"Bring it on!" Ryan rubbed his stomach. "I'm getting fat and sassy," he teased.

Shelly chuckled. "Nah . . . you work out too hard for that."

Enjoying the banter, Ryan prepared for a comeback, but was stopped by the telephone's ringing. Shelly stepped toward the kitchen wall phone and snatched it up before the second ring. She glanced at the screen and said, "It's mom's cell," while pressing the button that engaged the call.

Ryan tried to act as if he wasn't listening to the conversation until she said, "Dena? She wants to talk to me?" Then his attention riveted on Shelly, and he didn't bother to hide his interest.

Shelly's wide-eyed gaze held a question that Ryan didn't know how to answer. After charges had been dropped in lieu of Dena getting long-term care, Shelly hadn't mentioned her sister much—aside from a reference or two of having to work through anger over what happened. But then, Ryan had been dealing with the same issues.

"Well . . . okay, Mom," Shelly finally said with a nod. "I guess I can talk with her." Shelly moved into the doorway between the kitchen and living room, leaned against the doorjamb, and rubbed at her temple.

"Speaker phone?" Ryan whispered and moved closer.

She nodded and gripped his arm as he pressed the button on the phone system's base, which brought Dena's voice to both of them. Shelly set aside the handset.

"Hello, Shelly?" she said.

"Yes," Shelly replied, her fingers digging through Ryan's sleeve.

Silence permeated the line. Just as Ryan began to wonder if Dena might have hung up, she spoke again. "I'm—I'm back on my medication—this time, really."

"Good," Shelly rasped, her cheeks pale.

"And I-I just wanted to tell you . . . Mom told me everything. Some things I remember, some I don't."

"Okay," Shelly said.

"I'm—I'm sorry."

Shelly covered her mouth. Tears streaming her cheeks, she helplessly gazed at Ryan. He stiffened and determined to maintain control. "You want me to talk to her?" he whispered near Shelly's ear.

She nodded.

"Dena? It's me, Ryan," he said, keeping his voice even.

"Ryan?"

"Yeah."

She didn't reply.

"We appreciate your call. Thanks for the apology. The main thing now is just to try to get better, okay?"

"O-okay," Dena said. "I don't know what else to say. It's just that . . . I don't know why I sometimes do what I do. And then when I get on medicine, I feel so . . ."

"Yes, we understand," Ryan said.

"I won't ever try to get Sean again," she added.

"Thanks," Ryan said and eyed Shelly with a silent encouragement to engage in the conversation.

At last, Shelly said, "Dena, I've got to be honest. I've really struggled with what happened."

Dena didn't reply.

Shelly leaned against Ryan and continued, "But maybe one day we can sit down and talk about it more."

"Maybe so," Dena agreed. "But right now . . ."

"Yeah, I know you've got a lot on your plate right now," Shelly affirmed.

"Yes, and I've—I've gotta go," she said before their mother's voice came over the line.

"Shelly, thank you so much for talking to her," she rushed. "It's something the psychiatrist was saying needed to happen, but I didn't know if you'd even want to—"

"To tell you the truth, Mom, I didn't," Shelly said, an honest edge to her voice. "But I figured it was for the best . . . maybe for both of us."

"Thank you," Maggie said, her voice trembling. "I love you, honey. And one day, we're all going to pull out of this. Remember what we talked about last night?"

"Yes," Shelly replied. "And I'll keep praying for you and Dad— just like I promised."

Once the goodbyes were spoken, Ryan pressed the button that disengaged the call. Since Shelly didn't offer to pull away, he wrapped his arm around her and held her while she wept. Strangely, hearing Dena's voice had been a purging experience for him, and he expected the same for Shelly. Nevertheless, he didn't give into the emotions that went along with the purge. Instead, he stayed steady for Shelly until she backed away and reached for one of the napkins lying by their saucers.

Pondering the events of the last month, Ryan eventually said, "It's hard to believe everything that's happened. It all feels so surreal— almost like it was just a bad dream."

"I know." She sniffled and took another napkin. "That's what I was just telling Mom when she called last night. By the way, she said that Dena's doctor recommended they go to a counselor to better learn how to manage her. Anyway, they're starting to realize they're going to have to use some really tough love if she's ever going to get on her feet."

" 'Bout time, don't you think?"

"Yeah," Shelly agreed and laid the napkins on the table.

Even after such a traumatic moment, Ryan couldn't stop himself from admiring her simple beauty. Shelly never wore much makeup or went for dramatic hair. She always had just been who she was, and Ryan appreciated that from the start of their acquaintance.

"I've really wrestled with my anger toward Dena and what she did," she shared while slicing each of them a piece of pie.

"Yeah, I've had my moments too," Ryan admitted and took a seat.

"But talking to her somehow . . ." She served a piece of the lemon masterpiece onto Ryan's saucer.

"I know," Ryan agreed. "It was good—in a strange sort of way."

"Yeah." Her smile wobbled. "Maybe we can all just move forward. I hope she'll *stay* on her medicine. From now on."

"Sounds like your parents are going to see to it now."

"I hope they can." She settled in a chair and didn't bother to serve herself. Resting her elbow on the table, she placed her chin in her hand. With a sigh, she added, "I wish so bad life could be simpler."

Ryan ignored his dessert and debated whether to offer more intimate support, or continue to keep his distance.

"I've *got* to talk to you about something else as well," she continued, lifting her face to his.

"Okay," Ryan said, wondering where this was heading.

"I've been thinking about this off-and-on all month. Last night on the phone, I knew for sure." Her eyes earnest, she rushed forward. "I think I've realized the reason I so obsessed on my parents. It was because I was trying to make up for Dena."

"Oh man," Ryan breathed as Shelly's full meaning unfolded in his mind. "I can see where you might do that."

"I don't know why I couldn't see it before now," she admitted. "I think maybe I was so hurt over . . . over . . . everything that I couldn't see anything but the pain. And before we split up, when *you* tried to tell me . . . well, by that time Dena had disappeared and I was so worried about my folks and how in the world they could be holding up that I was blinded to anything else."

Ryan reached for her hand. "I just hate it, Shelly," he soothed. "I hate that you've had to go through all this."

"It's been hard having an unstable sister like this—really, really hard," she stressed. "It's hard on Mom and Dad. I see them so upset and I feel so sorry for them. They're nearing their retirement years! Like they need this burden!"

"And you were always trying to lift it by being the perfect daughter, right?"

"I guess so," she breathed. "I guess I was thinking that if I was perfect enough and attentive enough—"

"It would all just be okay?"

"Yeah . . . but I'm beginning to think no matter what I do or how I try, I can never fix it."

"And the more you try to fix it, the more it will tear your life to shreds." Ryan squeezed her hand and Shelly squeezed back.

"I know," she admitted with a nod and then added a dry laugh. "What a mess we've been."

"Yeah." Ryan smiled and didn't think he'd ever loved Shelly more than now. "Except you don't look like anything close to a mess," he said. "You're beautiful, Shelly. And the older you get, the more beautiful you are."

She narrowed her eyes, and the teasing light sparkling from her spirit belied any irritation. "I look like death warmed over, and you know it," she said. "You're just kissing up."

"Actually, no." Ryan shook his head. "If I was kissing up, I'd do something like this." Impulsively, he swooped in and planted a kiss on her lips. Only the second after he pulled away did he realize the implications of his compulsive action.

Shelly's gasp and her widening eyes accompanied the rush of heat to his gut and the flush of red to her cheeks. The sparks that had threatened to ignite all month exploded as if they'd just shared their first kiss. Ryan wondered what had possessed him.

He told himself he should back away, but the old flame immobilized him. Ryan's mind raced with the urge to pull her closer and kiss her in a way that would have her longing to say, "I do" all over again. Out of nowhere, a controlled voice transcended the urge and suggested he should make light of the kiss, laugh it off, and soon take his leave.

But when Shelly's gaze went from shocked to mesmerized, when her attention trailed from his eyes to his lips, he could no longer hear the controlled voice. All Ryan could think was that she'd gone from subtle hints to blatant ones. And in the face of her obvious longing, Ryan's resolve melted to weakness.

"Shelly?" he croaked, his heart pounding. "Are you serious about this? Because if you don't mean it . . ."

The memory of Sean's voice begging Ryan to stay, asking if they could be a family again, sprang up between them like a magnetic field pulling their lives together once more.

When the tension mounted to desperate, Shelly finally whispered, "I mean it, Ryan."

"Are you sure?"

"Y-yes, I'm sure," she replied. "I-I don't understand everything. I'm still working through the trust part. But I do know I love you. I-I still do. And I want to at least try, if you'll be patient with me."

"Oh, Shelly," Ryan groaned. "You know I love you." Standing, he reached for her and she rose into his arms. "And I'll be patient, I promise . . . if you will with me."

"I will," she vowed.

But the kiss that followed was far from patient. The feel of Shelly in his arms was sweeter than ever as the promise of the future sang through Ryan's veins. The heat that sprang between them testified to a union that might be nullified on paper, but in their spirits still lived strong.

When temptation pushed Ryan to the brink, he regretfully pulled away and was thankful Shelly understood the need to do so. "We aren't married," he said, wishing more than ever they were.

"Yeah." She nodded, but the message in her eyes couldn't be mistaken. "I don't know how I ever convinced myself I was in love with Tim Aldridge," she admitted and sealed Ryan's certainty that remarriage couldn't be far away.

Tempted to pull her close again, he backed off and moved toward where his jacket lay draped over a dining room chair. "I really ought to go now," he admitted. "While I can. I want to earn your trust, and you need to know I respect you so you can fully respect me . . . again."

Crossing her arms, Shelly nodded, but appeared more forlorn and bereft than convinced. Finally, she tore her aching gaze from his and said, "I don't want you to go, Ryan."

His ears roared with her words, yet he doubled his resolve and kept his distance.

"But we both know it's what's best, and what's right . . . for now," she added.

"Right," he agreed and tried to decide whether he should mention getting married or wait. Finally, he decided the imminent issue was putting some space between them. Popping the question could wait, at least until the morning.

CHAPTER TWENTY-TWO

Shelly stood in the kitchen until the front door closed, then she collapsed in the nearest chair. Never had she experienced the power of such a kiss, not with Ryan and certainly not with Tim. The old attraction, lying dormant for years, had intensified and erupted with a new fire that turned Shelly's bones to liquid.

"I can't believe this. Oh God, what are you doing?" she whispered and saw exactly what God was doing. Her spiritual eyes, once dulled by the pain, delivered a sharp image of a wrecked couple complete once more through the power of an almighty God who heals the brokenhearted through His unconditional love.

"Help me, Lord," Shelly pleaded. "Help me wholly trust Ryan again. I want to. I really, really do."

Sean's panicked cry drove Shelly to her feet. "Dad!" he bellowed. "Dad! I want Dad! Mom!"

Her heart throbbing, Shelly bolted down the hallway to nearly bump into Sean running from his room. When he spotted Shelly, he grabbed her legs and sobbed for his father all the more.

"Sean . . . Sean . . ." Shelly soothed while bending to pick him up. "Sweetheart, Mom's here. I'm right here."

His body writhed as he rested his head against her shoulder. "Dad . . . Dad's gone, isn't he?"

"Yes, he's gone." Shelly sighed. "He had to go home, just like he always does, but he'll be back tomorrow. I promise, honey."

"No, no, no. I want Dad *now*," he demanded. Ever since the abduction, Sean had begged to go to Ryan's nearly every night. Several times, Shelly had given in, especially right after he came home. But in the last week she'd begun to be stronger as she realized this could become a nightly pattern.

"If you go to Daddy's, you can't stay here," Shelly explained. "Don't you want to stay here with me tonight? You spent all last weekend at Dad's."

"Why can't Dad spend the night like he used to?" Sean pressed. "And it can be like it used to be—just us three."

"He just can't—not now, anyway," Shelly answered, moving to the living room where the rocking chair waited. Until the abduction, Sean had grown out of the need to be rocked. But in recent weeks, the old comfort had calmed him as nothing else could.

Once the rocking began, Sean went back to his former mantra, "I want Dad." And Shelly was reminded of the weeks following the separation when Sean begged to be with his father.

Her heart swelled with the weight of Sean's needs, and Shelly stated the first words that came to mind, "Daddy will be back home soon, honey. Very, very soon."

By the time Ryan pulled into his driveway, he was praying that God would complete his miracle within the week. *We could be married by next weekend*, he thought, and for the first time didn't think that would be rushing Shelly—not if her expression when he left was anything to go by.

Ryan parked his truck, invaded his duplex, and was stepping out of the shower when his cell phone rang. But Sonny didn't even give him time to say hello.

"Hey there, you lazy lug," his younger brother chided. "I'm here with a new friend. Why aren't you answering your door? Your truck's out here. Where are you?"

"I'm getting out of the shower," Ryan explained and didn't elaborate that he was tired and really not prepared for company. "Who's the friend?" he questioned.

"It's a surprise visitor. Trust me, you'll be *glad*!"

"Okay, okay," Ryan grumbled, his mind still full of Shelly. Grabbing his watch from the sink's ledge, he started to remind his brother it was nine o'clock but decided against it. "Give me five minutes," he promised.

"You got it!" Sonny crowed. "But make it a short five minutes! You know it's colder than ice out here."

"I know, I know," he agreed. "I'll be fast."

Ryan threw on some sweats and dried his hair with a towel as he walked down the hallway. Only when he opened the front door did his thoughts turn from Shelly to the present. For Sonny stood outside with a tall young man who looked suspiciously familiar.

"Surprise!" Sonny crowed.

"Blake?" Ryan roared, recognizing his nephew from the pictures Sonny had shown him.

"In the flesh," Sonny said, stepping into the apartment. "Meet my older brother, your uncle Ryan," Sonny explained.

"Yo," Blake said, offering his doubled fists in lieu of a handshake.

Ryan obliged him by bumping fists before closing the door on the frigid air. Dressed in a pair of baggy jeans, an oversized jacket, and a black toboggan, Blake reminded Ryan of dozens of other misdirected teens he'd encountered. Several conversations with Tanya had indicated that she hoped Sonny could influence Blake for the better. On first impression, Ryan understood her concern.

"Sonny, I had no idea Blake was coming for a visit!" he enthused and hoped he hid his misgivings. "Last I heard, you were just visiting him in Dallas some."

"I have been," Sonny explained, beaming like the father of a newborn. "But his mom's actually considering moving here. They're here for the weekend, actually staying with Tanya and me."

"No way!" Ryan exclaimed while Blake plopped onto the couch and looked around the place with an attitude as old as Sonny's adolescence.

"Yep! She thinks a smaller town will be better." He sloughed off his jacket, dropped it on the couch, and left the rest unsaid.

Noticing that Sonny's jeans were just as baggy as Blake's, Ryan hid a smile and scrounged through his memory for what he could offer his guests to drink. But he'd spent so much time at Shelly's this last month, he couldn't recall. Furthermore, he'd used his grocery money to stock her fridge rather than his.

"I don't even know if I have a Coke to my name," Ryan admitted. "Let me see what I can come up with. If nothing else, do you guys mind bottled water?"

"We just went to the store," Sonny said. "I've got a case of Dr Peppers in the truck."

"*Works!*" Ryan offered a thumbs-up. "I'll ice the glasses." Smoothing damp hair with his hands, Ryan tossed his towel on the breakfast bar. It landed near the answering system, and he noticed his message light blinking. Trying to remember the last time he checked his voice mails, he reminded himself to do so after Sonny and Blake left.

"So Blake, I hear you like basketball," Ryan called out as he removed three plastic tumblers from the cabinet.

"Yeah," Blake agreed, his footsteps nearing. "If we move here, Sonny—uh, Dad—wants to get me on his church's team. We just came from youth group and they were talking about it."

Ryan glanced toward the kitchen doorway to see Blake mimicking a long shot. The athletic swagger so matched Sonny's teenage cockiness, Ryan chuckled out loud.

"What?" Blake challenged.

"Nothing," Ryan replied. "You just look like Sonny, that's all."

"Yeah, we're weird like that," he admitted with a tinge of admiration in his voice. And Blake's fraction of a smile diminished Ryan's former worries.

He opened the freezer, plunked several cubes of ice in a glass, and said, "You're all right, Blake."

"I try," he said and moved closer. "Need any help?"

"Sure. Here." Ryan handed him a tumbler. "You set them on the table. As soon as Sonny shows with the Drs, you be the designated pourer, all right?"

He offered a thumbs-up and said, "Gotcha covered."

"Uh, Ryan?" Sonny's voice preceded his kitchen invasion by only a second. He plopped the Dr. Peppers on the table and neared his elder brother. His confused expression along with the disappointed droop to his eyes perplexed Ryan.

"Are you seeing Arlene again, man?" His urgent whisper accompanied an if-you-are-I'm-going-to-smack-you look that both annoyed and concerned Ryan. "I thought you and Shelly were getting back together."

Ryan stared into his brother's gray eyes. Once he got past the shock of Sonny's questions, he realized something significant had happened during the few minutes it took for Sonny to retrieve the soda. As Ryan grappled for possible scenarios, an unearthly dread numbed his mind and chilled him to his toes.

"Shelly and I *are* on. What makes you think I'm seeing Arlene again?" he questioned, already knowing he wasn't going to like Sonny's answer.

"Hi, Ryan," a familiar female voice said from the kitchen doorway.

His gut knotting, Ryan's gaze slid toward the voice to confirm that Arlene Marigold had just stepped into his kitchen.

"Arlene!" he gasped, noting she looked the same as she had the day he left her—same blond hair, same blue eyes, same sweater that should have stopped several inches closer to her neck than it did.

"Hi!" she said. "I'm sorry to barge in like this." Arlene glanced at Blake whose "teenager wow" expression contrasted with Sonny's stunned staring.

"Well . . ." Ryan replied and stopped himself from saying, *That's okay*. Because it *wasn't* okay! "What are you doing here?" he blurted.

"I left you several voice mails," she said and glanced down. "Grandma Marigold had a stroke. I've been in town several days, so I looked you up in the phone book. I said in my last voice mail that if I didn't hear back from you, I'd drop by." She shrugged. "So here I am."

"Holy Toledo," Sonny breathed.

Ryan shot him a silent SOS before shoving the other tumblers into his hands. Only one thing majored on Ryan's mind: *Get Arlene out of this apartment and make it clear that she is not to return under any circumstances.*

If Shelly finds out she's been here . . . He panicked at the very thought.

"Arlene," he said, gently nabbing her arm and steering her toward the living room, "I'm sorry but I never got those voice mails. If I had—"

"That's okay," she said. "I understand. Maybe this isn't a good time." She glanced over her shoulder.

"Actually, *no* time is going to be a good time."

"Ryan, if you'll just *listen* to me," she pleaded and gripped his arm until he halted. "I wanted to see you *so badly*."

"I can't help it, Arlene," Ryan replied. Her beseeching stare leaving him cold, he continued his trek to the door.

"But you don't understand—I-I . . . " She searched his face as they halted. Finally, her shoulders took on a dejected slant as her eyes reddened.

"Look, I'm on the verge of remarrying my ex-wife," he explained.

"So it was her all along," she accused, crossing her arms.

"Yeah, and that's the way it *should* have been in the first place. I tried to explain when I left, but you wouldn't listen to me. I can't go back to our relationship on *any terms*. It was wrong, Arlene. And this won't do—you're being here right now is bad timing. Really bad. I don't even know what possessed you." Arlene never had been shy about her feelings for Ryan. Truth be known, she'd aggressed him shortly after they met. Tonight's behavior wasn't far removed from their first date.

Ryan gripped the knob and paused before opening the door. When she dashed at a tear, he couldn't deny a thread of sympathy. He hated seeing a woman cry, and sometimes he wondered if some females fully understood the power of tears. Hardening his heart, he decided not to put such a manipulative move past Arlene. The last thing he needed to do was show sympathy and have her maneuver her way into his arms.

He backed away. Sensing he was being watched, Ryan glanced toward the kitchen to see two bug-eyed males shamelessly peering across the breakfast bar. Arlene darted a look their way and said, "Do we have to have an audience?"

Ryan opened the door and followed her outside. If not for the fact that he wanted to make certain she never returned, Ryan would have let her leave without the escort. But his desire to permanently end any chances of her return drove him to her side.

"I hate to be so blunt," he explained, "but I *really need* you to go for good. It's best if you don't ever come back."

She sniffled and lowered her head. "You haven't changed a bit," she accused in a petty voice. "You never did mind if you hurt me."

"I'm not trying to hurt you," he said, keeping his voice even. "But we don't seem to be communicating somehow. I told you two years ago we were through."

"Well," she shrugged, "I just thought maybe you'd missed me as much as I missed you." She lifted her gaze and shivered against winter's chill.

Ryan glanced down at his bare feet and wished he'd at least thought to put on his Crocs. "Look, it's cold," he said. "We're both going to catch pneumonia, and there's really nothing left to say."

The flash of headlights preceded a car's pulling into the parking lot, and Ryan strained through the shadows to see if he recognized the driver. The way things were going, his place was turning into a beehive. Once the car stopped near a streetlamp, Ryan's heart dropped to the concrete. He recognized the minivan all too well.

When Sean bounded out of the vehicle and started hollering, "Dad! Dad!" Ryan wished Arlene Marigold could disappear. On an impulse, he thought about shoving her back indoors, but that would only up his guilty appearance. After his mind darted in a thousand desperate directions, Ryan knew he had no choice but to stand like a zombie and helplessly watch as Shelly approached.

CHAPTER TWENTY-THREE

When Shelly exited her vehicle, she noticed Ryan outside his door, talking to someone in the shadows. Assuming it might be a neighbor, she forged forward and made certain Sean remained safe as he dashed across the parking lot. Only when Shelly moved within five feet of Ryan did she recognize the woman standing near him. She also recognized the cloak of shame covering Ryan's features.

Shelly never imagined she'd ever see Arlene Marigold again; she would have rather died than have to face Ryan's former mistress. The shock left her colder than the December air chilling her lungs. Shelly's spine stiffened to the point that she couldn't move. And while the white cloud of her breath testified that she was breathing, Shelly felt as if she'd stopped . . . as if something inside her had died.

Ryan had promised her . . . he'd made her believe . . . she'd even begun to think she could fully trust. Now . . .

"Dad! I've come to spend the night with you!" Sean crowed and ran headlong into Ryan's legs.

Stumbling to keep his balance, Ryan scooped up his son.

Shelly noticed Arlene's lips moving but couldn't comprehend a word she said. She was too distracted by that low-cut red sweater contrasted with bleach-blond hair.

When Arlene turned and strode across the parking lot, Ryan said, "Shelly, it's not what you think."

Shaking her head, Shelly backed away while Ryan held Sean and moved forward.

"It's really not. You need to let me explain!" he continued.

"No," Shelly croaked. "No!" She pressed the heels of her hands against her temples and frantically eyed her son. "He can't stay here if she's staying," was all she could think to say. "You know the terms of the divorce. No cohabitating in front of him."

"There's no cohabitating," Ryan claimed. "If you'll just let me explain!"

"I-I . . ." Shelly gazed toward Arlene. The shadows partially concealed her, but Shelly still detected that she paused by her vehicle, watching . . . waiting. And that's when Shelly knew. No matter what had happened here tonight or what might happen in the future with her and Ryan, Arlene would always be watching and waiting from the shadows. They'd never be free of her. *Never!*

Shelly debated whether she should make Sean return home with her or leave him with Ryan. Watching the way he clung to his dad, recalling the way he begged to come, Shelly decided that ripping him from Ryan would just add more emotional turmoil to an already volatile situation.

"As long as she's leaving, he can stay," she ground out. "But I will grill him when he comes home, and if he tells me that she came back, I will call my attorney. Do you understand?"

The shadows only intensified Ryan's dejected nod.

The tears that assaulted Shelly blotted everything else from sight, and she stumbled back to her vehicle.

Ryan stared after Shelly's departing van and decided Arlene's appearance must be some cruel twist of fate. *Or maybe it's my own negligence*, he thought, recalling those voice mails he never bothered to check. Only one returned call would have stopped her from ever coming over again, but Ryan had been too busy pursuing Shelly to think about mundane responsibilities.

When he relived Shelly's shattered look, a shiver started in his soul and spanned his body. Even now, Ryan considered chasing after her and not letting her get away until she heard the truth.

But would she believe me? he thought and already knew his answer. The issue went much deeper than Arlene's presence tonight. It involved Shelly's ability to trust him, period. She'd already told him she was still working on the trust and that he'd have to be patient with her. Apparently, working toward total trust had just hit a brick wall.

After another shiver, Ryan decided to give Shelly some space for now. If she couldn't come to a point of giving him the benefit of the doubt on her own, then there was nothing Ryan could do. He'd told her there was nothing going on between him and Arlene. Ryan didn't know how else he could convince her. Either she believed him, or she didn't. Again, it all went back to trust.

Holding Sean close, he endured another shiver. "Brrr," he said, trying to sound normal, but Ryan wondered how he could keep up the pretense when he felt as if his heart were being ripped out. "Let's go inside, okay?" he suggested, straining to catch a final glimpse of Shelly's vehicle.

"Okay." Sean squirmed from Ryan's arms, hit the ground, and opened the door.

When Ryan pivoted to enter, he glimpsed Sonny and Blake moving away from the front window. He didn't need a secret agent to tell him they'd been spying.

"Do you have a Coke?" Sean asked, and Ryan chuckled. "You're a Coke junkie, aren't you, kid?" He ruffled his son's hair.

"How about a Dr Pepper?" Sonny offered.

"That's fine." Sean dropped his backpack near the sofa and unzipped it.

Certain Shelly would not approve of his having a caffeinated drink at bedtime, Ryan didn't have the strength to protest. Leaving Sean to his backpack, he went into the kitchen, grabbed a glass, and dug a handful of ice out of the freezer. Ryan was plunking it into the glass when Sonny's whisper snagged his attention.

"Aren't you going after her, man?"

"No." Ryan shook his head. "I think she's already made up her mind. I told her nothing was going on. If she doesn't believe me, then she doesn't," he said, his words going stiff as an unexpected exasperation mingled with the depression. "It's really about trust, and that's not something she's throwing around these days."

"So that's it? You're just going to let it go?"

Ryan gazed eye to eye with his younger brother, whose candid appraisal pierced him to the core.

"I really don't know *what* to do right now," Ryan admitted. "I'd really like her to come to the point of trusting me without my having to coerce her. I've bent over backward to show her I've changed. If she can't see it by now, I really don't know what else to do," he repeated, his growing irritation spilling into his words.

"Hey, little dude. You got a Wii?" Blake's question floated from the living room.

"Yeah! Mom let me bring it," Sean replied. "I brought Mario Brothers."

"No way! Wanna play?"

"Sure," Sean replied.

Ryan shoved the cup into Sonny's hands and blurted, "I need some time alone. Would you make sure they don't burn down the place?"

"Uh, sure," Sonny agreed. "But I still think you should go after her. How would *you* feel in her shoes?"

*　*　*

After a fitful night and only a few hours sleep, Shelly awoke by seven the next morning. Feeling like she'd been hit over the head with a bat, she stumbled to the kitchen, made her coffee, and crawled into the shower. While the warm water momentarily revived her, it did nothing to wash her mind of the images that had haunted her all night—Arlene Marigold standing outside Ryan's duplex, looking like a she-wolf ready to devour Ryan.

After a good cry last night, Shelly had flopped onto her bed and fumed until past one o'clock, when she finally fell into a disturbed sleep. But dreams, assaulted by turmoil, had jolted her awake by three. The doubts had chewed at her troubled emotions until Shelly finally focused long enough to pray.

She'd drifted into the next round of sleep while talking to God: *Dear Lord, help me to see the truth. Show me what to do. If I've jumped to conclusions, please show me.*

The next time she awakened, it was to the echo of Ryan's desperate appeal, *Shelly, it's not what you think. . . . It's really not. You need to let me explain! . . . There's no cohabitating . . . If you'll just let me explain!*

Presently, Shelly teetered between believing him and dismissing the words as an act to once again cover his tracks. She closed her eyes and plunged her face into the spray, welcoming the warm sting that continued to awaken her.

What do I do? she asked on a half-prayer. *God, show me. Do I believe my eyes or listen to him?*

Shelly thought back to the early years of their marriage, before Arlene ever came into the picture, and wondered what she'd have done if she'd seen Ryan talking to an attractive woman in the shadows.

I'd have let him explain, she thought. *And, I'd have believed what he said because I trusted him.*

She pulled her face out of the spray and opened her eyes. "I trusted him," she whispered and wondered if she could ever get back to the way things had been. Shaking her head, she rubbed her face and couldn't answer that question.

But maybe I should at least let him explain, she thought, recalling the kiss that had left her weak. That kiss had been full of promises that Shelly could believe in. *Would the Ryan I've gotten to know again run headlong into the arms of his old girlfriend after holding me?* she questioned, challenging last night's assumptions.

Shelly turned off the shower as Ryan's words pummeled her mind anew: *Shelly, it's not what you think. . . . It's really not. You need to let me explain! . . . There's no cohabitating . . . If you'll just let me explain!*

"But I didn't," she mumbled. "Just like I wouldn't listen when he told me I had a problem with my parents." It had taken Shelly hours of praying to be able to voice this reality. While she hated the taste of the words, she couldn't deny the ugly truth.

"God help me," she squeaked and squashed a tear as it trickled into the moisture on her face. *I should have let him explain last night. Instead, I accused him. What if he was telling the truth? Would he have lied after everything we've been through?*

She slung aside the shower curtain, snatched a towel off the rack, and rubbed her skin red. Once she'd donned her jeans and shirt, Shelly swabbed at the bathroom mirror and gazed at herself through the haze. Her chalky skin and damp hair along with the dark circles under her eyes made her look destitute.

"If I go over to his place, I'm going to have to do something about the way I look," she said, not considering she'd just decided to go to Ryan's. Shelly flung open the bathroom door and invaded her bedroom closet. After a couple of minutes of digging, she pulled out the vanity case she'd purchased at a makeup party last year. Tim had given her his debit card and encouraged her to buy some makeup. She obliged by purchasing this starter kit, replete with everything. In retrospect, Shelly wondered if he was trying to tell her he'd rather she wear more makeup. Presently, she didn't care. Tim was ancient history. This was about Ryan.

By the time Shelly dried her hair and pulled it into a clip, she was pleased with her appearance. The light application of makeup hid her dark circles and added a rosy blush to her cheeks. Jitters dancing along her nerves, Shelly wondered if Ryan would notice the effort or even care.

"I was married to him for years," she reminded herself. *It's not like we just met and I have to impress him.* Throwing in a final prayer, Shelly marched from the bathroom, grabbed her purse, and opened the front door—only to see Ryan approaching the porch steps. Head bent, he studied the ground and seemed oblivious to her presence.

Shelly stopped, gulped for air, and fidgeted with her purse strap until Ryan glanced up and halted.

"Shelly!" he said, his eyes wide.

"Ryan!" she replied and blinked until she was certain she hadn't conjured him. "What are you doing here?" She gazed toward his truck. "Are you bringing Sean home? Where's Sean?"

"Sean's with Sonny and his son, Blake. They took him to Mc-Donald's for breakfast," he rushed. "Actually, Sean thinks Blake is the coolest thing going. They played the Wii last night until all hours." He waved his hand and then rubbed at his twitching eye.

"I see," Shelly said, helplessly staring at him.

The longer she observed him the more she remembered last night's kiss and the more she found herself longing for a repeat. She also longed to know that Ryan's explanation would completely exonerate him.

"I, uh, well . . . I actually came to see you—to talk to you," he said, his heart in his eyes. "Were you going somewhere, because if you were I can always—"

"No! I mean, yes. Yes, I was actually going to your place." She rubbed her dampening palm against her sweater.

"Oh." He wrinkled his brow. "Did you need to pick up Sean for something? Because if you do, I can call Sonny." He reached for his phone attached to his belt.

"No." Shelly shook her head and swallowed at her tight throat. "I was coming to talk to you, actually."

"To me?"

She nodded and wondered how she could be sweating when there was frost on the fields. "Yeah, I wanted to . . . to discuss l-last night," she stammered and scrutinized his jeans and boots.

An elongated silence gave Shelly enough time to consider half a dozen other things to say, only to dismiss them all. Finally, she blurted, "Well, you said you wanted to explain!" and snapped her focus to his.

"Yeah, I guess I did, didn't I?" he said, a relieved smile crawling across his face.

Shelly held her breath and waited while her heart thumped in her temples.

He ascended the steps, stopped on the edge of the porch, and paused to appraise Shelly to the point of distraction.

"Well?" Shelly prompted.

"Arlene dropped in on me out of nowhere last night. I had no idea she was even coming over," he explained. "She called and left several voice mails on my land line that I never got because I hadn't checked my voice mail in days because I'd been, well, with you," he said, his expression as guileless as a child's. "I listened to them this morning. You're welcome to listen to them as well. In her last message, she told me she was going to drop by if I didn't return the call. Since I never bothered to listen to the messages, I hadn't called her."

"And so she just showed up?" Shelly asked.

"Yeah." Ryan shrugged. "I had no idea she was coming and was in the process of essentially telling her to get lost for good when you drove up."

"That's all?" she croaked.

"Yes, that's all," he said on a sigh. "That's all, Shelly. With God as my witness, that's all. You've *got* to believe me." He laid his hand against his chest and that wedding band glistened in the sun. The longer Shelly observed the band, the more her eyes stung. Finally, she averted her teary gaze.

"I *want* to believe you, Ryan," she whispered.

"I have no interest in her whatsoever," he replied, stepping closer. "I lost all interest the day I went down to the altar that Easter Sunday. Something changed in me, Shelly. It was something supernatural. All I've wanted from that day is *you* . . . and my family back." He stopped only inches from her. "I love you, Shelly, and *only you.*"

She searched his soul for any signs of falsehood, any hint of wavering. All she encountered was unbridled love and blatant honesty from a man who had nothing to hide.

"I prayed all night," he continued, "and finally decided to swallow my pride and come over here. Did I do the right thing?"

In that instant, something within Shelly began to unravel. The tight wad of suspicion that had bound her from the second Ryan reentered her life gradually diminished until nothing was left but pure love. That's when she knew beyond all doubt that Ryan Mansfield really had changed.

The man she married was not the same one standing in front of her. This Ryan would never succumb to the guiles of another woman. This Ryan would be true to Shelly until death. This Ryan had allowed the Lord to transform him into a man of honor that would always put her best interest above his own. The conviction was so strong, Shelly didn't question its truth. She just knew that Ryan Mansfield was her man, and only her man, for the rest of his life.

"Shelly?" he prompted, a plea in his voice.

She nodded and whispered, "Y-yes, you did the right thing. The absolute, best, right thing," she added before wrapping her arms around him and burying her face against his chest. "I love you, Ryan, and I don't think I ever stopped."

"Ah, Shelly," he breathed. Squeezing her tight, he kissed her cheek and stroked her hair.

"I'm sorry I jumped to the wrong conclusion last night and that . . . that I didn't give you a chance to tell me what happened. I guess I just flipped out."

"It's okay," he encouraged. "In your shoes, I might have done the same thing."

Closing her eyes, Shelly clung to him until his rapid heartbeat matched her own. Only when she pulled away did Shelly realize he was trembling as much as she. The kiss that followed left her weak and again wishing they were married.

"We've *got* to get married," Ryan whispered next to her ear.

"I know," Shelly agreed. "What about next week?"

"Next week?" His eyes wide, he pulled away. "Are you sure?"

"I've never been surer of anything in my life," Shelly responded and drowned in another kiss.

Dear Friend,

The Bible is full of stories like Ryan and Shelly Mansfield's—stories of people who have blown it and a God of grace who redeems their bad choices. If we aren't careful, we can fall into the thinking that the "best Christians" never make mistakes or wrong choices and are therefore more deserving of God's grace. The truth is, without our mess-ups there is no need for grace. Grace doesn't exist in the absence of failure. It exists *because* of failure.

Likewise, God's redemption only exists in the presence of our having fallen. The Bible isn't about people who always made the right choices, but rather about failures that God redeemed and used despite their shortcomings. Moses, the great Israelite leader, was a murderer. So was Paul, the author of much of the New Testament. Peter, Christ's celebrated apostle, turned into a cursing traitor during Jesus' trial and crucifixion. These are but a few examples. As with these Bible greats, God uses our failures to His glory if we'll allow Him to redeem them.

Unfortunately, there are those who refuse that redemption. A variety of reasons play into this choice. Some people convince themselves they've blown it so bad that God is through with them. Others refuse to forgive those who have sinned against them. Then there are those who assume that God only works with perfect people and they "have to get their act together" before God will work in their lives.

The truth is, nobody alive fully "has their act together." We're all just moving through life by the grace of God and, with His help, "getting our act together" one issue at a time. For those who wholly turn their hearts to the Lord, He faithfully redeems every wrong choice, one at a time. As Scripture states, "And we know that in all things God works for the good of those who love him, who have been called according to his purpose" (Romans 8:28).

I hope that Shelly and Ryan's story has empowered you to accept God's redemption on a new level in your heart and life. Even if their sins aren't yours, each and every one of us is a product of God's grace and each and every one of us never moves away from the need for His redemption.

By His Grace,
Debra White Smith

DISCUSSION QUESTIONS

1. Most broken relationships happen as a partnership effort—two people each contribute a set of issues to complete a whole sin or problem. Individually, they hold only half the issue; together, it is made into a whole. Discuss how both Shelly and Ryan's issues contributed to their divorce.

2. How would Shelly's forgiving Ryan have been inhibited by her inability to place herself in her husband's shoes?

3. How is the ability to place ourselves in the shoes of another directly linked to the Golden Rule: "So in everything, do to others what you would have them do to you, for this sums up the Law and the Prophets" (Matthew 7:12)?

4. Ryan testifies that when he encountered Christ, he knew he couldn't continue living with Arlene. Why does a real encounter with Christ lead to such conviction?

5. Can someone have a real encounter with Christ but have no sense of conviction over willful, known sin in their lives?

6. Just because Ryan does have a genuine encounter with Christ, that doesn't mean all his issues vanish. Discuss why God often

uses the method of redeeming our wrong choices one by one over a period of time.

7. Discuss how our unwillingness to obey the Lord will halt His redeeming our bad choices.

8. As they did with Shelly, many times childhood issues play a part in the decay of a relationship. Why is it important to the health of any relationship that we be willing to sort through and find healing from any childhood issues?

9. God uses the trauma of Sean's disappearance to throw Shelly and Ryan together and ultimately bring about the answer to Ryan's prayer for reconciliation with his wife. Share those times in your life when God used a trial to bring about an answer to your prayers.

10. How is Sonny Mansfield's pursuit of his son, Blake, like the heavenly Father's pursuit of us?

11. How would Sonny's story be different if his wife refused to accept his son?

12. Discuss the redemption themes in Sonny and Blake's story.

Photo by Daniel W. Smith

DEBRA WHITE SMITH is a seasoned Christian author, speaker, and media personality who has been regularly publishing books for a decade. She has written more than fifty books with more than one million books in print. Her titles include such life-changing books as *Romancing Your Husband*, *Romancing Your Wife*, *It's a Jungle at Home; Survival Strategies for Overwhelmed Moms*, the Sister Suspense fiction series, and the Jane Austen fiction series.

Along with Debra's being voted a fiction-reader favorite several times, her book *Romancing Your Husband* was a finalist in the 2003 Gold Medallion Awards, and her Austen series novel *First Impressions* was a finalist in the 2005 Retailers Choice Awards.

Debra White Smith

BOOKS BY DEBRA WHITE SMITH

TEXAS HEAT
Lone Star Intrigue, Book One

ISBN 978-0-06-149316-4 (paperback)

Jack has harbored unrequited love for Charli for over a decade. When she's wrongly accused of embezzlement, as the chief of police, Jack risks everything to prove her innocence.

"Debra White Smith is a master storyteller whose way with words will charm, delight, and entertain. Her stories are not to be missed!"
—Tracie Peterson, author of the Alaskan Quest series

TEXAS PURSUIT
Lone Star Intrigue, Book Two

ISBN 978-0-06-149325-6 (paperback)

In the second installment of the Lone Star Intrigue series, a single mother joins forces with a private eye to keep her safe from the man who's trying to ruin her life.

"Blending faith, suspense, and romance, *Texas Pursuit* is a book you will not be able to put down until you've read the last word on the final page."
—Pat Ennis, co-author of
Becoming a Woman Who Pleases God

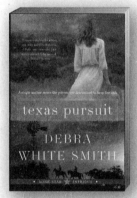

THE CHASE
Lone Star Intrigue, Book Three

ISBN 978-0-06-149326-3 (paperback)

In the riveting final installment of the Lone Star Intrigue series, Ryan Mansfield can't help the fact that he's still in love with his ex-wife Shelly when they band together to find their missing son. As they work together to track Sean down and bring him back home, can they find forgiveness and give their family a second chance?

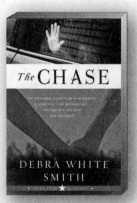